MW01244131

Also By Joshua Loyd Fox

Non-Fiction

I Won't Be Shaken: A Story of Overcoming the Odds

Fiction

The ArchAngel Missions:

Book I – Had I Not Chosen

Book II – Amongst You

Book III – To Build a Tower

Poetry Collections

I Don't Write Poetry: A Collection

Short Story Anthologies

The Tower and the Traitor

THE
ARCHANGEL MISSIONS
BOOK 2
AMONGST YOU

JOSHUA LOYD FOX

Published by Watertower Hill Publishing, LLC
Copyright © 2020 by JLFoxBooks, LLC
www.jlfoxbooks.com

Cover design by In the Blackwoods Design and Digital Art
www.intheblackwoods.com
Cover copyright © 2021, JLFoxBooks, LLC
Interior format by J.L. Fox.

Author's Note:
All characters and names in this book are fictional and are not
designed, patterned after, nor descriptive of any person, living or
deceased, except those used with permission.
Any similarities to people, living or deceased is purely by
coincidence.
Author and Publisher are not liable for any likeness described herein.

Library of Congress Control Number: 2021918456
ISBN: 979-8-9855562-0-9

Permissions: Quotes by King, Jr. Martin Luther. Used with
permission. Copyright ©2021 Estate of Dr. Martin Luther King, Jr.

This story is dedicated to:

All those who have lost their lives
at the hands of police brutality, racial injustice, and
hate.
If there was a quick fix, it would look like evil on the
face of it,
But a blessing in the end.

The end is all that matters.

"Injustice anywhere is a threat to justice everywhere. We are caught in an inescapable network of mutuality, tied in a single garment of destiny. Whatever affects one directly, affects all indirectly."

--Martin Luther King, Jr.
Letter from Birmingham, Alabama jail, April 16, 1963

Sickness is not an end,
A Fall is never fatal.
What belief pretends,
Is ever a truthful denial.
Book of the Tower and the Traitor—Strophe Two

Foreword

       Small town funerals were just the worst, the young man standing next to an open hole in the ground thought to himself. He stood in the shade of an old sycamore tree, its overspreading branches shielding the gravestones under it. A sentinel at watch, the young man thought, distractedly.

       But he was as miserable as the old women, sniffling next to him, smelling like dust sachets, everyone else dressed in black and lace. He looked around at those assembled and the angst of having to keep in his own excitement made the young man almost angry. Almost.

       He had been much angrier, in the past.

       The young man, with the unfortunate name of Harold Emory Higgsby III was happy that his old man had finally keeled over. Not that he ever had a thing against his father, but the man had been in his mid-fifties when Harry III was born and had never had much time to devote to his young progeny.

Harry III (or just "Three" as most of the rest of the family called him while trudging and grumbling during the brief visits they nonetheless made each year) grew up knowing more about his black nannies and the other African American staff around the mansion than he did his own father and lineage.

It wasn't his father's fault, however. Harry Higgsby II had been an often and oft-declared bachelor, having sworn off women many years prior to a single indiscretion with a young step-cousin of one of the scion's of his brother's adopted family.

The girl, truth be told, had beguiled the old man, who everyone assumed was homosexual, but who she knew more than anyone he most certainly was not. She, fortunately (to the rest of the family's way of thinking) had died in childbirth, leaving the genteel old man with a new baby boy to look after and raise.

And looking after a new baby boy was the purview of the staff, the tenable old man had said on more than one occasion during Three's early life.

That's how Three had grown up, and that's how it had been when his father had croaked at the dinner table, exactly one week before this unfortunate funeral on this hot and all too-sunny July day in the small town of August, Alabama, smack dab in the middle of Washington County.

The Presbyterian pastor was droning on and on about the fragility of life, and Three was hardly listening. But he caught the ending of the sermon — By a sense of divinity, his ears pricked up as the final sentences were muttered by the robed man much older than his own deceased father had been at the time of his death.

"In life, as in death, we must remember those who came before, who blazoned the path of the righteous to go forward and love in life, as the Creator loved us in His own death. We must remember the scripture from the Book of Romans, in the fifth chapter:

'Nor can the gift of God be compared with the result of one man's sin: The judgment followed one sin and brought

condemnation, but the gift followed many trespasses and brought justification.'

The wrongness of man, in sin, was brought clean by the sacrifice of the One," the pastor explained.

"So, Death begets Life."

I believe the Pastor has the right of it, Three thought to himself as he threw down a single white rose into his father's grave.

The ornate casket had been lowered minutes earlier, and now he could feel, with the tingling on his skin, that everyone wanted this over with, and to get out of the oppressive heat.

Three thought of the countless dishes of good Southern cooking cooling on the dining table back at what was now, he presumed, his mansion. The meeting with the family office lawyers was tomorrow, and there was a bit of fluttering in his belly thinking of what the old man's Last Will and Testament had stipulated for his only offspring.

And Three was hungry. For some reason, thinking back over the short twenty-five years he had lived on this planet, he always seemed to be hungry.

Three looked once more at the casket sitting in the bottom of the deep hole dug into the ancestral burial grounds of his family's personal cemetery.

It was at the back end of the estate grounds, a long walk from the large plantation home, which, like a lone oasis, was situated in the center of hundreds of good Alabama acreage.

Trees surrounded the grounds, but trees would get in the way of the fertile, flat, and prosperous land that had served his family for generations.

He said one last flippant goodbye to the father he never really knew in life and turned back to the mansion for lunch. He gingerly wiped his hands on his black suit pants and smiled to those around him.

It was a show he was used to giving outwardly to others. A show that was second nature to the young man who would go on to become the most prolific serial killer in United States history.

Two figures stood looking down upon a world much divided and full of strife. They were in the place where the material could not see the spiritual, and there was peace all around. But the world below knew no peace.

The shorter figure sighed heavily, his shoulders rising and falling slowly. There was no need for air in this place, but he breathed deeply just the same. The taller figure smiled down at his beloved son.

The shorter, pink-garbed figure looked up at his Divine Father and knew that what was to unfold, if properly executed, would change the world for the better. He also knew that the means hardly ever mattered.

What mattered were the ends. It had been the same way two millennia before, on this particular world. And the shorter figure knew that these ends mattered more than anything this world had seen yet.

Well, except the ends from the Son of the Divine, those 2000 years ago. That particular situation had changed the course of the Universe.

A sudden thought blossomed like a firework in the shorter figure's mind, and he found his own peace from it.

"DEATH BRINGS LIFE. IT HAS ALWAYS BEEN MY LAW. DON'T BE TROUBLED, MY SON," the thought boomed into the ArchAngel's mind.

Chamuel nodded and watched as the Divine Father slowly faded from sight. The Father would not be able to see, nor be a part of, what was to happen below. The Divine could be no part of the darker side of this reality. And so, Chamuel was alone. Alone to do what was right for the boy below.

But deep inside the ArchAngel's soul, he knew he was never alone. He was one of many. A host. A number of fifteen.

And so, he reached out with his mind, and connected with his sister Azrael.

He beseeched her, deep in the light which made up his being, for her help. He felt her reply in the positive. And he felt instantly better.

He felt his sister coming to this world in which he looked down. Looked down on a broken world on the brink of painful change. It was one of a multiple of worlds, but important, nonetheless.

And this world, a world that the boy below, and his friends, were to make. Or rather, unmake.

Again, the means never mattered as much as the ends.

Chamuel sighed heavily again and started changing the course of history as much as he was able, through the Choices the people involved would make.

It always came back to the Choices. Only this time, the Choice really was the difference between life and death.

He would enact the changes for life, and with the help of his sister Azrael, the death would be as mitigated and as poignant as possible.

How he hated this part of his job.

PART I

"You must share death amongst you in order to exhaust it and cause its dissolution, so that in you and through you death may die."

--Valentinus

Chapter 1

"Everything? Like…everything?" Harold III said to the beguiling and venerable old man who sat across what seemed like an acre of California Redwood from him.

The desk was the largest that Three had ever seen, which wasn't saying much, but he felt uncomfortable having to shout for the old lawyer to hear him.

"Before you, your father was the last in a long line of Higgsbys, and every penny that every one of those men owned, now belongs to you. It's a liquid-able amount of about three hundred fifty million to four hundred. And some change. Depends on what the accountants can do with it from day to day," Mr. Benjamin Rigsby, Esq., said to the young, but quite handsome man (he thought to himself) sitting across from him.

"The men of your family had a set-in-stone investment portfolio that spread the seed money into consumables and commodities, so as the farming community rose up out of the Great Depression, your family's pockets got quite deep," the old man was saying. But Three wasn't listening.

Plans within plans started taking shape in the young man's mind, and if anyone could see the way the wheels were turning in his quite remarkable mind, the future of the country would change drastically. But no one could read the young man's mind, which Three thought was a good thing.

Cutting the old man off, he asked what he needed to sign, did so with gusto, and departed the antique law office in downtown August whistling a tune he didn't outwardly realize he was whistling. He was now a very rich, very lonely young man, and the plans from earlier needed to start, and they needed to start that very day, he knew.

Since the dawning of the investiture of the small Alabama town known as August in 1785, the downtown two blocks had not changed much. So, Three walked across Second Street to the bank which his family had used for generations.

First Title Bank of August stood in a turn-of-the-century red brick three-story, and the rumor was that even in the Great Depression and Segregation, the bank had stood for white privilege and wealth for the white plantation owners within a hundred-mile radius.

It slightly sickened Three to walk through the glass doors and smell the racism in the lobby. But he had a job to do, and it started right now.

Glancing down at his cheap Timex watch, he saw that it was close to noon. He had about a half hour to get what he needed done here and was supposed to meet his team at 1 o'clock back at the house.

And he really was nervous about the first step of letting all of the family staff and the people he had grown up with go and making sure they were all taken care of. But he couldn't have witnesses for what came next.

Well, except for Four and Five.

As he walked up to the information desk in the old bank, he thought about his two boyhood best friends. They would be sitting in his ancestral home's gigantic kitchen at the moment, eating a lunch served to them by Dottie, the ancient black nannie who had raised Three, and his two best friends at the same time, by proxy.

Dottie had served his father and grandfather her entire life, and Three felt like shit for what he was about to do that afternoon, but there was no choice, and Dottie should be able to retire by now anyway, he thought. She was almost ninety years old for God's sake.

Three had to clear his voice twice for the pretty brunette secretary sitting behind the marble desk in the middle of the bank's lobby. She finally looked up, and when she saw that it was a Higgsby standing in front of her, she gave a small squeak, and asked in a singsong voice how she could be of service.

"Please inform Mr. Mathers that I am here, and need to perform a bit of business, and I'm on a time crunch," he said to the young girl.

The secretary made no excuses, she simply picked up the black telephone receiver on her desktop, dialed a two-digit number and spoke hurriedly into the phone. Three missed what she said as he walked over to the sitting area adjacent to the information desk and took a seat.

As he glanced around the bank proper, he saw that there were only two other customers standing in line to do business with the tellers, but the three or four desks for bankers were all unoccupied.

It made Three remember that his hometown was slowly dying, and there was nothing he could do to stop it. What he was about to do at this bank was going to make very large waves in the community.

His family had always kept their wealth locally, and that was both stupid and antiquated. Three was about to change all of that, and he was mentally gearing himself up for the barrage of counter-advice from the president of the bank.

Three was quite aware that his family's money made up the largest chunk of this bank's cash flow. He was actually trying not to smile at the indignation he was about to cause in this pillar of local systematic racism.

William Mathers, an older, finely dressed man walked out of a back door and his heels clicked across the marble floor smartly. He approached Three with his hand extended, and a fake smile plastered to his face. Three looked up, made the man stand there with his hand extended for two seconds beyond normative social cues, and stood up with his own fake smile plastered to his own face.

"Pleasure to meet you Mr. Higgsby, pure pleasure. I had the privilege of assisting your father for the last fifteen years, and I look forward to assisting you anyway I can," the older man said all in one breath.

"Please, call me Three, Mr. Mathers. The family stuck me with that nickname some years ago," Three affected a distinguished and white privileged air, which made him slightly nauseous. The older man just smiled knowingly at the younger man.

"Please, can we speak in your office?" Three asked as he let the older man's hand go and tried very hard to not wipe his own on his jeans. He didn't succeed, but at least waited until the older man asked him to follow and turned back towards the back of the bank proper.

Three followed the smartly dressed man's clicking heels on the marble floor back to the back part of the bank. A part of the bank that most customers never saw. But Three knew that his family's name granted him access to areas most families in

4

this town were not privy to. He also disdained that knowledge, but it was useful in some cases. Like today.

Walking into Mr. Mathers' very sophisticated designed and richly designed office made Three smile even more. He didn't think the man would have his job after today. And Three found it very difficult to care.

Mr. Mathers gestured at one of the two leather chairs in front of his spacious desk, and the two men sat down together. The top of the desk was spotless, and Mr. Mathers folded his hands on top of the leather desk blotter, waiting for Three to speak up.

"Mr. Rigsby informed me of my family's holdings at this bank, and I signed all of the necessary legal documents transferring control solely to myself this morning," Three explained.

"Yes, Mr. Higgsby, umm, Three, I was sent word not even ten minutes ago, and pending the electronic transfer of documents to our database, I am at your service for whatever you need," Mr. Mathers said with another fake smile.

"Well, I don't have much time, so I will cut to the chase, if I may," Three said, never taking his eyes off of the man across the desk.

"I would like to liquidate all holdings, investments, and cash accounts and move all of the funds from those transactions to this account," Three said, and pulled a slip of paper with several alpha-numeric lines on it.

Mr. Mathers spent several seconds longer than was socially acceptable blinking at Three. He finally cleared his throat and spoke in a strangled voice.

"I'm sorry, you want to do what again?" he asked. Three just smiled at him in return.

I want all of my family's money, I'm sorry, my money, out of this bank, along with all CDs, retirement funds, cash accounts, and liquid-able holdings. I want it all wired in one cash amount to the overseas account on this piece of paper," Three answered him, placing the slip of paper on the leather blotter.

Mr. Mather's looked down at the paper like it was a pit viper, ready to strike. He even unfolded his hands and jerked them away. Three just smiled again.

"I'm sorry Mr. Higgsby," Mathers started.

"Three..." Three interrupted.

Mather's cleared his throat. "I'm sorry...Three...but that is quite impossible and would take weeks to clear up. I'm not sure you understand the ramifications of what you are asking," Mathers tried to explain.

"I'm quite aware of the penalties for early liquidation, tax assessment penalties, and your fees for such work. I am willing to lose that money to remove my family's presence from this institution," Three answered matter-of-factly.

"Furthermore, with everything being electronic nowadays, and quite easy to do, you have one week to finish all preparations, at the end of which, I will return to sign any documentation needed, and the wire transfer will happen that day, if you want any future business with me and my holdings," Three said.

Mathers just gulped loudly.

"Now, if you'll excuse me, I have an appointment. Please call with any information or questions. I will leave my personal cell number with the girl at the front desk," Three said, rising.

Mr. Mathers did not stand with him, so Three let himself out of the office.

Walking back out to the main lobby area, Three walked over to the lone banker sitting at one of the unoccupied desks lining the west wall. He sat down and asked the middle-aged man if he knew who Three was. The man said he did.

"Good, here is my ID, and my passcodes. I have four cash accounts in my father's name, and now they should be in my name as well. I would like those accounts cleaned out and closed. Take the amounts from each account, and make a cashier's check, left blank, for each, with the cash in the accounts. Please." Three said.

The middle-aged man balked at the request but knew there was nothing he could do. So, he took Three's ID, and the other scrap of paper from the other pocket of Three's jeans, and walked to the back, where Three knew he was getting permission from Mr. Mathers to make the necessary adjustments.

Within thirteen minutes, by Three's Timex watch, the man returned holding four white, non-descript envelopes and handed them to Three, along with his ID and the slip of paper with the bank's passcodes on it.

Three looked into each envelope, smiled that no fees were taken out of the amounts for the bank's troubles, turned and walked away before the low-level banker could ask Three if he needed anything else.

Three only stopped long enough at the front desk to write his cell number on a yellow sticky note and made sure the starry-eyed brunette knew to give it to whoever needed it.

He turned and walked out of the building whistling and felt the heaviness of knowing what he needed to do to begin his plans lift from his shoulders as he again stood outside of the bank, glancing down at the two-block downtown area of August.

Three walked over to his dark green and tan Jeep Wrangler, a gift given to him from his absent father when he had graduated college.

It was his favorite possession, and he loved how the strength and sound of the V8 engine made him feel as he turned towards his home, and the meeting with his best friends.

As he drove away from the unusually quiet downtown area of August, Alabama, he turned on his stereo full-blast, and cranked the famous song from Queen, "We Will Rock You," as loud as he could. He couldn't help but burst out laughing as he headed towards his home.

7

Chapter 2

Three pulled into the long, tree-lined road that led to the middle of the grounds, and up to the large white, seven-columned plantation home which his great grandfather to the fourth power had built. And he had built it on the backs of slaves.

For generations, the plantation of the Higgsby family had grown cotton, corn, sorghum, and most recently, soy and grapes. Three had grown up learning the farming lessons of crop rotation, soil remediation, and managing fellow human beings.

Three was not fond of the later of those lessons.

He pulled the jeep up to the fifteen front steps leading to the giant red door. Floyd, his family's longtime carriage man, walked slowly to Three's driver's door and opened it for him.

"Thank you, Floyd. Thank you. Can you please have Dottie, Harmony, and Chester meet us in the parlor? I have some news," he told the much older man.

Floyd had never been a man of many words, so he just nodded to Three, and grunted. Three smiled at Floyd. He was going to miss every one of these wonderful people who had practically raised him. But he had a job to do. He shook away the encroaching depression and walked resolutely into the big house.

As he walked through the front parlor, down the middle hall, and into the bright and overly large kitchen, he stood in the doorway leading into the large, redone industrial room, watching the woman at the stove who had raised him.

She was short, quite thin, but stronger than any other woman he had ever met. Her tight curly hair was mostly gray under her kerchief, and her exposed forearms were strong and wiry. Her veins stood out against her jet-black skin, and Three thought that she was just the most beautiful creature he had ever seen.

He walked into the warm room and just nodded to his two best friends sitting at the eat-in breakfast table on the left-hand side, and walked over to Dottie, who was wiping her hands on her apron and turning, she smiled up at Three.

Three noticed how skinny Dottie was getting again.

He worried that she didn't have much longer, and he worried even more that the news he was about to give her would finally finish the job his father had tried to do for so many years by relying on Dottie to run the entire household, including watching after a growing and mischievous little boy, who she had nicknamed "Three" when he was a baby.

He walked over to his lifelong nanny and kissed her on the cheek when she motioned him to do so.

"Smells great, Dottie. What's for dinner?"

"Just rolled out some dumplins' sir, got 'em in the pot taking a bath," she laughed.

9

Three's stomach dropped, and he hoped that one day, this woman would understand what he was going to do. And more importantly, why he was doing it.

"You don't have to call me 'sir' Dottie, you know that," he told her as he walked over to the cutting board and started putting together a dry sandwich with the meats and cheeses she had set out for his two boyhood friends who had still not said a word. He looked up at the pair as he put ham on two slices of homemade bread and added a couple of slices of white cheese.

He nodded at the pair and patted his breast pocket. They both breathed out in relief and went back to finishing their own sandwiches. The last thing that Three did was pour a large glass of sweet tea from the pitcher that was never empty on the island of the large kitchen.

He could hear Dottie moving around behind him, getting dinner ready enough for ten people. Three sat down with his two best friends and tried to swallow the first bite he took of his sandwich. He almost threw it back up.

But he had his friends with him to face what he was about to do. They didn't speak a word to each other, just knew what was coming up, and they all felt the heaviness of the situation. But again, they had a job to do, and it started today.

A few minutes of quiet in the kitchen, punctuated by Dottie tapping the stirring spoon on the pot of dumplings and the three young men sitting at the breakfast table trying to not talk, Floyd walked in and whispered something in Dottie's ear. She whispered something back to the tall, strong man, and Three turned his back to her in shame as she took off her apron and glanced over at him.

She had a knowing look in her eyes, but Three didn't think she really knew what was coming. How could she? he thought. She just walked with Floyd out of the kitchen's swinging door and didn't look back.

10

Three looked at his two best friends, sitting on either side of him at the table. Their lunches finished, and the time was here to start what they had planned for so long. Three whispered to them both to be ready and said a thanks to the heavens that he wasn't alone in this.

The three young men, all close to the same height and build, walked into the front foyer, where the four members of the house staff were standing in a line, all of their hands slowly wringing in front of them.

Only Dottie had her arms crossed, and as the three young men walked into the room, all eyes shifted to them. The three men looked at each other, and they all felt the same feeling of being in trouble and were gearing up to get a lecture.

Three looked at the four people who, besides his best friends throughout his life, were the only real family he had ever known. This was going to kill him, but he worried that it would upset the four people in front of him even more.

He looked into each of their dark eyes.

The two men were as tall as Three, but thicker. They had carried him as a young boy on their shoulders, and he never knew stronger men.

Floyd was the quiet one, hardly ever speaking, but could break a two-foot log in half with one swing of an axe. And he had always been willing to show Three how to do it. Well, how to do just about anything the young boy had asked the older man to do.

Chester was bubbly and always had a joke for the young boy. He was portly in his advancing age but could still keep all of the lawns and landscape of the grounds in tiptop shape.

He took so much pride in what his hands could create, and many of the mantles in the large home were decorated with his wooden carvings.

Chester had whittled a running horse, mane flying behind it, for Three's fourteenth birthday.

It was the best present that he had ever been given. Three was going to miss Chester's bright white smile more than anything else besides Dottie.

And as Three looked into Harmony's eyes, he remembered the young woman as a teenager. He had only been a very small boy, but he looked up to her as his angel.

She had protected him from the adults of the house on several occasions, and she was always calling him "Little Sir" when people were around. When they were alone, she was the only person on the planet who called him Harry.

Harmony knew what he had dealt with growing up, and Three knew that when these four got news of what was going to happen over the next several years, she would be the one to understand.

She was tall, willowy, and her hair flowed down her back on most days. Today, however, it was done up in a bun and she wore her customary uniform of khaki pants, a silk blouse, and sensible shoes.

Three was going to miss her genius for keeping the house books. She knew more about the Higgsby fortune than anyone besides Three himself, and he knew that what he had done at the bank today had probably already gotten back to her.

Three stepped in front of his friends and cleared his throat. This was not going to be easy. He had been raised by the people standing in front of him, and had always seen them as his self-adopted family, and not just the help.

It had been a source of contention between him and his father, and on many occasions throughout his childhood, his father had made him act like more of a master to his self-adopted family, and not outwardly show the deeper connection he had with them all.

Those were lessons that he abhorred, and his black family knew it. This wasn't going to be easy because he had to put on the front of the employer, and not the family member in what had to be done.

He pulled the four white envelopes out of his breast pocket and held them in his hand while he started speaking.

"Dottie, Floyd, Harmony, and Chester," he said to the gathered group in front of him.

He looked at each of them, memories forming in his mind of each of them, caring for him, and teaching him all about their history, as well as his own. Chester had taught him how to hunt the wild grouse on the property. Floyd had taught him how to drive. Harmony, who was Dottie's daughter, had been his first big crush, although she was ten years older than him, and had changed his diapers.

"As you know, when my father died last week, everything was left to me. I have decided to sell the house, the grounds, and move away. That means that I am asking you all to retire, and I have something for you all to make that easier," he said all in one breath.

There were gasps from the four standing in front of him. And it was quickly followed by angry outbursts from each of them except Dottie. She just stood looking at the boy whom she had raised. She had one eyebrow raised, and Three couldn't take his eyes off of her.

The other's growing voices were drowned out by the weight of Dottie's stare.

To Three, the rest of the room faded from his consciousness as he looked deep into her eyes. And then she spoke.

"Ever 'one. Shut it. The master has spoken. Let's see what he has for us," she said to those standing with her.

Three had never heard her speak that way, especially calling him "the master." It broke his heart. But he just put his head down, and walked to the group, handing them each an envelope. They all looked inside and gasped again.

"Two hundred and fifty thousand dollars!" Harmony was the first to explode. "You cleaned out the four cash accounts, didn't you?" she said accusingly.

13

Three had indeed emptied out the four cash accounts that his father had kept for emergencies.

All four balances were the same, quarter of a million dollars. The top amount that the federal government would insure. His father had been no dummy. And Three had felt these four deserved the money a lot more than he did.

Dottie looked at her own cashiers' cheque. She folded the envelope and held it in one hand as she looked back at the boy in front of her.

"Well, guess I can say I ain't surprised none. I always known you wouldn't stay," she said to him. He just kept his head hung. He heard her approach him.

He kept his head down and heard the other three household workers who were like family to him walk away, to gather their things, and leave the home they had all known for at least Three's entire life.

But he saw Dottie's very comfortable shoes come to a stop in front of him, and he looked up into her eyes. He only saw love and kindness in them. He let out the breath he didn't know he had been holding.

"Three, I've raised you like my own. And you is my own. I know this day was a comin'," she said to him. She reached up and raised his chin, making him look at her.

"Whatever it is that you gotta do, go do it, son. We raised you right. You'll be ok, and so will we," she told him.

He felt the first tears fall, but he had to stay strong. If he folded now, it would be all for nothing. And he owed those not still with him to be strong.

"I love you, boy. You'll always be family. I'll write and tell you where we go," she said.

She gave him a hug, and he could feel her small frame and bones beneath her sensible house dress. She looked back up at him one last time.

14

"Don't you let my dumplin's burn now. Go stir them and add the chicken around 4. I can't stay and do no more," she said.

She knew him better than he knew himself, he felt. He nodded to her and watched her walk back to the servants' wings to gather her belongings.

He knew that he just needed to get out of the way and let the four leave. He felt like shit. And he knew that he would feel like shit for a while.

He turned back to his best friends who had stayed quiet the whole time he had been home. They had planned this months earlier, and in some ways, even years earlier. He walked up to the pair and put his arms around both of them.

"Let's go up to the office. We need to let them go, and I don't want to make the goodbyes any longer than they need to be. They need to just go, and not look back," he said to them.

"I thought you were very strong, Three," Four said to him. Four's real name was Christopher, but two years ago, when they started making these plans, they had decided to just use their childhood nicknames.

"Yeah, buddy, you did really well," Five said.

Five's name was Mark. Three looked at his two best friends and shook his head to dispel the depression again. That was happening more and more he thought as the trio walked up the carpet covered grand stairway to the second floor, and into his father's mahogany lined office.

Three didn't want to touch anything in the office, as he had not been permitted to come into this room much as a child and teenager.

But it was his office now, and he was damned if he was going to be scared to enter his own office. Still, though, it felt completely alien and weird to sit in his father's large executive leather chair behind the large desk.

He felt like an imposter.

And he thought to himself that that was a feeling he was going to have to get used to.

Because he was about to set off a decade-long plan that would force him to be an imposter every single day in that whole time. It was daunting, and he was suddenly very scared.

He knew that this plan was required to make the changes this country needed. He had watched, for years, the divide this country shared amongst people of differing backgrounds. That divide needed to be broken down in the strongest, and most permanent way possible.

And as he listened to the commotion coming from down on the first floor over the rest of the afternoon, he knew that he was going to feel very lonely as well.

Chapter 3

Three sat behind his father's desk and looked at his two best friends sitting in the shorter leather chairs across from him. They were silent for the most part, the only sound in the room coming from the laptop in front of Five. It was beeping, and when the sounds went away, Three knew that things could start moving.

"So, it will take at least a week for the bank to liquidate the funds in the mutuals and the certificates of deposit. The stocks and bonds should go next, with huge penalties. But, correct me if I'm wrong Four, but by this time in two weeks, all of the funds should be in the bank in the Caymans, right?" Three asked his best friend.

"That's right. I have my guy at the Grand Cayman Bank waiting for all of the wires. He texted about an hour ago that the cash deposits were already wired," Four said.

"Routing through the Suisse Banke, it should be very difficult to track. And I've filed all of the IRS forms for offshore holdings. You are going to take another big hit with those taxes," he went on.

"So, you should be covered as far as all the money leaving the States. After that, there is no trace of the wires from the Swiss to the Caribbean. That's just how international financing works. No one knows shit," Four finished up.

Five was studying the figures appearing on his laptop, and the beeping was sounding further and further apart.

Five spoke up.

"It looks like First Title of August has informed the Suisse Banke that there would be three wires today, two more tomorrow. And the final one by next week. That's the one you will have to go back into the bank here and sign the forms. I'll let you know what the Swiss say," he said.

He spoke across the desk without taking his eyes off of the laptop.

Three had no idea what Five could do on that computer but had learned years earlier never to ask questions. Five was a born hacker, and had only gotten in trouble one time, early on in high school, when he was a part of a hacking group that was trying to take down the IRS.

It didn't happen, and Five was only marginally known in the hacker group. He was both a minor, and not a central player in the group, so got off virtually scot-free.

The truth was, he was the real brains behind the group years ago and was able to mask his movements to a degree that he was never really discovered.

Only the IP address of the high school library, and he was known to sit in there for hours on end, hacking on his computer.

And now, he was one of the foremost hackers in the world, and no one knew anything about him.

They had often joked about their shared height, good looks and general positive nature. All those things had made them all popular in town, and the fact that the three had been juggernauts on the playing fields of August, Alabama hadn't hurt.

And since early childhood, they had been inseparable. Three looked over at Five and knew that Five was extremely happy with Four, and that Three didn't mind their love for each other, as it had been apparent since they were all at least twelve or thirteen.

When the pair had hit puberty, and realized that they were both homosexual, that they were both in love with each other, and that they were soulmates, the group had grown even closer.

Five had shaggy dark hair, and wore glasses, but Three had seen him hundreds of times without them, so he wondered if the tall skinny man really needed them.

Three looked over at Four. He had a hundred questions, but he trusted Four to know what he was doing. Four had graduated from The University of Alabama, "roll tide," with highest honors and went on to Law School at Harvard.

By the time Four was halfway finished with his education, this plan was in place, and so he knew that he would be coming back to August to work in his father's local, small-time law firm. As a Harvard educated lawyer, he was massively underutilized at his father's firm, which was perfect for this plan.

Four was extremely handsome as well. If he hadn't been born gay, the women of August wouldn't have let him alone for a second. He was blond, tall, and had a cleft chin.

As a very well-educated lawyer, and so very handsome, the women of the town just shook their heads and mumbled under their breath about the 'waste of a great man.'

19

That had always made the trio laugh uproariously.

And then there was Three. He had received a degree from Alabama State in cultural studies and spent most of his college years protesting for equality and racial discrimination reform, and marched every month against police brutality.

He wasn't liked or very much accepted in his hometown, and the residents had always whispered that he was a bit too liberal for their tastes.

Oh, if only they really knew, Three thought to himself.

But, what saved him, and had saved him since high school, were his athletic abilities. At August High, he was a record-breaking athlete in several sports. He even led the 2A football team to their first state competition. Although they hadn't won the final game, he was still lauded as the best athlete to ever come out of August.

So, the residents let him have his "hobbies," just as long as he kept throwing the football and running quickly around the track.

It was the same in college, and Three, every single day, had felt like the largest fraud in state history. He secretly abhorred sports. He hated competition. He had just always been completely physically gifted. Just like his ancestors.

His father had been a renowned football player as well, so it was expected in the community that with his family a little eccentricity was allowed, even expected.

The beeping from Five's computer finally settled for the day. All of the initial money was in the Swiss account that he had given the bank president earlier in the day, and he knew that more wires would fly across the Atlantic in the days ahead. But for now, they had the seed money in the account to start the plans.

"Alright Five, what do we have for schools and IDs?" he asked his hacker best friend. He saw Five and Four exchange glances and knew that what passed between them was concern.

20

"There is no going back after this Three," Five said to him.

"I'm aware. Once I'm in the system with the fake IDs you've procured, there is no going back. We didn't plan all of this out to back out now, Five," Three answered him.

"There are five schools, over the next year. The first is in Arizona. It's for four weeks, and it's run by Dan Forrester. He's a retired FBI agent, and was on the team that originated the forensic profiling the FBI is famous for now.

He teaches seven to ten students at a time. The brochure online says that it is a school for patriots who want to know advanced FBI techniques for home defense and for students of crime forensics," Five answered him. He continued.

"The ID for the Arizona school is under the name David Franks, thought the matching initials could come in handy to get in close and ask deeper questions. He is also an ex-NCAA football standout but was never drafted. You guys should get a long swimmingly," Five said.

Four snickered. Neither Four nor Five had never been much of an athlete, although they had all played football and basketball together at August High School, "Home of the Wildcats."

The pair could hold their own, but their real gift was backing up Three. That's why they had all been so successful. Three was the star, and Four and Five backed him up and made him look even better.

It was such a successful relationship between the three friends that no one in all of their lives could penetrate the circle. Well, Three thought to himself, except for One and Two.

Three had found the real family that he had always yearned for, and the other members of the group had the support, acceptance, and sustained love that they themselves had yearned for as well. A group of separate misfits had found themselves in the group of best friends.

21

Four spoke up, looking over at Five, who was busy punching keys on his computer.

"Three, are we absolutely sure here? You've let the staff go, true, and you've moved around the money. But after next week, we are going to disappear. Are you ready for that?"

"Are you? What do we have here? We have made this plan solid over the last three years. We aren't stopping now. We have a very long ten years in front of us, guys," he said.

"And at least you have each other. I don't have anyone to share this with romantically, or as a couple. But that's okay. Not much different than before, actually," he said wistfully.

"Not since One," he whispered after a quiet pause.

The other two men in the room were still able to hear his final, mumbled musing.

All three were silent as they thought about One. The person who had brought them all together as kids. No one sitting in the office wanted to think about her, and the tragedy of her life, so they soon began to make preparations to move to Arizona after all the money was in the bank.

They all knew, it was time to start making alibis. And to start the next phase of the plan.

Within a year, Three thought to himself as they walked down to serve themselves the chicken and dumplings that Dottie had started cooking earlier in the day, the killing would start.

And he had that year to get to a point where he could actually do it.

He thought back over so many past conversations with those he loved the most, and what could change this country. What could bring about acceptance of others. Love of people not of your skin color. Acceptance of people that some outdated religious systems told you to judge and throw asunder.

He looked over at his childhood best friends, who were smiling secret smiles at each other and still touching as much as possible even after having been together for so long. That was

22

true love, Three thought, and who in the world could judge that negatively?

He had never understood that kind of hate, but then again, he had been brought up by such amazing black people, who had had to fight against that hate their whole lives.

He understood completely what needed to be done now.

And it was a good plan, he thought as his childhood best friends served up the classic southern dish. But it all hinged on him being able to pull the trigger, so to say.

And as he thought back to One, and seeing her broken body sprawled out in front of the Dairy Queen in town, he knew that he owed it to her to do it.

He just had to remember why they were all doing this.

In the coming years, that would be all that would get him through.

Chapter 4

"When the two-man team would go into the interviews, they always knew that they had to press the psychological advantage. ," Dan Forrester said to the informal group of students sweating in a large trailer in the Arizona heat.

"But they all had a weakness," he said.

"The agents knew the killer's triggers and would use psychological tricks to bring out the illicit responses they were looking for. After all, serial killers were as smart as they came. We knew that," Dan told the rapt audience sitting before him.

"It was those weaknesses, those obsessions, which the agents would use to manipulate the subjects into telling the hard

24

truths. And it was typically those same triggers that would get the serial killer caught in the first place," he said. He then paused and looked at the crowd of eager faces looking back at him, hardly breathing.

He continued.

"They were like dogs with a favorite treat. The FBI would use those triggers to train and condition the killer into getting caught. Quite brilliant if you ask me," he snickered.

"Whether it was women's shoes, perfume, dark curly hair, or in one case, Snickers candy bars, these memories, these triggers, would take the killers back to their crimes, and they would reveal the motivations, the perversions, even the techniques, so that we could better understand the minds of the serial killer in those interviews," Dan said.

"And that knowledge, those dirty and gross triggers would show us that serial killers are usually all alike in some ways. They all had two or more of three main traits from childhood. We will talk about the Macdonald Triad this afternoon," Forrester concluded.

The eight students, all male except one lone woman, who no one really wanted to mess with, gathered up their notes, and moved to walk back out into the scorching sun of the Arizona desert.

They had been at this school on the outskirts of Phoenix for the last eleven days, and they had all learned so much from the ex-FBI Special Agent, Dan Forrester.

Most of the students were taking this school because they all wanted to join the FBI, and this obscure school on the back end of the world was their introduction to that world. Most of the students, except one.

"Mr. Forrester, I was wondering if I could ask you a question," the tall, dark-headed student approached the teacher after all the other students had filed out to the only other building at this little school, the joint dormitory and chow hall. He was pushing up the dark, horn-rimmed glasses on his nose as the teacher looked up at him.

"Sure, son, what's your name again?" Dan Forrester asked.

"Umm...David. David Franks. But my friends all call me DF," the student answered the teacher.

"That's funny, my brothers at the Bureau called me DF as well," the teacher said, smiling. "What's your question?"

"Well, if every single serial killer had some obsession, and that's how a lot of them were caught, what would you guys in the Bureau do if there was NOT an obsession? If the killer did not have some kind of kink or fantasy?" the student asked, looking down.

The teacher assumed that this student was painfully shy, but it was a great question, he thought.

"Well, that's the thing, son. All serial killers have an MO. A modus operandi. And when we learned what it was, things like they only killed women, or only young women, or only dark-haired prostitutes, or hitchhiking young men, we could use that information to track and capture the killers," the teacher explained.

"It was one of the basic tenets that we learned from all of those interviews with the captured serial killers back in the 60s and 70s," the teacher answered.

"So, without a doubt, all serial killers have some sort of repetitious routine in picking victims, or how they used and disposed of the bodies?" the student asked.

"Yup. And it's what gets 'em all caught, eventually," the teacher answered, ending the conversation.

The teacher left the student in the room alone, and when the door to the trailer classroom he was standing in closed, the student spoke into the two-way earpiece in his left ear.

"Did you get that, guys? Even the FBI wouldn't know what to do if there was no pattern," he said.

The answer came back into his ear and made him realize that maybe this whole thing would work.

"They wouldn't know what to do if there was a common calling card, but no MO. And that's kind of scary," Five said into the microphone.

The pair of lovers was camped out less than a mile away, in a chrome gulfstream camper attached to a large pickup truck. The camper was full of communication equipment and foodstuff.

Four and Five were enjoying their four-week stint in the camper, listening to everything that Three was learning at the school. All the information was recorded, digitally stored, and would be brought back out when needed.

They were looking forward to the next school, where Three would use a different alias and would learn shooting and counterterrorism activities, taught by a retired Boston PD lieutenant, who had started the school after the events of the Boston Marathon bombing.

That school was in the mountains of Colorado, and the weather would be much cooler, the scenery would be nicer, and the group would learn more about how to get away with being the most prolific serial killer in US history.

This education was turning out to be a lot more fun than anyone in the group had figured. It was almost scary fun, Five thought as he listened to Three set off for lunch.

At the school, Three walked back out of the trailer, into the hot sun, and squinted up at the haze caused by the beating sunshine through his non-prescription glasses.

He absently scratched the curly dark hair wig covering his now-bald head and started sweating under the latex glue holding the wig on. He was looking forward to not having to wear the heavy disguise for the next two schools.

As he walked into the chow hall for lunch, he wondered if any of the students he was sharing this school with would go on to be in the FBI, and if they would be on the task force that would be created to chase him, and hope to catch him before he completed his long checklist of victims. Three felt more quizzical then afraid at this point.

He wondered if he would see any of these classmates again.

It was a scary thought.

Chapter 5

Marc Bruce, otherwise known as Three, crouched down behind a dumpster in a deserted alley, which smelled very much like rotting flesh. His long gun was gripped in both hands tightly, but his breathing was regulated.

He closed his eyes, mentally preparing to take out the two dark-clothed adversaries who he knew would move into this alley within the next two minutes.

Opening his eyes, he checked his sights on the long gun for the hundredth time and controlled his heartrate. He was made for this. His sight narrowed to the mouth of the alley, and he knew that his trained pupils were dilated in the darkness, seeing everything all at once, while also focusing on where he knew that the two-man team was soon going to appear.

He could hear his heart beating in his ears, but it wasn't so loud that he didn't sense everything around him.

The man and woman who had been following him through the deserted streets of the town in the mountains moved stealthily and swiftly into the mouth of the alley, but he had seen them easily. They didn't know he was there, but they suspected.

They had successfully cornered him in this alley, and he wanted to even the playing field by removing at least one of them. He was going to do that right now.

He got down on his knees, moving ever so slowly. In the shadows, he was invisible to his adversary's eyes. They had not adjusted to the darkness like he had. They were still sun-blind.

He was also dressed in flat black clothing, black camo paint smeared on his face and hands. The only thing that could give him away would be a flash of light on his shiny long gun, so he kept it down at his side.

When his two adversaries moved into the center of the alley, thinking they may just very well be alone in it, he raised the gun to his sight-line and fired at the shorter woman first. He scored a hit, center mass.

The taller, swifter man moved to his left instantly, and Three got off a shot, but missed. The man was protected behind a large metal trash bin. Damn it, the man known as Marc, thought. Now it was going to be a standoff.

He stayed where he was, his training replacing his instincts to retreat. He knew he could wait the man out. After all, the man had just lost his partner, and he was sitting silhouette to the sunlight coming from the head of the alley. For now, Three had all of the advantages.

So, he waited.

He glanced down at the woman's body, laying still in the middle of the alley, about ten feet into it.

What a waste, Three thought to himself. They had been so sure of themselves.

Four minutes later, by the muted diver's stopwatch on his wrist, he heard shuffling from the left side of the alley, where he knew the man was waiting him out as well.

The smart move, Three thought to himself, would be for the man to change the paradigm, and therefore the landscape of the coming conclusion of this hunt. And, as if on cue, the man crab-crawled out of the alley and took off running with his sidearm held in front of him.

Three caught a glint of sunlight off of the top slide of the 9mm handgun as the man retreated to find a better ground to die.

He waited two minutes, and then started slowly walking down the alley, left foot in front of right, watching the mouth of the alley for an ambush.

He stepped over the prone figure of the woman he had dropped with a shot to her chest several minutes earlier, and as he geared himself up to pursue the man with the 9mm, a hand reached out and grabbed his ankle.

He let out a small yell as he fell to the hard ground of the smelly alley, and the woman who he had thought he had dropped with a single shot to the chest stood up behind him and shot him in the back. A loud beep sounded in Three's earpiece.

"Not fucking fair! She was dead!" he yelled into the microphone attached to his black shirt's collar. The woman snickered behind him.

All at once, lights came on, lighting up the fake alley and the trash bags piled up everywhere filled with crumpled papers and non-biological trash. Three got to his feet, giving an ugly look to the woman who stood behind him, a half-grin on her face.

The other man, dressed the same as the two students staring each other down, walked into the alley, holstering his laser-ammo sidearm. Three dropped his long gun, and the gun

31

strap pulled taunt as the long gun swung around to rest against his back.

He was not happy.

The rest of the class soon joined the three students at the mouth of the alley. Three looked around at the mock city street around him, now seeing the signs that showed that the city block was fake, and mostly a shell. The teacher, Dom Franco, walked up to him, asking him what went wrong.

"She was dead. How could she trip me up like that?" Three asked, again giving an ugly look at the pretty blonde woman who didn't seem very apologetic.

"You can never assume anything in urban warfare. If she had been wearing a flack vest, or Kevlar, you wouldn't have ended her. She could be playing possum, sacrificing herself to ensure her team's victory. You did well drawing the pair in, but the lesson here today is that you can't assume anything. Nothing will make sense once the first bullets fly," the older man said.

Three once again thought the man was made from a tree stump. His skin was dry and rough, his features sharp and severe. A mostly gray flattop haircut brought the whole look together, and Three knew that this man was not one to mess with. He was the scariest man Three had ever met.

"When we first went into Baghdad, every citizen of that city was our enemy. We had to watch our backs every second of every day. One engagement in particular sticks out in my memory. I have nightmares about it to this day," the teacher said.

"We were clearing buildings in a section of the south side of the city. As we went into each building, our troops started getting picked off. We didn't know why, as intel told us that there were no hostiles in the area, and the bulk of the standing army was way to the south. But we were dying, and it took losing at least ten soldiers before we figured out what it was," he said.

32

He closed his eyes with the memory. The entire class was quiet, all eyes on the old teacher.

"The government had armed the children of this neighborhood. As we cleared the buildings, we ignored the hundreds of small children, until we couldn't ignore them anymore.

You people don't know what it's like to have to pick off children who are trained to shoot you first."

"Don't ever underestimate the number of eyes on you in this kind of situation. The more you can control those eyes, the easier it is to dictate the rules of your engagement. When the adversary is playing by YOUR rules, you will win the engagement every time," the teacher concluded.

"Assume everyone is your enemy, and you will never be surprised."

The students broke up into groups then, walking back into the coolness of the now overcast day. The sun, which had been shining bright all morning was hiding behind quick-moving clouds.

Three loved the vastness of this country, where large mountains ringed them in, and the sky really was just as big as he had been told before coming here from Colorado.

He was in a bit of heaven, and he didn't look forward to leaving the school in a few weeks. He was learning so much, and he was loving every minute of it.

They were on a ranch in Wyoming. Three had been at this Urban Survival School for over four weeks.

It was by far the most advanced, and most fun school he had been a part of. His cover for this school was Marc Bruce, and it was becoming increasingly difficult to keep the identities apart. But with the help of Four and Five, he was getting the hang of it.

Both of his best friends, and the other members of his team had gone home to establish the cover of them slowly moving away from August, Alabama.

Four had casework to do at his father's firm, but not enough to distract him from the plan. Five was always more reclusive in his work, so he was just sure to be seen many times around town, sitting at various public places, laptop always humming along.

He was actually working on solidifying the sale of the Higgsby plantation and grounds to the shell dummy company he had established several months earlier, which really led nowhere.

There was no trace back to the three friends, but to the general public, it was as if an agriculture testing company had bought the hundreds of acres and the home.

The plan was to let the grounds become overgrown in the next decade, but the team would still use the home as the ground base for the plan.

They couldn't help that the citizens of August would see lights on at various times, or hear loud noises coming from the several buildings scattered around the grounds, which would likely be chalked up to the "company" using the property for nefarious reasons.

Luckily, no one would think to poke around or trespass once the chain link fences were installed all around the perimeter of the estate.

As the weeks went by, both Four and Five would start dropping hints to friends and family about moving to the East coast for work, and to be together in a state where they could now legally become a married couple.

The truth was, they would never really leave August, but the town would believe that the couple had moved away from the home that mostly shunned them for their sexuality anyway.

Meanwhile, Three was happily ensconced at the Wyoming ranch, where four square acres of the over one hundred acres that Dom owned had been turned into an urban battlefield, complete with dummy enemies, and laser-controlled weapons.

Dom was a retired US Marine officer, who had been heavily decorated in a couple of the African campaigns, as well as the first Iraqi war. He then had gone on to a very distinguished career as a military consultant in Hollywood.

He had been the advisor of almost every major, high budget war movie in the last twenty years, making it possible for him to afford the Wyoming ranch outside of Cheyenne and staff the elite school that had been frequented by the best of the best in every major police department and law enforcement agency in the country.

Dom had become a legend in warfare tactics, and almost every major metropolitan SWAT team leader had taken his course.

Three felt a real kinship with the man, though. Over the last four weeks, Dom came to know Three as Marc, but he really had gotten to know him by his natural ability in the types of engagements that the school taught.

Three never had to be told something twice, and he had won every single engagement he had been placed into over the last week of practical scenarios. Even the five-on-one engagement the day before, in which Three had stalked and then killed the other team one at a time.

Today's practical, in which a double-man team had been hunting Three, was the first one where he wasn't a clear and decisive victor. But he had learned something very valuable in this lesson. He needed to remember to always try and control the environment around him. Or, in the very least, to be aware of everything he could.

He had learned the hard way to make sure that someone whom he thought was dead, really was dead.

He thanked the skies for the lesson. Somehow, he knew, he was going to need it in the years ahead.

"This afternoon we are going to spend a couple of hours at the range. I want three full fifty-round sets with both your long gun and chosen handgun. And Jeff, not your god forsaken Desert

Eagle. Use a damn 9-millimeter or a 40-cal. I'm tired of my teeth rattling from every shot of your damn gun," Dom told the class, and in particular, the large man at the head of the group.

They walked up to the dormitories to change and get ready for the afternoon class.

The biggest man that Three had ever seen, whose name was a simple "Jeff," smiled at Dom and nodded. He wasn't a man of many words, Three knew, but Three was still slightly limping from the week two hand-to-hand training where Jeff had unceremoniously pile-driven Three into the practice mat.

Three now kept a wide berth of the jolly big man. But Three's pride, as well as his knee, still smarted. In his mind, Three had called Jeff "Lenny," but never out loud.

The big man was strong as a bull, and slower than Three, but he was far from simpleminded. Three did get satisfaction out of the one-on-one engagements in the mock city block where his death time against Jeff was less than two minutes.

It didn't matter how big and strong Jeff was, Three knew. A gun made every man equal.

The ten-person class shuffled into the locker room of the dorms, men to the left, women to the right, although there were only two of the latter, and they all took off their black khaki uniforms and wiped the camouflaging makeup from faces made more tanned by the Wyoming summer sun.

Once dressed in civilian attire, the class walked over to the large shooting range, which was separated in three sections. One section, on the far left, consisted of simple shooting lanes. Twelve of them. The middle section was an open expanse for distance shooting.

Targets were placed at intervals of every twenty-five yards up to small ones which represented a thousand-yard shot. The third area, on the far-right side of the large live-ammo area, was the smaller mockup of roof-less rooms and blind corners for close-encounter practice.

That section had several dummy targets dressed up as adversaries and civilian victims. It was by far Three's favorite place to practice with his chosen handgun, a Glock 9-millimeter. During the time he was at this survival and training school, Three had had felt his first feelings of having a natural ability for something he actually enjoyed.

He had always been a gifted athlete, but this stuff, he just got. He actually enjoyed it. The teachers, on several occasions, had remarked that Three would make a natural soldier and battlefield leader. It was praise that almost derailed the entire plan. But Three stayed the course.

However, he felt an almost kinship and brotherhood with the ex-military and retired police instructors who had trained him during the entire eight-week course.

Three almost asked to take the school again but knew that that would raise suspicions.

As the lessons and practical engagements wound down over the next four weeks, Three became even more adept at urban warfare and showed an above-average aptitude for weapon use, earning the highest score in both the final sniper competition and the close-quarters time trials.

As he packed up his gear and clothes on the last day, several students congratulated his success at the school, and the positive rivalry between them all made Three happy.

But it was Dom's last words to him that stayed in his consciousness over the next week when he went home for a short break and to meet up with Four and Five.

"You are one of the best students that ever come through this school, Mr. Bruce," Dom said to him as he was leaving.

Dom Franco had stopped Three and extended his hand outside of the main building as Three was walking to his car.

"I would hate to go toe-to-toe with you on the battlefield. I know I'm a scary sonofabitch, but you, kid, you could do this for a living, and your body count would make mine look like peanuts."

Chapter 6

Three sat in his father's office at the deserted plantation home with his head between his knees. His eyes were closed, and his head was buzzing with the sound of the laser printer at the far end of the room slowly releasing pages of the printed Plan that he had just completed.

It had taken every ounce of strength he had to finish it. He felt that there was no turning back now, and he had never been so frightened.

"It's October 6, Three. The fourteenth is next week. We have to pick a target. We have to leave in the morning," Five was saying to him from one of the leather chairs between the large desk and the printer at the end of the room, printing out Three's doom.

"I know," Three said, his voice masked by his knees. He still couldn't make himself straighten up and face the daunting task in front of him.

Over the last year and a couple of months, Three had become a deadly, fighting machine.

He had taken every privately owned school around the country, and two across the ocean in Europe, to learn everything he could about survival, killing, police tactics, forensic psychology, the newest profiling techniques, and he still felt like he was going to be behind the curve from just plain manpower.

But the task he had before him was, by necessity, a solo job. Only his small team had all of the details and knew why they were doing what they were set to accomplish.

"Hey guys, I think you need to come see this." Four came into the office and grabbed the remote to the large TV they had installed early last year.

He switched the set on and changed the channel to CNN. The screen lit up with a group of masked people in the streets of a city, lighting a police car on fire, and looting buildings.

"Civil unrest has resulted in mass protesting, looting, and hysteria in several cities around the United States. All of this is in response to the reports we received yesterday about the death of Breonna Taylor, a young black woman in Detroit," the CNN anchor was saying.

"She was killed during a botched search and seizure raid on her home by Detroit SWAT," the news anchor was saying.

The three friends watched the screen as the story unfolded about how the Detroit police department's SWAT team had broken into the wrong house, thinking they were busting up a drug and gang den, when they had actually broken into the home of a young black ER nurse and her boyfriend.

As the black clad police officers threw in flash/bang grenades and swept through the home, Breonna Taylor rushed to the room next to her own, where her two-year-old daughter was asleep.

As she ran through the hallway, a trigger-happy SWAT officer opened fire.

Breonna Taylor was killed instantly.

And the country, especially the Black community had gone, understandably, berserk.

On the screen, there were thousands of protesting people carrying signs with "Black Lives Matter" on them, bold, and in black print.

Three watched as the young communities around the country exercised their right to protest. But he also saw so many looting, destroying property, and fighting against the police who were lining up, protecting the communities.

Three completely understood and agreed with the movement of the people on the screen. He wished that he was there, causing the same kind of rage-driven violence.

But, he had to be about the Plan. It was the only real way to exact the change those on the screen were begging for with their own actions.

It was a powder keg ready to explode, and Three knew that the time was right for what he was aimed at doing.

The country was ripe for a change, and that change would come in the form of fear.

Several years earlier, Three had had to write a paper in college about the social impact of the terrorist attack on September 11th.

What he learned from studying the results of several sociology reports and experiments, was that for a short time, the attack on 9/11 had caused such widespread fear and pain in this country that it had actually acted like a lodestone, bringing all peoples of this country together.

It hadn't mattered about race, creed, religion, color, or any other dividing characteristic. Fear had brought humans together, Americans together, all people together.

But, like anything else, it had not lasted long enough. There was no real, lasting change.

So, the idea had begun in Three's mind, and in the minds of his small team, that real fear, long lasting fear, fear that the country couldn't control, would cause the kinds of change that those looting and rioting on the screen in the office of the abandoned plantation home, were trying to make.

So, the plan had started taking shape. And, spurred by events that had transpired when the three-man team had been five strong, they were now ready to start it. But Three was so damn afraid! He knew how it was going to end.

He could feel it in the most visceral of ways.

But his biggest fears were taking his best friends down with him. Taking his family down. He didn't fear prison. He feared Four and Five losing each other.

And at the end of the day, if he was completely honest with himself, he really feared that the Plan wouldn't work the way it was supposed to, that it would end prematurely. That they wouldn't make the changes needed, and he would let One and Two's memories down.

A voice brought him out of his internal angst.

"Washington DC. We have to start at the Capitol, Three," Four was saying as they watched the riots all around the country, late into the night.

The next day would bring the preparations for the first killing, and it was time to nut up or shut up, Three thought to himself.

So be it, he thought.

He turned off the TV, and they moved off to their rooms, ready for a night of restless sleep, and the coming test of all of their abilities. The difficult days ahead would prove if what they were doing, what they were sacrificing, was worth the price.

Four and Five slept together more peacefully than Three did that night, wrapped up in each other, and praying for the strength for what was ahead.

None of them were exactly religious men, but some small prayers for strength were whispered that night.

They all felt that they were dooming themselves, but they were doing it for a very important reason, and the sacrifices of a few would marshal in the change for the many.

It was a shitty math equation, but a necessary one.

It had been necessary throughout history, and it would be necessary once again for this great country.

Every war on this planet had been justified by the same equation. The sacrifice of the few for the benefit of the many.

It was a law of nature, as strong as gravity, Murphy's Law, and death and taxes.

The atmosphere was silent and moody the next morning, as the three-man team met in the kitchen for a small breakfast, and to start the preparations and precautions for their trip to the Capitol.

Three had not slept well at all, and he couldn't eat much. He had an ache in his gut, and no amount of aspirin or drinking water seemed to ease the pain.

He was just going to have to live with it, he knew. If he could get past the first one, the first sacrifice, he would feel somewhat better.

But the first one was going to be the hardest.

It had to make the biggest impact, and he still wasn't sure if he could do it. Several times throughout that day, as they loaded up the RV, and made sure they had everything they needed for the night of the 14th, Three shook his head, dispelling the depression and panic that was trying to set in.

And as the team got on the road from Alabama, north to Washington DC, he felt a little better from just moving.

He was finally going to start the plan that he had promised himself, his team, and most importantly, to One and Two, to avenge their own deaths, which had come at the hands of the authorities who needed to fear for change more than anyone else.

Chapter 7

Hunter still didn't understand the messages on his phone. And that wasn't a surprise. He was drunk off of his ass, once again, and had just left the Asian massage parlor that he frequented at least once a week.

As he had walked back to his government issued car, tucking his shirt into his slacks, he checked his cell phone, and saw that he had missed thirteen messages. They were garbled, something about *coming home soon, be careful, take it easy,* and *call the office.* The last one was from his partner, Red. That one just read: SOS.

As Hunter got into his car, his cell went off again. It was Red, and he simply texted for Hunter to meet him at Hunter's home in Alexandria, Virginia. Hunter was currently across the

Woodrow Wilson Bridge, on the Maryland side of the beltway, but he could be home in about ten minutes.

He turned on the flashing red and blue lights built into his unmarked car and raced as fast as his alcohol-addled brain would let him. He very narrowly missed taking out a small SUV as he crossed over into the Virginia side of the District.

He was starting to panic. Why would Red need to meet him at his home? He kept asking himself that question over and over. But he also had a million other thoughts swirling through his foggy mind. He could never quit control the noise in his mind, but the alcohol usually made the million thoughts into a pretty, colorful tapestry of lights that he could handle.

Not so now, as he wound his way through his neighborhood.

And as he pulled onto his street, he could see all of the revolving lights, and the rushing around members of both the Alexandria PD, and his own FBI cohorts. So many uniforms, they looked like ants to Hunter. Shit, he thought.

He screeched to a stop behind the yellow tape, strewn across his street, about three houses down from his own. A small group of his neighbors were milling around, and when they saw Hunter exit his car, a babble went up between them.

Hunter hardly noticed his friends and acquaintances amongst the group, instead focusing on the Alexandria PD officer who was trying to block him from moving behind the tape.

He lifted his FBI badge to the young beat cop, and as the man lifted the yellow tape barrier for Hunter to step under, Red strode up behind him. His tall, overly large frame was taking up the entire street, to Hunter's drunk eyes.

The white patches of skin on Red's dark face and neck stood out sharply in the bright white light coming from the spotlights.

"Holy shit, H, where have you been? We have been texting and calling for a half hour," Hunter's large partner said to him.

The large black man grabbed Hunter by his arm, and dragged him over to the side of the residential street.

He whipped Hunter around to face him, which Hunter did not want to do at the moment. He was still wondering why all the hustle and bustle around his house, which should have been making him piss himself, but which he just felt strangely detached from.

Red physically shook him out of his mind trap.

The two older men starred at each other in the alternating bright lights of the cop cars and the spotlights set up in the street in front of his home. The home he shared with his wife, Karen.

"What the fuck, are you drunk again?" Hunter's longtime friend asked him.

The large man sighed and looked back at the house, which was lit up with large spotlights from portable trailers brought by the police department. Hunter knew they only did that for homicide details.

What the fuck, he asked himself.

"Well, maybe that's for the better. Listen Hunter, this is going to be hard. It's Karen, Hunter. She's gone man," Red tried to break it to him gently, but failed miserably.

Hunter had still not found his voice. He had already known. He knew as he had driven breakneck across the Wilson Bridge.

He had known as he listened to the static on the police band in his car, and he had known when he saw the looks from his neighbors.

Word had gotten around fast.

"What happened, Red?"

He finally raised his red-rimmed eyes up to his best friend and partner.

"It's not pretty H, not pretty at all. It looks staged, and it looks frightening as fuck," the large man said.

His shoulders were shaking, and Hunter realized that the large man was crying, but was keeping it in as best as he could.

The big man and his wife, Renee, had spent countless days and evenings over barbeques and drinks, and game nights at Hunter and his own wife Karen's home. His wife of over thirty years. His Karen.

Oh shit, Hunter thought, right before his knees went out from under him. All of the last half hour of panic and feelings of doom overcame him suddenly, and on his knees, he broke down completely. Tears and snot fell from his face onto the concrete of the sidewalk under him.

Red stood above him protectively, and Hunter let the sobs shake him until resolve replaced his grief. He would process all of this later, he knew. And it would take a shit ton of whiskey to feel normal again.

Several minutes later, Red helped him get to his feet. Hunter wiped his eyes on his sleeve and told Red that he was okay. He needed to see the scene.

This was his gift, and if there was anyone who deserved his full attention, it was his beautiful wife, Karen.

Red, also, knew that Hunter needed to get in and see the scene. No one in the country could do what Hunter could do at a crime scene.

Hunter shook himself, mentally and physically, and felt the effects of the several whiskeys that he had consumed before getting his happy ending earlier in the night fade away, and he got ready to do what he did best.

He walked with Red up to his front patio. He purposely didn't think about Karen's plants on the front steps, or the rocking chairs that Karen had hand-sanded and painted, restoring them to their original shape just last fall.

He purposely did not look at the home as his home, or the life that he had shared with Karen over the last thirty years.

He put it into his mind that he would think of all of that later, but right now, he had to access the scene like all the others. All the thousands of others.

He was suddenly weary in his soul, but he put that behind him as well.

A technician he knew from the office handed him gloves, booties, and a dry paper suit so he did not contaminate the scene. He could hear Red off to the side, arguing with the brass about letting Hunter in to see his slain wife's body.

But everyone knew the absolute truth here. Hunter was the best at this.

If anyone could turn this scene into the truth of what had happened, it was Dr. Hunter O'Connor, PhD. This was his gift from God ¯and how he fucking hated it.

He walked through his house, not noticing the surroundings. The lights were strongest from the rear of the home, and he knew that she was on the sun porch. She would be surrounded by her plants, and she loved nothing more than her plants, he knew.

He felt a tear fall down his face, but he brushed it aside. Later, he thought.

Police officers and FBI agents were moving out of his way as he walked through the spotless kitchen. He knew that their presence in the home meant that it had been swept for evidence already, and there was nothing in the home proper.

It meant that the scene was relegated to the sun porch, and that was nice of the killer. Made his job easier, he thought. A tight scene.

But as he opened the screen door leading down to the porch, he stopped midstride. Fuck, he thought as he saw the scene.

This was not going to be easy at all.

His wife's body was obviously staged. She was laying in the middle of the porch, but she looked asleep. At first Hunter couldn't wrap his mind around what he was seeing, but then it hit him. She was half-naked, but not her bottom half.

If the killer had raped her, he had put her slacks, her shoes, and her socks back on the way they had been while she was alive. From the waist down, she looked serene, and her legs were placed together, straight out from her body, toes pointed skyward.

But from the waist up, it was a completely different story.

His wife had been thin, beautiful, and had aged gracefully. He had always been proud of how much she kept herself in shape, and her body looked quite the same at the age of fifty-one as it had when they had met when she was eighteen.

So it was quite a shock to see her upper body exposed for the whole world to see. As Hunter stood on the top concrete step leading down into the porch, the other members of the scene re-creation team moved to the sides, allowing him space to see his wife completely.

He couldn't move, not until his curiosity overtook his horror at seeing his wife so exposed. What caught his curiosity was what was written on her chest, and what was sticking out of her mouth.

He finally moved. He stepped down to the concrete floor of the sun porch, and hardly noticed the team shuffling to get out of his way. The porch was large, decorated with white wicker furniture and all of the many plants of which Karen had been so proud.

He had often joked to her that she was becoming Tom Bombadil, the green thumb caretaker of the Olde Forest, from the *Lord of the Rings* books.

He walked over to his prone wife's body and looked down at her for the last time. He knew in his heart that after this, he wouldn't be able to look at her beautiful face again.

But he needed to do his job, and he needed to do it the best that he could. So, he shook off the malaise, and squatted down next to her.

The pictures had already been taken of her body, so he could study them later, but the photographer was the only one who had stayed behind. She was going to take pictures as Hunter removed the piece of paper peeking out about an inch from her slightly parted, blue lips.

But it was the number on her chest that really made him think in circles. In large, broad, and black lines, the killer had written the number "120." It was emblazoned across her upper chest, right above her breasts. It was harsh, and stood out starkly against her pale, white skin.

Just those three numbers. "120."

The numbers were written right below the ugly black marks around her neck. A little blood had welled up in the black marks, and Hunter knew exactly what the marks were. She had been garroted.

The fucker had snuck up behind her and strangled the life out of his wife with a metal wire that had bit into her soft, perfect neck. Hunter couldn't think about her death at that moment. He had to finish processing the body. He had to get the answers only he could usually find.

He still couldn't make himself look at her face, but he knew that it would be slightly bloated, and bloodless. He didn't want to see her blue eyes, bloodshot from the strangulation. He couldn't stomach that.

So, he asked over his shoulder for a probe. The team knew that he usually asked for tools like a surgeon on a scene, and they were usually ready with what he needed. This was by far not their first rodeo.

He was handed a long-handled metal probe from the photographer, and he used it to pry open her lips enough to remove the paper there. The flash started going off as he pulled out the paper.

It distracted him momentarily, but when he saw what the paper was, the surroundings vanished from his sight. And as he pulled the yellowing paper from her mouth, where it had been wadded up and pushed in by the killer, his heart quickened.

He was suddenly more confused than he had ever been at a scene of a murder.

He pulled out a single yellowed page from the Bible. He smoothed it open and saw a single highlighted verse on the back of the page when he turned it over in confusion. He saw that it was the first page of the *Book of Revelations*.

The verse that had been highlighted was in the first chapter. The killer had underlined the verse in black ink. Hunter saw that it was verse 18.

Hunter got a sudden ache in his gut when he read it. He knew what it meant.

And as he looked at the numbers written so boldly across his deceased wife's upper chest, he knew what it all meant.

It meant that this was just the beginning.

"I am the living One; I was dead, and now look, I am alive for ever and ever! And I hold the keys of death and of hell."

Chapter 8

Three could not stop vomiting. He felt like everything he had ever stuck in his mouth and swallowed had come up in the last two hours. And the stomach cramps!

But he wondered, as he dry heaved into the RV bathroom, if he deserved it.

The RV hit a bump in the road as it traveled south, and Three was thrown off balance in the small bathroom, hitting his head against the wallpapered wall behind the small portable toilet.

He straightened up, wiped his mouth with the hand towel on the sink, and walked out to the bedroom at the rear of the RV.

He sat on the edge of the full-size bed and put his head in his hands.

He remembered back to two days earlier, when the trio had approached the Capital District on I-95. Along the three-day trip north, Five had put his computer sleuthing powers to work, picking out just the right person for sacrifice number 120.

Looking through old news clippings and hacking into unauthorized databases of police files, they had found their Subject #120.

Hunter O'Connor.

Before Three was to set off, Four asked him, once again, why 120 victims.

"Because, the proven number of victims of the current highest body count of an American serial killer belongs to Samuel Little, who confessed and was linked to over 103 victims. If we aim for 120, over a period of ten years, than we will hold that spot, and the public, knowing all along the total we are shooting for, will have unspeakable fear instilled," Three had explained.

And, as he looked over the dossier of Mr. Hunter O'Connor, he knew they had the perfect first victim.

It looked like old Mr. Hunter had been a bad boy when he was a young FBI special agent in the Washington DC office. According to unreleased FBI files from deep in their Internal Affairs Office, Mr. Hunter had been on the firing end of a government-issued firearm which had taken the innocent lives of two black teenagers in southeast Washington DC in 1985.

The resulting investigation had been practically swept under the rug, with even a high up Co-Deputy Director signing off that the killings of the two youth was "a negligible byproduct of the gang warfare going on in SE DC and Special Agent Hunter

O'Connor was justified in his actions, protecting the lives of himself, and his partner."

After that, Mr. Hunter had steadily, and quite swiftly moved up the ranks in the FBI, earning himself quite a reputation as a crime scene analyst, and earning medals and commendations along the way.

To the trio in the RV heading north, Mr. Hunter was the perfect candidate to make their initial public statement. He was a part of the broken system, a rather big part, and he deserved retribution for what he had done.

There had been no marches, no protests, and no memorial plaques for the two teenagers that Mr. Hunter had gunned down in cold blood. So, Three was going to perform the only memorial that would serve to make a difference.

But to Three, it wasn't quite that simple. He was going to be taking an innocent life, and it wrecked him inside. He prayed that he would grow callousness, or at least some numbness, as the months went by, and the plan was brought into fruition.

As the trio pulled into a KOA Campgrounds in northern Virginia, Three was determined to accomplish the first step of the plan, but inside, he didn't like it one bit. He shook off the horror of what he was about to do and prepared to accomplish step one.

Three packed everything he would need into a black duffle bag, made sure that the communication equipment he took with him was in perfect working order, and as he waited for a car to pick him up from the gas station that he had walked to, he radioed to the RV, making sure the connection was secure.

Five answered in his ear, giving him comfort that he wasn't alone in this, and Five further verified that he had finally hacked into the Alexandria public video system, and the police response database.

As Three rode in the back of the non-descript car into downtown Alexandria, he kept his dark sunglasses on, his hat low on his head. It wouldn't do to leave any kind of evidence behind. He would take the car about three miles from Mr. Hunter's home, and walk the rest of the way, finding a place to change into his tactical uniform on the way.

The car pulled up in front of a Starbucks near Oldtown, in Alexandria, off of Route 1.

All financial transactions for the car ride were done electronically, on his cell phone. He left a normal tip for the driver, knowing that assured he wouldn't be remembered, even if somehow the driver was found out.

Three glanced around at the semi-busy street, and looked down at himself, making sure he didn't stand out. He was wearing blue jeans, a polo shirt under a black pea-coat, and sensible tennis shoes. Nothing that stood out. He shouldered the black duffle bag, and started walking, making sure to keep his head down.

Five would track him on public video, whenever he crossed in front of any cameras mounted high on poles, or sides of buildings. Three made sure to know his surroundings, and to watch the eyes that could be watching him.

He made it into a residential section without causing notice. The day was just chilly enough in early October that most people just kept their heads down to go wherever they were going. Three used that to his advantage.

And then he was in the alley behind the O'Connor home. He glanced around, making sure no one was near. Five verified, when asked, that there were no public, or private video equipment in the alley. It was secluded, and the tree cover made the alley a deep, shadowy pathway between close quarter housing.

But Three was always careful, and he moved swiftly to get into position. He would have to be still for several hours, and he was not looking forward to the discomfort of his wait.

He disrobed, exposing the skintight seal-skin suit under his clothing. He took his civilian clothing off quickly, placing the shirt, pants, and jacket into another, smaller, black duffle bag he pulled out of the black, non-descript duffle bag he had carried in public.

He stored the clothing deep in a hollow of a dead tree trunk several meters down from the back fence of the O'Connor home. He would retrieve it later.

He moved swiftly back to his staging area behind the O'Connor's fence, and pulled the remaining items from the black duffle. The biggest item was a fall leaf-colored gilly blanket.

The camouflaged cover would allow him to wait patiently in the O'Connor's large, tree covered back yard for the proper moment to perform the deed he was here to do. He swallowed hard with that thought, but he was here, and nothing would stop it now.

Once, while he was preparing his equipment, a car drove slowly by the mouth of the dark alley, sun glinting off its windshield. Three made himself as small as he could between several trees, but the car went by, and no others came by while Three was preparing.

He was shaking slightly, and he knew what was at stake. It wouldn't do to be caught on the first victim. He had too long of a row to hoe to get to where he wanted to be, ten years from this day.

He slid his arms into his tactical harness, 9-millimeter Glock resting on his right thigh. The heavy canvas harness gave him access to several pockets and slings that allowed for equipment storage and the silent removal of things he would need, and several things he hoped he wouldn't need, including the firearm. But you prepared for the worse, he thought.

He slid the tight seal-skin hood over his head and placed the advanced optic goggles over his eyes. He was sweating inside the seal suit, but the moisture wicking material made him comfortable while keeping him cool. He was ready. As ready as he would ever be.

He slipped into the back yard of the O'Connor home silently, and stealthily. The intel they had on the couple who lived alone in the large colonial home was that neither would be home in the late afternoon of October 13.

Three would have to wait for almost fifteen hours, without moving. While he would be lying prone, waiting for the proper time to accomplish his goal, Five would keep him entertained by speaking in his earpiece, reading books, playing music, anything else to pass the time. Three simply had to not be found out.

And he couldn't move the entire time.

He moved quietly and speedily through the large, shadowed back yard, and moved close to the house. The trees grew right up close to the home, so he was able to mark a place amongst a pile of dead leaves, in an even more shadowy corner of the privacy fenced-in yard, and lay down prone, covering himself with the fall colored, multi-leaved gilly blanket.

He made himself comfortable, and checked his forearm mounted mini tablet to ensure that the small, unobtrusive, wireless cameras that he had first placed on the back fence and close to the sun porch of the home were in working order. It was how he would watch his surroundings, while he was blind under the camouflage blanket.

Three lay there for the rest of the thirteenth, overnight, and into the morning of the fourteenth. He watched the couple arrive home separately the evening before. He watched as the middle-aged Hunter and equally aged Karen interacted woodenly in the kitchen, preparing dinner, and eating at the dining room table together.

Hunter watched through the wireless camera while the couple ate at separate sides of the table in the lit-up windows of the dining room, but looking at their cellphones the entire time, hardly talking. And he watched as different lights in the home went on, stayed that way for a little while, and then went out.

57

He could almost see the domestic lives of the couple in their evening and then nightly movements. At a quarter to 11, the final light in the home was extinguished, and there was no further movement until 6 am on the 14th.

During the cold night, Three was rather comfortable under the large gilly blanket. He ate a snack of a protein bar and drank from the small flask of water he had strapped to his left side. He didn't leave any evidence behind, and he didn't move.

At one point in the night, as his earpiece was silent, and the night around him was serene and heavy, his eyelids drooped, and the only thing that woke him from a surprisingly fitful sleep was Five asking him to check in at 0500.

Three jerked awake, silently thankful for the deep darkness he lay in, and he quickly checked the cameras to ensure no movement anywhere around him. A dog barked in the distance, and he could slightly hear traffic from somewhere off to the south.

But around him, all was still and quiet.

It was October 14th, and this day had always been hard on Three. He said his traditional silent prayer for the loss of his best friends when he was thirteen years old, and mentally prepared himself for what was going to happen that day.

The sooner he accomplished his task, the quicker they could all head home for a month. The only thing that got him moving that day was focusing on the task being finished, and the RV driving back south that afternoon.

He watched the morning activities of the couple in the house. Mr. Hunter was out of the house by 0730 hours. He knew that he would have a very small window of time to accomplish what he was going to do before the Mrs. left for the day as well.

He couldn't risk staying in his location for another day. He already had to urinate, and he knew that that was impossible for a little while longer. His stomach was also rumbling, and he knew that his nerves would overtake him if he focused too much on the task.

So, instead, he kept the memory of One in his mind, and the first time that he had kissed her.

She had tasted like strawberry lip gloss, and the memory was both sad, and made him angry. The life they should have had together...he thought, not for the first time.

Instead, he was laying on damp ground, under a camouflaged blanket, about to murder an innocent woman. He shook himself, and watched as Karen O'Connor ate breakfast, and prepared for her morning chores.

He watched as she filled up the metal watering can she would bring out several times to the sun porch, to water her plants.

On the third trip, Three started stretching his legs, moving his arms around him as he still lay prone. He would get to the sun porch door in fifteen seconds, he would approached her in five seconds, and a minute and a half later, she would be dead.

As the woman filled the water can back in the kitchen for the fifth time, Three rose from his prone spot, hearing his knees pop with the movement.

He stood up, out of the woman's sight, and dropped the gilly blanket. He would have time to come back to it. As the woman walked down the three concrete steps into the sun porch for the final time, Three ran for the screen door leading into the porch.

He was at the door in less than thirteen seconds by the counting in his mind. He threw open the door, thankful that it was silent.

Within three seconds, he had the garrote up in front of him, wooden handles easy in both of his hands.

He moved silently behind the woman, hearing her humming as she bent forward, watering a large green plant. She never turned around as Three wrapped the wire around her throat.

As he pulled the wire tight, he performed a movement that he had practiced over and over.

He put both handles in one hand, right behind her neck as she jerked up, and in less than a second, he spun his back to hers, reaching his other, empty hand to his full one, and grabbed the other handle.

He was much taller than the small woman, and as he bent forward, both hands back over his shoulders holding the handles of the garrote, he pulled her off of her feet, and against his back.

He could feel her feet kicking, but her hands were not able to reach him, and he didn't have to watch her die.

He stared at the concrete floor in front of him, until she stopped kicking, and he waited an additional minute, not moving at all, until he knew that she was gone.

He stood up, letting her weight pull the garrote from his suddenly numb fingers. Her body crumpled behind him, and he still couldn't look at her.

He still had to prepare the message, but his stomach was threatening to empty on his shoes. He quickly reached into a hip pocket and pulled out the vomit bag that Four had pressed on him before he left the RV the day before.

He had laughed it off when Four mentioned the bag, but he was eternally grateful at this moment to have something to vomit into. He couldn't leave any trace behind, and vomit was the worst thing to leave.

So, he opened the large bag, emptied his soul into it, and when he was finished, he sealed it back up, using the built-in glue tabs. When he composed himself, and checked his forearm tablet, saw that nothing was disturbed in his immediate surroundings, he finally turned and looked at what he had done.

The woman's body lay at his feet where it had dropped like a sack of meat, and he put what he was doing out of his mind as he set about staging the scene. The entire time, he had kept his tactical gloves on, and his head covered. There was to be no risk of exposure, of witnesses, and he had to control the entire environment until he exited it.

He pulled her surprisingly light body over to the middle of the sun porch. The light from the early sun poured in through the greenhouse windows surrounding him, and he was glad for the light. It made him feel slightly better doing what he was doing.

His thoughts scattered as he prepared the woman's body to be found, and he thought more about his exit than what he was doing.

He assumed her husband would find her body later in the day. And if not him, then anyone else who happened by. He didn't go into the house, and he didn't leave tracks.

So, it was up to fate how this woman would be found. But he knew, from what her husband did for a living, that he would certainly be a part of securing the scene.

And so, Three left the prick a message.

Taking off the woman's shirt, he stuffed it into the empty pocket against the small of his back that was there for that purpose. He made sure to get some of the woman's blood on it first, however. The ligature marks around her neck were deep, and a line of blood spilled onto her pure white skin.

As Three removed her shirt he embarrassingly looked away for a moment. He did not want to sully this moment by getting aroused by the woman's exposed breasts. She had not yet put on a bra, and he didn't want to spoil the respect that this woman deserved for being an innocent in his plan.

But he passed his own little test for himself by being able to look back at the woman's body and felt nothing.

He breathed out a breath he had been holding. He quickly finished his work, writing the large numerals on her upper chest, and finished by balling up the Bible page that he had previously marked upon, and gently pushed the wadded paper into the woman's mouth.

He didn't like this part, but it was essential. He reached between her teeth and pulled a corner of the paper out, so that it would be seen first.

All of the supplies he had needed for this message had been in various pockets on his tactical harness. His mind went to Batman's accessory belt in the comic books he had loved as a child. But the memory did not bring a smile.

Three stood up and looked down at the scene.

It was exactly as the team had planned out. He looked around at the porch and made sure he had left nothing behind. Even microscopic evidence wouldn't do. That was why he had not removed any part of his coverings, exposing any part of his skin or body.

Under the seal-skin suit, he was completely shaved of body hair, but even skin cells could be collected. That just wouldn't do at all.

He took the time to ensure there was no evidence, based on his own training in crime scene science. He was sure that he didn't know all of the tricks and technology at the FBI's disposal, but he left nothing to chance.

Except for some leaf fragments near the door, which would be collected and analyzed to show they had come from the back yard of this home, there was nothing else to show that he had been on the porch.

Even his footprints would show nothing. The soles of the tactical boots he wore were solid rubber, with no distinguishing marks. The footprint analysis would just show solid prints, and the only information they could gather from the boots was his shoe size, which was a very typical size twelve.

He had made the soft rubber soles himself, so the purchase of these specific boots could not be traced.

Satisfied that he left nothing behind him, and no noise had been made to bring witnesses, he silently moved back out into the back yard, and gathered up his gilly blanket, and the cameras he had placed in three places around the backyard.

He scattered his resting place with dead leaves and knowing that he couldn't make it look perfectly like no one had been there, he at least tried.

He moved back into the alley and repeated the movements he had made the day before, but in reverse. He placed his civilian clothes back over the seal skin suit, and walked back out of the neighborhood, taking a different route this time.

Two and a half miles further on, he caught back up with the RV at a predetermined location across from Reagan International Airport, with no witnesses and no cameras.

Within a half hour, the RV was on I-95, heading south, and Three was vomiting his guts out in the bathroom.

He lay back on the bed as the RV bumped along, and Four and Five rode in the front, talking quietly, giving Three his space. They hadn't asked details, and they knew that Three would talk when he was ready.

At the Virginia-South Carolina line, they stopped for gas at a roadside gas station that was so large, more than twenty semi-trucks stood in line to gas up. Ensuring their features wouldn't be seen on cameras, Four and Five got food for the road, filled the RV gas tanks, and let Three hide in the bedroom.

They were back on the road in a matter of minutes, and nothing was said until they pulled into the now-abandoned looking plantation home of the Higgsby Estate, a day later.

Three had slept much of the trip and had not eaten a thing. Four and Five knew that they would need to be there and support Three over the next week, and that in a few short weeks after that, Three would have to do it all over again.

There was no end in sight for the plan, but they were all determined to accomplish what they had promised they would finish.

But over the next several days, it was apparent that it would eventually turn Three into someone that the pair hardly recognized. And by Christmas, they could tell that Three wanted it all to be done with.

With each consecutive month, Three would retreat back into his own version of hell for the week or two it took the friends to pull him out.

They just had no idea how all of this would end, and who and what Three would be when it was finally over, many years from now.

It would be weeks before Three would smile again.

And as the two friends watched Three, even when he would rarely smile or laugh, they knew that something had broken inside of him in Virginia.

The couple would look at each other in these moments and realize that they never would have the old Three back.

Chapter 9

Hunter felt like he had been hit with a dump truck. Not *by* a dump truck, but *with* a dump truck. There was a marked difference, he knew.

His head was splitting, and his eyes were crusted over. As he came slowly awake, he could feel the soreness in his body, and he realized that he was laying on something very hard and uncomfortable.

He could hear distant, muffled voices. He reached up with one hand, to rub the crust from his eyes so that they would open, but his hand wouldn't move independently from the other one.

What the hell, he asked himself mentally.

Then he realized that that his hands were handcuffed together.

Shit, he thought.

So he used both hands to rub the crustiness from his swollen eyelids. He opened them both gingerly, trying to look around. When his blurry vision became sharp enough, he suddenly and overwhelmingly wished that he hadn't woken up at all.

He was in a jail cell. He knew that fact instinctually, without needing more information for his foggy mind than the concrete walls and the hard bench under him. He slowly raised to a sitting position on the scarred, wooden bench, and again felt like his head was going to explode.

He also almost lost whatever was in his stomach. He couldn't remember the night before, or if it was even morning. There were no windows where he was sitting.

He heard the voices again, arguing outside of the steel door closing him away from the world. He recognized one of the voices. It was Red. That was not good, Hunter thought to himself as he gathered himself together and looked down at what he was wearing. A suit, for some reason. His gray suit.

And it looked like hell. Like he had, in actuality, been hit with that dump truck.

He needed water for the horrible taste in his mouth. A toothbrush and toothpaste would be better. Hell, a shot of whiskey would disinfect his mouth perfectly.

His stomach almost flipped over again at the thought. This was turning out to be the shittiest hangover he had had in a very long while.

Karen will be pissed, he thought, distractedly. Oh shit. Karen. It all came back to his foggy mind again, but he shed no tears. He felt completely dried out, and there was no moisture in him for tears. He was a desert unto himself, he thought.

A desert that was full of hot sand and glaring hatred.

He didn't have time to think about that anymore, because the scraping sound of the key in the steel door jarred him from his mental aerobics.

The door swung open and his partner walked in, wearing a jogging suit and a very unpleasant look on his face. Red instantly railed at Hunter. In a very loud voice.

Hunter winced as he started speaking and winced again at each activity Red described from the night before.

"You drove drunk, wrecked your car into a tree, almost killed some late evening walkers, and then passed out in the middle of Constitution Avenue, almost getting yourself killed, Hunter," Red said to him, hands on his hips and glaring down at his longtime partner.

"Alright, alright. Not so loud, please. I need some water," Hunter said up to his friend. Red sighed heavily and reached down and pulled Hunter to a standing position.

"And you smell like vomit and shit, man. I know it's been a hard couple of weeks, but Hunter, we have to clean you up. You aren't the dead one here," Red said, none too gently.

One thing Hunter knew about Red: the large man was never gentle. He said what needed to be said, regardless of how it made other's feel. Hunter could always count on his best friend to cut to the chase. Painfully, most of the time.

"Listen, Hunter, the people upstairs want you in rehab. At least long enough to dry out," Red told him as he walked Hunter out of the holding cell, and down to the front desk to gather Hunter's belongings.

They stopped at a metal water fountain in the hallways so that Hunter could get some water into himself. After wiping some spilled droplets off of his chin, and standing again, he felt a little better. His mind was starting to un-fuzz itself.

Hunter assumed his friend had soothed things over with the DCPD, and that he could go on his way with a promise to clean up his act. He waited for the tongue lashing from the desk sergeant, but it never came. Nor from any of the uniformed officers they passed along the way.

They all just looked at Hunter with lightly disguised pity and remorse. He certainly didn't need that shit, but he was in no position to argue and complain. He had fucked up royally, and he knew it.

"Alright, alright. I'm assuming St. Joseph's?" Hunter asked Red as they walked out of the front doors of the police headquarters in Downtown D.C, the sun sending rusty nails stabbing into Hunter's eyes. He looked over at Red who just nodded.

"Right now?" He asked. Again, Red just nodded.

Hunter nodded in return, resigned.

He knew he needed help. He couldn't much remember the last two weeks. Not since they had bagged up his wife's body and took her to the morgue. Hunter didn't even remember the funeral.

That fact alone made him realize that he needed to dry out, and today was as good a day as any to start. His genius mind went through all the information he knew about medically assisted detox. He knew he was in for a really bad three or four days.

He squared his shoulders in the front seat of Red's new Cadillac SUV and nodded again. He was ready. Already, he knew that vengeance and finding the bastard who had killed Karen would give him purpose and clarity. He had moped around long enough.

He was starting to get pissed off, but the nagging feeling in the back of his mind that he needed a drink was still there.

That was the problem, Hunter thought for the remainder of the ride across town to the Catholic Recovery Center, known around town as St. Joseph's.

Hunter had called it correctly. Over the next several days, he suffered horrible withdrawal and his body almost didn't handle it. Hunter felt, more than once, that his body had betrayed him.

His heart was weak from the effort, and Hunter almost lost the challenge a couple of times.

But Hunter had always been a fighter, and something as small as alcoholic recovery wouldn't stop him. Not now that he had a purpose again.

So, he suffered the night sweats, the body tremors, the nausea, and the overwhelming weakness. Once he was through the worse of it, the next step was intense therapy, twelve steps, prayer time, and exercise. He learned yoga in two days. He learned meditation in one.

He found it impossible to clear and quiet his mind, which had been a lifetime struggle for him. He had accepted that fact years ago. But as his mind cleared as close to complete as he had ever had it, he was able to start focusing on what he needed to focus on.

He contacted a young agent in the office and had the case files for his wife's murder brought to him. He might as well use his downtime to do some work, he thought, laughing to himself.

But as he looked over the reports, and studied the scene pictures, he lost any humor he had found. The murderer was a professional. There was absolutely no trace of him anywhere at Hunter's home.

The techs had found a spot in his backyard that looked like where the guy had waited for the proper time. That meant that the guy was clean, meticulous, the scariest kind of killer, to Hunter's estimation.

There were a thousand more items to study in the reports, Hunter knew, but he couldn't get a good read on the perp from them all. It had been clean, professional, and dispassionate.

Two weeks later, he checked himself out of the hospital, and felt like a new man, with a new purpose. He had even lost fifteen pounds, but that was due more to the fact that he didn't eat during the detoxing. His body couldn't handle it. But Hunter felt lighter, faster, and ready to fight.

As he walked down the front steps of the hospital, with Red waiting for him at the curb, Hunter had a new spring to his step, and he was ready to get started on his wife's case in more detail.

Red's first words to him almost made him explode in sudden emotion. Later, he couldn't figure if it were positive or negative emotion, but he suddenly felt slightly overwhelmed. He gulped visibly and listened to the details.

"He killed again. Same set-up. Not strangulation this time, though. It was a stabbing. But there were definite similarities." Red explained. "The victim, a sixty-nine-year-old pediatrician, had a big number '119' on his chest. And a Bible page shoved in his mouth," Red said as Hunter got into the front seat of the SUV.

Hunter wasn't happy that someone else had lost their life, but he was excited because solving a single murder was very difficult, but solving two, done by the same person, was much easier. You could start comparing things. Start seeing the bigger picture. Start seeing the murder's intent.

The job just got a little easier for Hunter, and he was impatient to start the challenge.

"When?" he asked Red.

"Last night. Arizona. Little town called Snowflake. And Hunter, it was exactly one month since Karen. November 14. I think the perp has an MO," Red said.

"The date, and the countdown numbers. And those damn Bible pages."

Hunter wondered why that detail seemed to bother the big man. But Hunter agreed with the fact that this seemed to be the killer's modus operandi.

70

Two deaths, half the country apart didn't make for a serial killing spree, but you could draw some conclusions from the similarities.

His mind began moving at a million miles an hour while Red expertly wove through traffic. Hunter directed Red to take him home and gave him three hours to meet at Reagan Airport. They were headed to Arizona. He didn't need the powers that be upstairs at the Hoover Building to give him permission. Everyone knew that this was Hunter's case. And Hunter hadn't lost one yet.

"One last thing," Red said, as he dropped Hunter off at his home.

Hunter turned and looked impatiently at his partner. The sunlight was glinting off of the sunglasses that Red wore, and the white patches on his face and neck looked paler than normal, Hunter thought.

He waited for his partner to speak. Then the words chilled Hunter to his soul.

"The media linked the two deaths by the details someone leaked to them. And that did not make anyone at the office happy," The big man said, sighing while he said it.

"But it gets worse, Hunter. The media jerks gave him a moniker," Red told him. Red's voice dropped an octave.

"They are calling this guy '*The Preacher.*'"

Chapter 10

"What do you mean, a cult following?" Three asked Five.

Ever since they had returned to Alabama from Arizona three days prior, Five had been all over the internet, looking for signs of Three's first two targets.

They had been trying to establish an ideal of impartiality early on, but one in which they would have to mix up, fortunately. The team certainly didn't want to be celebrated for their actions. Not when they were trying to spread fear to every corner of the country.

"Just what I said. There is a small but growing group of followers that are singing your praises. They are calling you '*The Preacher*,'" Five said, as he pounded the keys of his laptop.

He had a sideways smile on his face, but Three couldn't bring himself to smile, and had not for a while now. He also missed Four, who had to make an appearance with his family for an early Thanksgiving.

Four had made excuses to be with Five during the actual holiday, but showing up for the entire family beforehand maintained the cover story.

Three got out his own laptop, sat down at his father's desk, well, his desk now, he thought, and started a Google search for *The Preacher*.

There were hundreds of hits, and the top link was a website called DeadX.net. Somehow, the moderators of this particular site had gotten copies of several pages of the local police reports in both Alexandria and Arizona.

Three sat for most of the morning reading about himself, and his dastardly deeds. Luckily, the police had very little to go on, and it looked like, as far as he could tell, that they had not the first clue who he was, or where he was going to strike next.

That would become much more important as the plan unfolded. They had to be careful to not establish any kind of pattern at all. But they also knew that the lack of a pattern was a pattern in itself. Like the old montage, failing to make a decision *is* a decision.

Three was convinced that for maximum effectiveness, this entire country had to live at a level of fear that would enact change. That meant that every citizen had to think that they would be next.

As Three read through the DeadX website, he saw the bio for the moderator and creator. Her name was Colbie X. The accompanying photograph showed a short, dark haired pixie of a girl with dark freckles across the bridge of her nose, and Three was slightly smitten.

But there was no way that he could interact with this woman. Even if she was his declared "number one fan." Three certainly realized the juxtaposition of a smart, attractive girl, with an obvious future, being a fan of a burgeoning serial killer. He had heard of it happening to several of the killers that he had studied to understand how the public would react to his actions.

He once again got the feeling in the pit of his stomach that had kept him awake for several nights now. He closed his laptop and let the emotions ride over him.

He once again realized that what he was doing was real, it had actually happened, even if he wanted more than anything to separate and exercise himself from the reality.

He needed to remember why he was doing what he was doing. He would walk out to the cemetery this afternoon.

For now, he needed to remember Arizona. And how he had killed a doctor.

Snowflake, Arizona was a small mountain town in the northeast side of the state. It was surrounded by mountains, hard terrain, and if he had tried to do what he did even a month or more later, the snows would be too deep to get away with it.

But, he had killed the doctor in November, when the wild grasses and the wide swaths of pine trees were just beginning to fall into winter slumber. He could still do what he needed to do, without a trace.

Alexandria had gone so well that he was a little cocky going into this month's day 14.

But he would find that he couldn't control every situation, no matter how hard he tried.

As the trio drove a rented Chevy sedan into Arizona on the 11th, the sky was darkening early, and they had to find a place to stay. Five had already made them reservations at different hotels in the area, but it was at the trusty KOA camp that they ended up.

They had just wanted to throw off any similarities from this part of the plan, and what they had successfully accomplished in Virginia.

Four rented a wooden cabin on the KOA website, and he had checked in alone that evening. He drove the rented car back around to a secluded spot in the woods and picked up Three and Five.

Together, the trio drove up to the cabin overlooking the valley of Snowflake, and Three felt a calmness in the air that he hadn't felt in a while. It settled him enough that he could sleep through the night of the 11th and woke up refreshed on the 12th.

For some reason, the trio had not talked about Thanksgiving this year. Four and Five had been invited to their family's celebrations but had not verified if they would make an appearance or not.

Four had made a promise to show up to the family home at some point after this month's death, if only to further the cover story.

The families for both men still thought that they were living in New York State, as it allowed for same-sex marriage. Little did they know that the couple was right down the road the entire time.

Planning for the fourteenth took up most of the rest of that day. The trio drove to downtown Snowflake, where the pediatrician had his practice.

Dr. Tomas Shipley, MD. A sixty-nine-year-old single white male. He had been accused of several abuses to his young patients over the years but had gotten off scot-free each time. Until the final victim: four-year-old Emmanuel Brown.

A black boy who had been under the doctor's care for sickle cell anemia. The boy had gone through several treatments from the aging doctor and had succumbed to the illness after six months.

An autopsy revealed that the young boy had actually died from a prolapsed and exploded rectum, and the doctor had tried covering up his crime with sutures and a fake cause of death on the boy's certificate of death.

75

Of course, he had gone to prison for twenty years after his crime was discovered, and had been released three years prior to this day, the approaching final day of his life.

He had then gone on to change his name, his history, and his medical license so that he could practice medicine again. This time, in Snowflake, Arizona.

It had been a fluke that Five had found the man in Arizona and had linked him to the murderous doctor from twenty years prior, during the time in between the murder in Virginia, and this new mission, but it had been a lucky fluke.

And a lesson had to be taught, nonetheless.

So, over the next two days, they scouted the doctor's offices, his route home, and his proclivities for stopping at the diner in downtown twice a day.

He gave special attention to the young daughter of a waitress who had had to bring her to work every day and couldn't afford a babysitter.

Three sat at a table two down from the good doctor, and Four sat at a table three down the other end and they both listened as the doctor offered the young waitress a place in his office where her daughter wouldn't be underfoot all day, and could play to her heart's content while her mother worked. The kind doctor would watch over the young girl, and it was "no bother at all, dear."

Thankfully, the world-weary young mother felt an off-putting vibe from the good doctor, and gave various, benign excuses to keep her lovely daughter close by.

The waitress saw herself as a bit of a mystic, and knew a bad person from sight and smell, more than any actual aura he or she gave off. But Three wondered if the young waitress was onto something more spiritual than she realized.

He put it out of his mind and was sickened by the doctor's too-forward advances.

The trio had a plan down, and they would perform it perfectly on the night of the fourteenth. And again, Three didn't know completely if he could do it or not.

This one was going to be a lot bloodier, and a lot more difficult, given the doctor's size and strength. Three knew that he could over-power the older man, but when adrenaline and the flight or fight system kicked in, you never quite knew what one was capable of. Still, Three had a job to do.

On the morning of the fourteenth, the weather did not cooperate. It started raining — big, fat, cold drops that soaked anyone caught in it.

Luckily, Three had prepared his equipment for this eventuality, so he was as prepared as he could be. It was still cold as a witch's tit though, he thought, as he found his waiting spot, in the side street next to the doctor's two-story office building in downtown Snowflake.

It was still quite dark in the pre-dawn, and Three watched the growing light bounce off of the underneath of the voluminous cloud cover that appeared to his eyes as the first rays of false dawn light appeared from the east.

He was quiet, settled, and felt a lot better this time around than he had in Virginia. Maybe it was because this victim was not innocent, but rather, needed a lesson to be made out of him. The righteous anger started in his belly, and as the day went by, with him waiting patiently in the heavy shrubbery at the side of the narrow lane bisecting the buildings around him, the anger grew up into his chest, and finally into his eyes.

By the time the doctor appeared at exactly his routine time of 4 pm, Three only saw red.

Three was dressed all in tactical black, head to toe, and the old man never saw him coming.

The doctor was walking along the bisecting narrow lane just as he had done the previous three afternoons. He was heading for a dinner at the diner around the corner from his offices, and the team had decided that this ambush site was perfect.

There were no windows looking down into the lane from the buildings surrounding it, and at 4 pm, it was already drenched in shadows, let alone the darkness from the relentless rain that had fallen all day.

A dank, dark, dismal day was exactly what the doctor ordered (pun intended), Three had thought to himself throughout the day, as he waited patiently for his opportunity to strike.

The doctor carried an umbrella and wore a light jacket over his usual uniform of a starched white collared shirt, khaki slacks, and black suspenders holding up the pants under his overhanging belly. The doctor was a man who enjoyed overindulgence.

That fact alone made Three feel justified in his next actions. That, and the fact that this doctor, who had made it his life's mission to care and treat small children also used that position to satisfy his base, carnal desires.

So, as was becoming habit on the fourteenth of every month, Three crept up behind the unsuspecting victim, and ended the victim's life in a very dramatic way.

As the doctor walked down the middle of the dark lane, heading for another meal, and another chance to talk the young waitress into letting her beautiful daughter spend the day in the care of the wonderful doctor, Three snuck out of the shadows, holding the blackened blade of a serrated K-Bar knife in his gloved right hand.

The knife was a tactical military issue, and the handle was roughened Kevlar, and wouldn't slip in Three's hand, no matter how much blood spilled out from under it.

He approached the doctor in under three seconds, his soundless boots muted on the wet pavement, and quickly grabbed the shorter, older man around his ample throat with a headlock in his left arm, and in less than a second, plunged the razor sharp, ten-inch blade into the man's body, right under his right armpit.

Three slammed the sharp knife home into the doctor's lung, knowing that blood would bubble up into the man's mouth, and drown out any sound the man could make.

Three had practiced this maneuver several times under his teacher's critical gaze and knew that his muscle memory wouldn't fail him.

He held the dying man from behind for the minute it took for his body to stop kicking, quivering, and shaking.

The heavier doctor's body slumped to the wet pavement with a meaty sound, and Three quickly went to work.

First things first, he thought as he pulled out the K-Bar, placing it, dripping blood, into the side pocket made for this very purpose with a waterproof inner lining.

He stripped the dead man's shirt off and placed it in the large pack on his lower back, and pulled out the black felt marker. It was waterproof and would stand up to days of wet weather, let alone the couple of hours it would take for others to find this body.

He wrote the victim number on the fat man's meaty upper chest. As he finished, he toggled a switch on the small radio on his hip. The other two members of his team would pull the rental car up to the head of the small lane within a minute.

Three then took the Bible page out of a side pocket and opened the man's jaw. He shoved the page into the dead man's mouth, stuffing it in deep. He didn't care if it took longer to find this time. The right people, Three knew, would know to look for it. Even with two victims, it didn't take much to establish an MO.

And Three distractedly thought about who those right people were for the few seconds it took him to finish what he was doing.

He finished up with the doctor's body, positioning it just right, and ran to the waiting car. The entire murder and staging had taken just under three minutes.

There had been no cameras in the narrow lane, and no witnesses. No one had walked by the narrow street during those three minutes, and the heavy rain earlier in the day made assurances that no one would be rambling around the downtown area on an evening stroll.

The threat of the heavy clouds overhead promised the trio that fact.

They all knew that it wouldn't always be this easy, especially when the country became aware of what the 14th meant every month. But this day, it had been easy. And that made everyone feel lighter. And a lighter mood was just what the team needed on this dark day.

And as the team drove out of the small town, with no one noticing, and no one paying attention, Three couldn't get the highlighted verse now stuck in the dead doctor's throat out of his own mind. The words bounced around in his mind, making him feel somewhat better about his actions on this day.

As he undressed in the back seat of the rented car and put on the lounging clothes for the drive back to Alabama, the verse loud in his mind, he felt lighter than he had in several weeks. He smiled, and looked towards the road ahead, the darkening town left behind forever, and the promise of the verse in his mind:

"The people dwelling in darkness have seen a great light, and for those dwelling in the region and shadow of death, on them, a light has dawned."

80

Chapter 11

This asshole was a professional, Hunter thought to himself. He was crouched over the body of the pediatrician, and he wanted a drink. He wanted it more than he ever wanted anything in his life, but he suddenly thought about the way that Karen would look at him with disappointment after a long day at a scene, and a longer evening at a bar, and he swallowed the need.

Barely.

Red was standing behind him in the cold of the November day in some bum-fucked town in Arizona. But Hunter knew that the choice the town was important, somehow. He didn't know why, just yet, but he would find out. He already felt three steps behind the man who had murdered two people, a month apart, and Hunter didn't like the feeling. He had to get ahead of this guy, and he was as sure as shit a man, he thought.

He had to stop the killer counting down any more victims. Who the hell counted down their victims, he wondered. A fucking professional, and one who was personally fucking with him, Hunter thought, starting to get angry.

He purposely kept his wife's face out of his mind. But the need for a cold drink hit him in the gut. He had to steady himself somehow. So, he started focusing on the scene.

Putting the scant pieces he had together, a picture started to form in his prodigious mind. And like his wife last month, the man had laid in wait.

Hunter looked at the bushes next to the doctor's office building and knew that they would find disturbed branches within the tall, dark hedge. He motioned a plain-clothed officer over and instructed the man to check on the area.

Hunter looked up and around him at the buildings surrounding the narrow lane. A perfect ambush site, he thought, distractedly. Like he had thought earlier, this guy was a professional.

There were too many signs of a prepared and determined mind. Everything was thought out, every angle covered, every possibility mitigated. Well, Hunter was a professional as well, and he was going to nail this guy to a cross of his own making.

And, trying to distract himself from needing that drink, he thought about the Bible verse. What the guy was trying to say, he wondered.

Red brought him out of his mind twists.

"The stab wound, Hunter. Clean, neat, fatal within a minute or so. Where would this guy learn that? Medical training?" Red asked, from behind where Hunter still squat over the large body.

Hunter didn't have an answer, but he had seen these kinds of wounds before. Military targets, keeping guards and

82

perimeter sentries quiet as they died. Special Forces in the desert kind of stuff, he thought. If this guy wasn't a medical professional, then he had advanced special ops training.

Hunter wondered if they were giving this guy too much credit. He may be just the luckiest SOB there was. It was too early to know anything concrete, Hunter thought, but damn it if he wasn't intrigued.

There just wasn't enough at either scene to give him anything to go on. There was no information to get them ahead of this guy.

At that moment, Squibb, or at least, that's what Hunter called the kid, ran up to the pair of FBI special agents with a piece of paper in his hands.

"Sir, sir, I've found something on the doctor," the kid said, breathless. Hunter wondered for the tenth or so time why they needed this kid on the team, but then remembered that he couldn't even check his own email without looking at a written out how-to on a piece of paper he kept in his wallet.

This kid knew computers like no one else. They needed him, but he still annoyed the shit out of Hunter. How old was the kid, anyway?

"Alright, kid, alright. What do you have?" Red stopped the MIT-educated young man from stepping in the thick line of blood running from under the body to the center of the lane where it naturally drained down into the shadows of the dark road.

The kid looked down and gulped loudly. Hunter just smiled at him.

"Well, for one, he wasn't supposed to be a doctor no more," the kid said. That got Hunter's attention.

"He changed his name after he got out of prison, and paid for a whole new black-market identification," the kid finished.

"Slow down, what are you saying? You can do that? And this doctor was in prison?" Hunter was intrigued. This could be something.

"Yes sir. I ran his prints and facial scan through the system and got two matches from the California Penal Control. Guy's real name was Randal Gray. Inmate number 14325. He was a pediatrician in San Francisco, and sexually assaulted a kid to death back in the 90s," he said.

"And now he is dead. What's the connection, Red?" Hunter looked up at his partner. Red shrugged.

"How can you connect this guy and Karen?" Red said. Hunter didn't have an answer, but something nagged at the back of his mind. Something was there. He just had to connect the dots. Goddamn he hated feeling three steps behind.

The crowd around the police tape at the end of the alleyway was cold and grumbling, but rubbernecking a crime scene in their little town was worth a few cold hands and feet.

Unbeknownst to the two FBI agents looking over the scene, and the young man trying not to step in anything, one intrepid young woman was standing close enough to hear what they were saying, and she was happily writing her next exposé piece for DeathX in her mind.

This information would put her on the map, figuratively speaking, she thought, bemused.

Unlike the two agents, she had pieced together what *the Preacher* was doing, and she was proud of him. Or her. Now, that was intriguing, she thought.

Colbie romanticized the murders, but she saw the mission behind the slayings, even if the cops didn't. And, as she looked over at Hunter and smirked, she realized the idiot didn't even realize that he, himself, had gotten his wife killed. Evil begets Evil, she thought, as she slipped away, mentally chewing on a new title for the piece she would write later that night.

Colbie was excited to see how far this was going to go, and if she had figured it out correctly, there would be a lot more killing. Perhaps for years, to ride this train all the way to the conclusion, she thought to herself, still mentally writing the piece about Snowflake, Arizona.

She wondered just what that conclusion would be, and if she would be there for it. She was a planner, and a decisive young woman, and she knew that this story was going to change her life.

No one yet had figured out what she had, and she had known for quite some time that something like this was going to happen.

She wondered if the killer was young. It made sense, she thought, as she walked back to her hotel room that she had hastily arranged when she had stumbled across the online travel orders for Hunter and Red.

She had a backdoor access into the FBI's ternary files, and she wasn't going to lose THAT. It was the only way that she could track *the Preacher*.

He had to be young. Only her generation gave a damn about how the world was turning to shit, and only someone in her generation had the balls to do something about it, she thought, arriving back at the shitty motel room.

She booted up her laptop and started typing on her website. She noticed, with pride, that her website counter had skyrocketed over the last three weeks. She was up to over 15,000 views now, but she knew that with the next article and connecting opinion piece, that number would continue to climb.

She was quickly becoming the online expert on *The Preacher*, and she knew that in the months and years ahead, the killer would skywrite his own ideals, and she would be the voice of her generation to make sure that his movement gained the traction that it needed to succeed.

She gave no thought to the people who had died. Or the others who would. Her generation had seen everything on a TV

85

screen, and online, and nothing shocked her anymore. She only cared about the changes that she knew in her soul that *The Preacher* was trying to teach the world.

She would make sure he did his job. And in the years ahead, she really had no idea what that would mean.

If she had, if she had had even an inkling of what was ahead, she would have closed her laptop and immediately moved back home to the parents who loved and missed their little princess.

And since the suicide of her twin sister three years prior, they had known that they had really lost both of their beautiful and gregarious girls. One to an unfair death by her own hand, and the other to an obsession with death and making some kind of difference.

And they also had known that they couldn't save either one of them.

Chapter 12

<ColbieX> *Well, sure, you think he has strayed from his initial mission, but the reality is, I think, he has taken it to the next stage.*

<HH3> *But how can you think this guy is doing a good thing? He is literally killing people, and now the entire country knows, and it hasn't stopped or changed anything.*

<ColbieX> *Harry, you can't think like that! The Preacher is doing what the rest of us in the movement can't do. He is causing change by being the change. It doesn't matter the way he does it, just that it works. My whole army of Deathheads, knows that. The sacrifice of the few for the greater good will always cause great change.*

<HH3> *I still think that you can't hero-ize a murderer. Those people had families. Now it's what, six victims? In six months? When will it stop?*

<ColbieX> *We don't make him a hero in the movement, Harry. We know what he is. But he IS making a difference. I read an article yesterday about how police forces around the country are stepping up changing their procedures to try to partner with their communities rather than fighting against them. What you don't understand is that The Preacher is being the hero we all need, like in Batman, The Dark Knight. Batman wasn't the hero they wanted. He was the hero they needed. The Preacher is making social, systematic changes. Not a lot. Not yet. But it will get better because he will get worse. Mark my words, kid.*

Three logged off his encrypted laptop after that last comment on the chat link with Colbie.

He had started speaking to her off and on for the last two months. He couldn't help it. It had begun with an initial post on her third article. He had written into the heavy chat link earlier than the thousands who were on there now.

So, he had stood out to Colbie, and she had kept up the weekly chats with him. He liked to challenge her on her beliefs that *the Preacher* was doing good, rather than evil.

Her prose on his plan, and what he had been doing the last six months was sometimes the only thing keeping him going.

The rest of the world held him up as the evil that he took himself for, and Colbie's words were like a sweet balm on an open wound.

So, he went against the plan to speak to her. Of course, she had no idea that she was speaking to the real *Preacher*, but the short exchanges had been just what he needed.

He looked around at the hotel suite he was staying in. He had just finished a good seafood dinner, and the plates and silver were still on the cart at the other end of the large suite. He would place it out in the hallway before bed.

He looked down at himself and knew that he needed to get to the gym in the morning. He was still in tiptop shape, of course, but the next bit of the plan called for him to extend his stamina more than normal. His mind wandered.

He had started making it a habit that the last two weeks of every month were spent on vacation. This trip, he was in Key West. He was staying in a suite in the hotel across the street from the Ernest Hemingway House.

The setting sun and the sound of the ocean outside of the double French balcony doors, with the breeze blowing the wispy, white curtains back into his room were all soothing and calming. Colbie's words would help him sleep.

But he knew that this short vacation would come to a close soon, and he would be heading back to Alabama, and meet up with the team for the next mission. Six months in, and he was already weary in his soul in a way that he couldn't put his finger on.

Sleep never helped. Only being able to talk to someone about his actions helped. And he could never tell the truth to anyone about that except the team. And the guys had been great, but he couldn't burden them anymore than he was burdened himself.

But they always made it a habit to open up as much as they could to each other so that they could see this damn thing through. But Three was tired. He was bone tired, and it had only been six months.

The six faces popped into his head as he looked out at the crystal blue waters on the other side of the tan sand outside his balcony. The sun was almost completely set, the sky to the west pink and purple with the bruising that this day brought to it.

That was how Three saw the beautiful tapestry of the sunset. It wasn't an innocent, colorful display of God's grace and mercy on this earth.

It was a bruising of the perfect horizon, slashed with the deeds of humanity on this single day, and all of the evil that humanity brought to each other.

His thoughts turned darker.

It always started with Karen. She haunted him. And then the doctor. But the fat pedophile doctor didn't bother Three as much as the others.

After him, things had changed, and escalated. The next victim had been Sharon King. A young black mother of two in Chicago. That one hurt him more than anyone except Karen.

Then there was Ian Shoto. A middle-aged Chinese national who was working in Silicon Valley on a work visa. He fit the criteria, but he was just an unlucky dart throw on a board of faces.

The team was shooting for variety, throwing off the hunters. And hunters there were. There was no mistaking the law enforcement efforts to catch *the Preacher* before his victim number count came to a close.

After Ian, the team threw off the hunters even more by linking the next two victims as people who had known each other, but who couldn't be connected to Three and the team.

They had been neighbors and co-workers in upper state New York, near the Canadian border in a small hamlet called Old Forge, in the town of Webb, NY.

The small Hamlet was the front door of the Adirondack Mountains, and as spring warmed the air, terror had gripped the small community.

The first victim had been a middle-aged white male who owned a backpacking guide company in Old Forge. His name was Charlie Chapman, and Three had ambushed him on a trail leading up McCauley Mountain on a clear spring morning.

Afterwards, the team had watched the news and the warning reports that were given out on all major news networks now.

They made sure that DeathX had covered the death and read every instance that they could about where the country thought Three would strike next. But they really had no clear idea.

Only that it could be anywhere.

By March, no one could guess that Three would strike right back in the Hamlet of Old Forge. And the victim, this time, had been a teenage girl who had worked with Charlie Chapman as another one of his guides. Charlie had hired her because he lived next door to her family and had watched her grow up with his own teenage daughter.

The victim's name was Crystallyn Smith, and she was seventeen years old.

As Three snuck into her second-floor room, right above where her parents slept, and next door to her little sister, Maryrose, he almost couldn't accomplish the mission for the first time since the plan started.

He stood over her bed, completely dark, not moving, and couldn't bring himself to end the life of the promising young woman. She looked regal and beautiful in the moonlight showing through the skylight above her second-floor bedroom.

But Three shook his head fiercely, and jumped on her, overpowering the sleeping teenager easily, and without a sound. He wrapped his gloved hands around her slender throat, and watched her eyes as she panicked, knowing what was happening.

Her dying eyes haunted him still. At first the terror in them made him weak, and then the resignation at the end made him weep for the next two days.

And just three days ago, in the panhandle of Florida, he had killed a Muslim student at FSU in Tallahassee.

The man's name was Omar Numeri, and he was a naturalized Islamic American from Lebanon. Three had strung him up with six-gauge thin metal twisted cord, raising Omar's body up over the common grounds of the college he had made his family so proud for having been accepted, and attended.

Three had lifted the young man's body quite easily, using a thick, overarching light pole in the middle of the grassy area in the middle of the campus.

It had been four in the morning, and Three knew that at least four separate cameras captured what he had done that night.

First, he had ambushed the student as he had walked back to the dorm from the night job he had had in the library, restacking books, and cleaning. The team had watched the student's routine the last three days and knew his every move. He had been too predictable to survive.

They had planned the next part on purpose. The country needed a visual cue to see that this was really happening. And the video from that night had played thousands of times on the news, internet, and chat groups all over the country.

A grainy video shot showed a tall man, completely dressed in black tactical gear, covered head to foot, and not showing any discernable details, hoist the body of the dead student from a prone position under the light pole, using the wire cord.

The dark clad man used the light pole as a fulcrum and the dead student's body was hoisted twelve feet into the air, and left there, swinging.

Three had looked up at the direction of the camera from which the video had been taken, and stood there, without moving, next to the body for a minute and a half. After which, he had disappeared into the shadows and gloom at the corner of one campus building and the next.

They had achieved what they had set out to do.

The country was a hornet's nest of fear. Every second week of the last three months, the country prepared for the worse, and they received it, every time.

The stakes kept raising, and the team was prepared each time. The hunters, or so the team called the coalition that had been formed to catch Three, still had little to go on, and as they were finishing up collecting all data from one crime scene, the next murder would have them scrambling to get to the next.

The team kept the hunters on their toes, and they never got ahead. Three knew that as the plan mutated and evolved, they would have to get craftier and smarter with their planning and their execution of the plan.

But law enforcement, led by Hunter himself, had scant details to go on. They would keep it that way.

Three walked in bare feet out on the balcony, breathing in the clear, chilly evening air.

The faces were replaced in his mind with a mantra he had been meditating on. It surprised him each month how very easy it was to take a human life. Life didn't mean much to him when he saw it extinguished in a matter of minutes so many times.

The fragility of this life made his thoughts darken, and deepen, constantly. He was in that place again now. The beauty of the setting sun to the west of the keys did nothing to bring him out of his darkness.

And he knew, over the next nine-and-a-half years, that he would live in that darkness. He was only six months into the plan, and he already wished for the release that the final victim would bring him.

He yearned for it, suddenly.

And that yearning brought him enough peace that he could fall asleep, a few minutes later. And as he closed his eyes, his head settling into the soft pillows, the gently breeze wafted over him from the still-open balcony doors, he heard two sounds.

One from without, and one from within: The whispering of the billowing, gauzy, white curtains, blowing in the gentle ocean breeze, and the gurgling sound of the teenage girl's windpipe being crushed under his strong hands around her neck.

One sound soothed him into sleep, and the other gave him a chill down his spine.

And as sleep overtook him, his final thought of the long, quiet day was that he couldn't differentiate which sound was responsible for which sensation.

Chapter 13

The hotel room was hot. Swelteringly hot. Hunter couldn't understand why. But inside, he felt so feverish, he was almost chilled on the outside.

He sat on the edge of the hard mattress, looking at his purchase from the convenience store, which was a block from the hotel. The purchase was what was making him sweat and feel goosebumps all over his arms and chest.

The frustration of the previous year was taking its toll. And he was staring at a bottle of Wild Turkey whiskey, and a six pack of Budweiser.

They were perched on the hotel room's only table, and they looked like demons, staring back at him, whispering into his mind that just one drink wouldn't hurt anyone. He watched a condensation trail work its way down one beer bottle neck. His pupils dilated; his breathing started to labor. He needed the release.

Hunter took his eyes off of the booze, and over at the bedside table. Stacks of manila folders, loose papers, black and white 8x10 crime scene photos looked back at him, whispering his failures back at him.

A whole damn year. Twelve victims. A spring of death, followed by a routine summer of the same, and now they were close to Halloween again, having passed the one-year anniversary of his Karen's murder.

Hunter had hardly stepped back into his home in Virginia. Her ghost was in every picture, every piece of her clothing still hanging in her closet. In the small blood stain that he swore he could still see amongst the dead plants in the sun porch.

He didn't have it in him to remove any of her things, or her smell radiating in that house. So, he stayed on the road, chasing lead after lead, evidence after evidence. Waiting for the killer to make just one small mistake. But the fucker had been perfect, twelve times in a row.

Hunter felt mocked after each senseless slaying. He felt emasculated. Nothing else mattered but *the Preacher*. Nothing. Hunter was going to be the man who brought *the Preacher* down, but so far, he was in the same place today, as he had been a year earlier, and it was that fact, more than any other, that was bringing him down. So far, he had not touched a drop of alcohol, but it was a close, close race, which no alcoholic wanted to lose.

Especially tonight.

He was hearing the whispering from the booze again. It was getting louder, and he was getting more and more thirsty.

And then suddenly, like a guardian angel coming to protect him, Red banged on the hotel room door. He yelled

Hunter's name, and Hunter sprang to his feet, rushing away from his demons sitting innocently on top of the table.

He opened the door a crack, and then further when he saw the look on Red's face.

"They found something. We need to go," Red said to him, impatiently, like Hunter should have already been out of the door.

Hunter just nodded at his partner and asked him for one minute. He closed the door so Red couldn't see what was sitting on the table and rushed over to the side table.

He clipped the leather holster onto his leather belt, feeling the weight of the Glock 9-millimeter reassuringly on his hip. He put on his FBI black service jacket and slipped on his loafers. He was ready.

He opened the door to a still-impatient Red standing in the hallway, waiting for Hunter to appear. He nodded at his partner, and together they walked down to the rental car, and away from the demons waiting for Hunter to come back and try to avoid later on.

They were in Seattle. The trees around the city were turning from dark green to autumn reds and yellows and oranges. But everything was dark as Red drove them to a dirty, rundown part of downtown.

Hunter wished it were daylight, so he could feel peace in the mountains and the trees around the city. Instead, the glaring neon lights, and the passing strobes of streetlights made him feel a depression which had been setting in over the last several months.

In fact, it was that depression that had made him make the convenience store purchase earlier in the evening.

Passingly, he realized that he wasn't even hungry, and he wondered when the last time was that he ate more than a drugstore sandwich or fast food. The depression set in further.

Red pulled up to a rundown home that would be perfect as the façade of a crack house in a crime movie. The yellow siding was bowing in places, and the wooden front porch looked like it could fall with a hard fart.

He sighed as they got out of the car and met a uniformed Seattle PD officer at the foot of the sagging stairs leading up to the dark front door. The officer didn't have much to say. He just looked up at Red and motioned into the dark opening leading into the crack house. Red nodded, and together, he and Hunter walked into the gloom of the home.

The smell hit Hunter first. It was coppery. He knew it was the smell of blood.

He wondered at first why that was. If this were a *Preacher* killing, the timing was off by a week, he usually never let enough blood spill to make this strong of a smell, and, although *the Preacher* could and would strike anywhere with no discernible pattern, this didn't seem quite like his normal scene.

Hunter knew that nothing about this felt right, and he wondered why he and Red were there, if it wasn't a *Preacher* killing.

And then he walked into the kitchen and he knew why they were there. The body was in the same position as a *Preacher* killing, and the number on the body's chest was the same number as the one on the body from last week.

The one that had brought them to Seattle.

"108."

"This isn't right. If this is victim 108, who the hell was the girl down by the train tracks?" Hunter said to the room.

The room was empty besides him and Red, and then he wondered where the crime scene techs, and the lights were. He pointed out their absence to Red.

Red replied. "They wanted you to see it first. This is fucking weird, and against the last twelve months. Everyone stayed away until you got first look," he said.

"Well, people are getting smarter, at least," Hunter answered back.

But the scene wasn't right. And then he figured out why. The footprints. The footprints throughout the kitchen made in blood. *The Preacher* would never be so sloppy.

"This wasn't *the Preacher*. This was a copycat," he said to his partner.

Hunter didn't even want to process the scene. If this wasn't *the Preacher*, he didn't know why he was even there.

He turned away from the dead teenager laying on the white linoleum floor and wanted to get out of the stuffy house.

But then he stopped in his tracks.

He turned back to the body and tiptoed past the red footprints all around the scene and bent down to the body. He saw the red-tinted Bible page peeking out of the boy's mouth.

It had triggered his subconscious, and he just figured out why. He reached into a pocket and pulled out a single latex glove he always kept there. He slipped it on, pried the dead boy's mouth open, and pulled out the rest of the page.

"This page matches the others, Red. We never released the Bible type or age. The red edged page shows it. This killer knows *the Preacher*," he said back at his partner.

Shit suddenly changed. Hunter's mind cleared. He started really seeing the room for the first time. His mind clicked into its familiar pattern of seeing things others couldn't see.

They needed to call in the cavalry. He needed his team of hunters. His hearing became attuned to the sounds around him, and the temptation to have an alcoholic drink or twenty, to feel the numbness it brought, suddenly vanished.

He felt the tingle of the hunt, and he was ready to do what he was born to do. To find the killer.

And he said out loud what he had been waiting to say for over a year:

"This fucker slipped up!"

Chapter 14

"What in the actual FUCK, Four? You just jeopardized the ENTIRE plan!" Three screamed into the face of his best friend, spit flying out of his mouth, hitting Four on his left cheek.

Four absently wiped his face with the back of his hand and looked back down at the ground in abject guilt.

"Why, Four? Why now?" Three calmed down a little. He did not want to cause a split in the team. They were teetering on a cliff's edge as it was, but this was almost unforgiveable.

Four had gone against the plan in Seattle. And there was no way of knowing how this would affect the future, if at all.

Three could almost swear he heard police sirens coming down the county lane towards the abandoned looking family estate again. They were phantom sirens this time, but they stuck in his mind, nonetheless.

Three took a deep breath. He looked over at Five, who was purposely looking down at his keyboard, but not typing. They were following up on the newscast from the night before, which had almost ended everything.

Three looked back over at his other best friend, who looked on the verge of tears in front of him. And then when he saw a tear fall from Four's eye, he calmed down completely. He took Four by the shoulders and hugged him briefly. He led him over to the breakfast table.

They were in the spotless kitchen. The room where his beloved Dottie had cooked for so many years.

Three missed his other family suddenly, and the feelings were sharp, and painful. He took another deep breath, completely calming himself. When he felt sure that his anger was under control, he spoke again.

"Four, I'm sorry. I'm wound tight, and this could end everything. But it's okay. Tell me what happened. Take me back to Seattle," he said.

He sat down and motioned Four to do the same, across from him at the breakfast table where they had shared so many meals and memories. The feelings were there again inside Three, but they were fading. He had more important things to contend with.

Four began, brokenly. And as the narrative unfolded in the spotless kitchen, Four became braver, more sure of himself, and for once, he felt like he had done what he needed to have done. The abject terror from the night before was gone.

"It was the day that you were taking care of the victim in Seattle, and Five and I had that argument, again," he began.

Three glanced over at Five, and saw that Five was listening intently, but was still looking down at his computer screen. His ever-present companion, besides Four.

Three knew the argument. He knew it well. Were they really making the differences they thought they were making, and should they continue? Especially knowing that they could get away scot free, for now.

Prior to the previous night, the police had known nothing, had no leads, and had no way to find the team. The three of them could walk away free, and not look back. And enjoy the money that Three had been making over the last year with the help of Four and Five, and a good international financial strategy.

But the crux of the argument stemmed around the fact that the other two members of the team felt like they weren't doing anything to further the cause. Four, especially, had felt like he wasn't pulling his weight for the Plan. And it was a pressure that was bubbling up in everything that Four did.

"I was in the market, down by the harbor. The smell of coffee was strong. So strong, that I had to get a cup, even though you know I hate coffee," he said.

Four had been just another tourist in the bustling town center in Seattle. The docks were packed with families, and Four was getting some sun, and some peace.

He and his longtime love, Five, had had the same argument that morning, but it had been more heated than usual. This last year had been such an emotionally heavy year, that nothing was the same anymore. And it shouldn't be, but Four didn't know if he could go through the next nine years like this.

And with the changes they were going to be making now, after Year One, his ability to adjust to the pressure was being challenged in ways he had never faced before.

So, they had yelled at each other, and Four had thrown a flower vase against the hotel room wall. That was not good. They couldn't be so conspicuous.

He had stormed out against the accusing looks from his lover. And Three was off, killing a teenage girl.

Four needed fresh air. He needed to DO something.

So, he had found himself at the docks, and as he stood in line at Seattle's best coffee stand, he saw the boy.

There wasn't anything different about the teenage boy. He looked like he was hungry and didn't have any money. Four absentmindedly thought that that fact made people desperate, even dangerous.

But as he turned to the barista to place his order, he heard a scream. He turned with the rest of the crowd around him and saw the teenage kid pull out a gun and put it in the face of an older white man.

The kid demanded the older man's wallet, and once the man reached into his back pocket and handed it over, begging the kid not to do anything rash, the boy did something he didn't have to do.

He aimed the gun, point blank at the man's leg, and shot out his left knee.

Four flinched at the sound of the gun's report, and again at the sound of the older man's screams. The older man fell to the ground, gripping his bloody and mangled leg while the boy ran away. He ran so fast that no one could grab him or was in the frame of mind to know what was really going on.

So, the teenager got away. But Four WAS in the frame of mind to ignore the old man screaming and continuing to bleed on the boardwalk's wooden planks.

Four ran after the kid, forgetting his coffee. Forgetting anything else except doing the right thing.

He followed the kid from a distance. He could hear the sounds of ambulance and police sirens behind him, but they were soon lost to distance and time.

Four watched as the teenage kid moved through the shadows of several alleys, ran across city blocks, and finally disappearing into a dilapidated house.

The home's yellow siding sagged, and the barely white painted front porch groaned in protest as the kid ran through it and disappeared inside.

Four started making plans almost instantly.

He knew that he didn't have a part to play in the events happening that day between Three and Five. They were teaming up to take out the newest victim, and Four was just a lookout, more or less.

He had felt useless for months now. Three was so proficient in killing, he didn't need help with that, and Five could get him out of any situation. So, they made the perfect team, and Four was left with his hands in his pockets, doing nothing.

His anger bubbled up to the surface as he watched the sagging house from across the street. No one came or went from the old home.

Four was convinced after a chilly hour of watching the home that the kid was in there alone. So, he made his move, before he could think of the consequences. Before his better judgement could take over and stop him.

Before he thought about what he was really doing.

Four ran across the narrow street and up the broken stairs of the dilapidated home. He burst through the thin screen door covering the entrance into the home.

Luckily, the kid had left the front door open, and as Four entered the stuffy front hallway, he realized why.

The house was crazy warm and stuffy, even though the outside temperature was around fifty or so. The open front door had let in a breeze.

Four quickly moved into the interior of the home, stepping over broken furniture, not hearing any sounds. He moved to the back of the small house, and into the kitchen. There, he found what he had been looking for.

The kid was alone. He was bent over the table, obviously high on the drugs that he had shot into his arm.

Four saw the evidence of a heroin hit. The blackened spoon, the dirty syringe, the tubal rubber band still around the kid's upper arm.

The teenage boy's head was on the table, and if his eyes were still open, Four couldn't tell.

The boy's face was turned the other direction, but Four could see his chest rise and fall. The kid didn't even know that Four was in the room with him.

Four looked around and saw a pretty normal kitchen for what he had assumed the house was used for. It looked like someone had kept it somewhat clean and used it for its actual purpose.

There was a faint smell of grease in the room, and Four wondered suddenly if someone would come home soon. He didn't want to be here if that happened.

But his anger had not dissipated at all. He still saw the kid shooting out the knee of the innocent man at the boardwalk, and his vision turned slightly red. He needed to DO something.

And as the events of the last twelve months flew through his mind, coupled with the pressure of what the plan was exacting on the team, he needed a release.

He walked around the unconscious boy, examining the room. He opened several kitchen drawers, finding normal cooking implements. He opened one drawer and found several butcher knives. He picked up the heaviest, feeling the weight in his hands. And then he heard a sound.

He spun around, expecting to see a new person standing in the doorway, maybe holding groceries, maybe holding a child.

These visions entered his mind suddenly and were replaced with the image of the young teenage boy holding the black gun from earlier, now pointed at Four.

But the boy's eyes were unfocused. The gun was shaking in his unsteady hands. Four wondered if he was still so high that he didn't see the reality around him.

Four only had a split-second to act before the kid pulled the trigger in a heroin-induced panic.

So, Four moved first.

With his empty left hand, he swiped the gun down and away from where it had been pointed at his face, and with the

105

heavy chef knife in his right hand, he stabbed the kid in the throat.

Blood sprayed out and hit Four in the face and upper chest. The boy didn't make a sound. He didn't make a move for at least three seconds.

His eyes glazed over, and he looked down at the black plastic handle protruding from the front of his throat.

He didn't even bring a hand up to the knife. Four wondered suddenly if the boy even felt the pain of the stab wound.

The teenager's legs simply went out from under him, unsteady as they already were. Four flinched back from the boy's body dropping, and the loudest sound was the wet, bloody gurgling coming from the boys open mouth. His lips moved up and down like a fish dying on dry land.

And then the boy stopped moving all together. The silence grew louder, and Four could hear nothing but the racing pulse of his heart in his own ears.

Four panicked. He didn't know what to do. But he had to get the hot, sticky blood off of him fast!

He ran to the kitchen sink, turned on both handles, and started throwing water onto his face. The blood was in his eyes, his mouth, all down his neck. He felt sick, but he didn't throw up. He was made of harder stuff than that, he thought, as he cleaned the blood off of his face.

He felt in a hurry, but he knew, from Three's stories about how he reacted right after killing a victim, that he needed to slow down, start thinking clearly, and try not to panic. The shock of the event from just a minute and a half earlier started to leave Four, and his movements started to slow down.

He began to breathe a little steadier. He hadn't realized that he had been holding his breath. His body felt heavy and slow, and then suddenly it felt tingly and light. His mind was flooded with endorphins and the adrenaline left him so suddenly that he felt both hot and fast, and slow and heavy.

106

He got suddenly and overwhelmingly lightheaded. Bright light flashed on the peripherals of his vision, and he had to grab ahold of the back of a padded chair to steady himself.

He stayed there, breathing heavily for some time, trying to get back to the scene. When he felt like everything was back to normal, and he had accepted what he had just done, he started to think about how to clean up his presence in the house.

Four looked over at a window that had the sash pulled down. He moved the sash aside and saw that it was dark outside. That was good. Luckily, it was late in the year, and darkness came earlier in the day.

Now he had to cover up his role in the death of the teenager. But he got sudden inspiration. He knew that Three had killed a female teenager that they had been following for three days.

What if, he thought with sudden clarity and spark of genius, they threw off the hunters even more by giving them two bodies, killed by *the Preacher*? And in the same city, nonetheless!

So, Four started looking for a couple of things. First off, he was extremely lucky that he had a wad of Bible pages in one pocket of his blood-splattered cargo pants.

He had shoved them in there after Three and Five couldn't decide on which verse to leave with the young girl across the city. They had picked one out, and Five had shoved the wad of other Bible pages into Four's hands. He had absently shoved them into a leg pocket on the cargo pants and forgotten about them.

Until the moment that he just so happened to need one. Lucky, indeed.

He found a black magic marker in what he assumed was a junk drawer in the kitchen. Luck was with him again when he saw that it still wrote as he rubbed his thumb over the black felt tip.

107

He got to work. He saw that he was leaving tracks from his boots in the blood on the white linoleum floor, but he was cognizant of time, and worried someone would come home to discover him, crouched over the kid's body, writing a black number on the boy's hairless chest.

He wadded up a page from the short stack of Bible pages in his pocket and shoved it into the boy's open mouth. He had to kick the boy's teeth closed around the page and could then barely pull one corner of the page outside of the boy's lips, which were quickly changing color.

He stood up, looking over his work. It was a good approximation of *the Preacher's* work, he thought. He was giddy, and he felt it was in poor taste if he giggled, but he was seeing the situation as comical, suddenly.

He stifled a laugh, and instead, felt a tear fall down his cheek. He was so far out of his element; he was still in shock. But he still needed to move quickly.

His mind cleared enough for him to clean up the way that Three had told him to, if he ever needed to help his best friend clear a scene.

He found cleaning supplies in a hallway closet outside of the kitchen, and his estimation of the use of the home changed once again. He felt like this kid may have had a parent who lived there, but only came around once in a while. Or maybe had been gone for a short time.

Whatever the case, Four wanted out of that stuffy house, and fast. But he had work to do first.

He found a white bottle of Clorox Color-safe bleach, and a spray bottle that held a blue liquid. He smelled it, and knew it was glass cleaner. So, he opened the cap of the bleach, and poured some of it into the glass cleaner. He prayed suddenly that the glass cleaner was ammonia free.

When there was no poisonous chemical reaction, he breathed a sigh of relief, and capped everything up. He walked back into the kitchen and started rummaging under the kitchen sink.

He found a used pair of yellow rubber gloves and slipped them on over his hands. They were too small, but they would work for the time being. Beggars couldn't be choosers, he thought as he turned to the scene in the middle of the kitchen floor.

His bloody footprints were everywhere. He thought he had been more careful. But he hadn't. So, he started spraying every surface with the bleach/glass cleaner blend.

The hard, porous surfaces got a scrub with a moldy smelling sponge from the sink. The hard surfaces and the boy's body got a general spraying.

Four knew that the chemical mixture would wash away any oils, skin cells, or fingerprints he had unknowingly left behind.

As Four cleaned the kitchen, his mind cleared even more. He had the presence to thoroughly clean the crime scene, leaving nothing of himself behind.

He went into the rest of the house, tracing his own steps throughout the home, and cleaned every area that he had touched, or had been. He wanted to make sure there was no physical evidence of his presence. He only wanted to leave behind the scene, and when it was found, to befuddle law enforcement even more.

He was actually proud of himself for what he did. When he left the home a short time later, not seen by anyone in the dark, and leaving nothing of himself behind, he thought that he had gotten away with another perfect *Preacher* killing.

They had arrived back in Alabama, and the newscasters were shouting with the news that *the Preacher* had slipped up and left something behind him that law enforcement could use to finally end the year-long killing spree and social changes happening all over the country.

The team watched the newscaster on CNN describe the evidence that had been left behind at the scene of the murder of a fifteen-year-old boy named Jerome Willingham, a slightly autistic teenager who had lived with his uncle.

And whose body it had taken a week to find, when his uncle had come home from a work trip to Colorado to find him, and the evidence of another *Preacher* slaying.

The evidence was damning, the newscaster said, and law enforcement was closing in on the suspect.

The newscaster pressed the microphone in his left ear with his left hand, the age-old signal that pressing news was coming in, up to the minute, just for the viewers of CNN. The screen switched over to a quickly contrived press conference.

Standing up on the stage, between two flags, was the head of Seattle Police, and the black jacket wearing FBI agents in charge of *the Preacher* Manhunt. Most noticeable to the team was Hunter O'Connor, standing to the right of the police chief, a half-smile on his ugly face.

The police chief was already speaking as the camera's turned on to his press conference.

"...and with this evidence, we are convinced that this murderous ordeal will quickly come to a close," he said to the cameras.

Several reporters started yelling questions, but the chief held up both hands, and indicated to Special-Agent-in-Charge Hunter O'Connor to take over the podium. As the now famous FBI agent stood in front of the cameras of the world, flashes going off in his face, and every sound picked up by the dozens of microphones in front of him, he lifted both hands up, palms forward, stopping the barrage of questions.

He spoke only one sentence, but it was the sentence that stunned the team, sitting in the office of the family home of Three, stomachs crashing to the floor, shock registering on the faces of the three best friends.

And as Hunter clearly spoke the sentence that made the team feel like its doom was upon them, a black-and-white picture of Four, walking down a Seattle neighborhood street flashed from the screen over Hunter's right shoulder.

"We believe the man in this picture is the serial killer known as *the Preacher*, and we know who he is, and where he is at this exact moment."

The crowd in front of the smiling hunter burst into loud shouting, which was ignored by the team in Alabama. They all looked at each other and panicked at the sound of a wailing police siren, coming down their country road.

Chapter 15

"A fucking mistake of identity? Are you kidding me?" Hunter screamed into the room of Seattle PD officers.

The officers in the room started to look around and acted busy so as not to be the one who would catch the rage of the FBI agent. Several officers looked at each other and then started writing nonsense doodles on a paper or on the wall.

An uncomfortable silence fell over everyone, but it was soon upset by a phone ringing, and a drunken criminal getting processed burped loudly at the rear of the large room.

"How in the hell did we mess this up? Can anyone tell me that?" Hunter continued.

No one would answer him, but they all knew the answer. It had been the beard.

Three days prior, as Hunter stood up on a podium, telling the world that the murderous reign of *the Preacher* was drawn to a close, several SWAT members burst down the door of a home in Boca Raton, Florida.

The sole occupant of the short and squat, lime green home shot out of his lazy boy chair, and spilled the cereal he had been enjoying everywhere.

The police officers threw a flash grenade at the poor man, and as his eyesight was obliterated temporarily by the flash and the smoke, they pushed him to the floor and cuffed him.

He was screaming in terror, not knowing what was happening, and mostly because of the ditch weed that he had smoked most of the morning. The house was searched, the property put into custody. Every square inch of the dumpy house was searched and nothing connecting it with *the Preacher* was found.

When the joint teams of Boca PD and the FBI got the accused into the closest FBI office in Tallahassee, they positively identified the man as one Preston James Jefferson.

Jefferson was a twenty-five-year-old pizza delivery driver who had just gotten back to Boca from a trip to see his aging mother in Seattle. He had shaggy blonde hair, a short, unkempt beard, and no future to speak of.

But what Preston James Jefferson did have was an uncanny resemblance to a lawyer in August, Alabama, who was on a team supporting the killing of innocent people every month.

The two could have been brothers.

And since Four had grown out his beard over the last year, the two were almost indistinguishable, especially from a grainy, alleyway camera which had been purchased and hung behind a store by its business owner in 1998.

After the picture of Four had come out over the airwaves, Four quickly shaved his own short, scraggly beard, and even went so far as to dye his hair a dark auburn brown. Five remarked all day long that he enjoyed the change.

Over the next twenty-four hours, Preston James Jefferson's story unfolded his entire life, but most especially his trip to Seattle, which was then confirmed with an uncle, several cousins, and one aging great aunt who came out on the news, declaring that it "was really the President of the US who was killing folks, and stirring up the country 'cause votin' season was a 'comin."

Three days after the most-watched news report in US history took place from Seattle, Washington, the second most watched news report in US history took place, declaring that law enforcement embarrassingly got the wrong guy.

But, the agents stated bravely and quite strongly, they would continue pursuing the man in the photo, and find *the Preacher* once and for all.

Back in Alabama, the team breathed a sigh of relief. Three nights ago, in an awful coincidence, an abandoned barn several large plots south of the old Higgsby plantation had somehow caught fire, or had been set ablaze by derelict teenagers.

The sirens that had caused the team to panic were just the August fire department responding to the smoke and a frantic call from Mrs. Freeman, who lived alone across the street from the now fully burning wood barn. She had worried about her cows getting burned.

The news, the picture of Four that had been spread all over the country, and the fact that the team did not have everything under control like they had thought, had all felt like an extremely close call.

The entire team was aware of just what it could and would look like if any of them were caught. They were in this dastardly Plan, and they were in it together. Until the end, the team said to each other over the following weekend, in an

114

attempt to solidify the rocky ground they suddenly found themselves on.

The bonds of the team strengthened even more, and they re-vowed to each other and to the friends lost in the past, to see this thing through. They had made some changes, but not enough. Not yet.

It was now Halloween time again, and it was time to change the rules, once again.

But there had been some positive changes.

In a year of terror and death, with twelve victim's dead and no further information or clues to go on, the country was a powder keg ready for real, systematic changes.

Speculation had already begun and talking heads on several news stations all had their own opinions about which changes needed to be made to assure safety against a ghost who killed indiscriminately and disappeared into the night, leaving nothing behind.

Most of the police departments around the country at first instituted an early curfew on the 14th of every month, and for two days on either side of it.

This got people off of the streets and made it easier for the police to canvas their areas. But that wasn't enough.

Next, they started working with neighborhoods, and with individual citizens to start a program of informants and watchers. The police couldn't be everywhere, but there were enough concerned individuals in most states and cities, down to small communities, to help the police watch their areas.

This had the unforeseen side effect of police approval going up. And over the previous twelve months, it had risen exponentially, each month.

Now, children and adults alike helped the police. Outreach programs like "Coffee with a Cop" and "Crime Stoppers" were attended by more people than ever, and the biggest surprise was that the majority of those attending these outreach programs were young people.

A renewed ideal of police coming from the community, rather than the age-old idea that the police were made up of unknown faces, hungry for power, started to emerge.

Even police television programming like *Law and Order* received renewed interest and their numbers of viewers skyrocketed.

Community relationships all over the country strengthened, but not enough to enact real change.

Not yet.

And as Three watched these events unfold, and people's overzealousness grow, his conversations with ColbieX changed as well.

<ColbieX> *Do you think he has done enough yet?*

<HH3> *I don't think so. I think this will go on until he is caught.*

<ColbieX> *But why do you think he is wrong, if these changes are happening because of what* the Preacher *is doing? Why are you so against what it is taking to enact change?*

<HH3> *Because we are forgetting the victims. Are their deaths necessary to make these changes? At what point is it too much? Do you think that Tiffany in Seattle's parents are happy that because their daughter was murdered on some train tracks, now that police have a higher approval rating?*

<ColbieX> *I can't answer for them. But I can tell you, I feel a whole lot safer walking around my city now. And he did that.*

<HH3> *Yeah, you're safer, unless* the Preacher *jumps out and kills you.*

<ColbieX> *Well, yeah, there's that.*

And now, going into the first month of year two, with 107 victims left on the list, Three had gotten his second wind.

As the leaves changed color once again, and the breezes around him turned chilly, he once again found himself down at the graves of his other childhood best friends.

116

One and Two.

The pair that the team never spoke of, but from whom all of the plans had come from. Or rather, because of.

He found tears in his eyes as he stood over her gravestone. A stone edifice which hardly expressed the wonder and joy that she had brought into the world. He put the purple ribbon-tied bunch of white lilies, her favorite, into the cup made for that purpose, removing the dead bunch he had placed there a month before.

He again promised her that he would keep going. That now that things were starting to change, he would make sure that the changes became permanent.

He knew that he could never get rid of law enforcement, or the system that killed discriminately and got away with it. But he could change the people in that system. And he would use the fear of the community to enact that change.

He had nine years left to go. He would make it. And nine long years from now, he could finally rest. He could rest knowing that he had done the right thing, because the ends would justify the means.

He just had to get there. And he had to make sure that the country knew why he had done what he had done.

They wouldn't understand. Not at first. He was okay going down in history as an evil killer, but the changes to the country would be left behind.

And people like One wouldn't be senselessly murdered by those sworn to protect her.

He walked away from One's gravestone, a lightness in his chest finally, and a renewed vigor to see the plan through to the end.

And then, on the seventh of November, he killed his thirteenth victim in Sonoma County, California.

The country was again in an uproar. Understandably.

Because the rules had changed.

PART II

Chapter 16

It was becoming increasingly difficult to accomplish their goals. And as the team gathered together in the updated "Information Room," as they had nicknamed the office, they were once again tasked with the difficult planning of the next mission.

It wasn't the actual killing of the victims that was difficult to plan. That was something that Three was quite accomplished at. No, the challenge was how to enter the mission area and then extract from it without a trace.

They could leave nothing behind, and they had to be aware of all of the angles. For the experienced team, it wasn't the known quantities that were bothersome. It was the unknown. And most importantly, it was all of the eyes.

119

Three now often thought of himself as a sort of Batman character. He had perfected getting into the mission area unseen, accomplishing the goal, and getting out like a ninja. Not seen, not heard, not noticed in any way.

But that was becoming the most difficult part, because now everyone was on the lookout. The country had become one big community watch program, and it was increasingly harder and harder to stay unnoticed.

The team had accomplished that feat now for almost two years, but they really had to start thinking outside of the box.

"I'm telling you, Three, you need help on the ground," Four said.

"It's too risky. I know you are capable, and with a little training you would be as good as I am, but where one person can slip through unnoticed, two will get seen, every time," Three answered him.

"Then just make it one person on the ground like always," Four said with sudden inspiration.

"What do you mean?" Three asked.

"I mean, what do you need a person on the ground to do? Like, really do?" Four asked in reply.

"Umm, I'm not following," Three said in confusion. He looked over at Five, who just shrugged.

Four answered them both.

"Three, you use that fancy sniper rifle you bought and haven't been able to use, and once the victim is on the ground, another team member can swoop in, plant the Bible page and write the number. Easy-peasy," he said with a smile.

He was very proud of himself.

Both Three and Five looked at each other and back at Four.

"Holy shit, that just might work," Three replied, incredulous.

"I like it. Keeps only one person in the kill zone, and if the report from the gun is silenced somehow, then the man on the ground will have quite a while to do what needs to be done to stage the area," Five said.

They were all impressed with the idea and wondered how many missions they could use this new strategy. Like all of the other plans, they had had to change tactics when the task force, as well as the community overall, became aware of their moves. And watched out for them.

The paradigm had had to shift many times already.

"They will know the victim was sniped. They will look for the shooting nest, so that needs to be properly scouted out as well, and nothing left behind," Three was saying.

He was already formulating shooting angles, weather concerns, and cover for both him, as the shooter, and the guy on the ground. That guy would be all alone, with only digital backup, while he planted the scene, and supplied the verse and number.

The difficulty with this plan is that it was actually two different entrance and extraction plans in one. Five would be the busiest team member during the mission, covering for the others on the way in and on the way out.

But as Three looked over at Five, he just saw determination and a little excitement in the eyes of his other best friend.

"This could really work guys," Three said with excitement.

He was thinking over the last several months, and how close he had come to being discovered, almost every time.

One mission, in Oklahoma City, he had been caught on closed circuit camera, once again, and thankfully, nothing could be seen from the video other than his black-clad countenance, and no other verifying or identifying attributes could be garnered from the grainy images.

Thank goodness that public video equipment had yet to reach the level of sophistication as those used in government installations or on public highways to charge tolls. Those cameras were some of the best in the world.

For now, every time he was caught on camera, it didn't give anything away other than the chance to scare the public and make them realize that Three was in some way superhuman.

The public needed to be reminded frequently that this was ongoing. Twenty-two confirmed victims, and no traces left behind. Other than that last grainy video.

It had still made its way around the news shows and on the internet, with the viewer numbers in the tens of millions.

Oh yes, he thought, they needed to change the paradigm, once again.

He wondered vaguely how long this strategy would last before they had to change the rules, once again. They would see, he thought, as he pulled up satellite images of the next mission area, now looking for cover for a clear shot on victim number twenty-three.

Four was very impressed with himself. He had been trying to think up a way to change the rules again like they had done with the change of the date.

After Year One, changing the date had made the country shut down even more than the previous year. But they had all known new rules would need to be made.

Four had been racking his brain for a week now for how to do that. And then, the thought of having an accomplice plant the evidence, while the killer got away somehow, had just made sense to him.

Secretly, he was still smarting from his mistakes in Seattle last year, and he wanted to both make up for that, and to still be a bigger part of the plan than just pushing the paperwork through, arranging the money transfers, and having to use his overseas contacts for financial investments.

He wanted to be Three, but ever since they were kids, he had never measured up. This way, he could have his feet on the ground, with Three somewhere else, climbing out of a tree, or walking away from a heightened building across town from the victim.

Four could make a real contribution now.

He sat, smugly, looking over the images on the large screens mounted against the far wall, showing topographical and traffic information of Vernal, Utah. The next victim was going to be someone a little more important. They were about to ratchet up the pressure, and change the paradigm, once again.

Time to kill a politician.

And he wouldn't be the last politician they took out, but he would be the most memorable.

Four was ready for whatever he needed to do. He then looked over at the one screen that they never turned off and smiled.

On the screen was a rolling clip of a documentary showing the headquarters of *The Preacher* Task Force.

In the docuseries, the self-proclaimed "Hunters" tried to gain more public support by showing all the hard work they had been doing in chasing the serial killer across the country.

It had been a three-part series, played over three different nights about six months before. A famous newscaster narrated the documentary, and the team never turned it off. They kept it playing on a loop on one specific screen in the Information Room.

And at the end of the series, the camera zoomed in on the office of Hunter O'Connor, and showed the man sitting at his desk, a phone pressed to his ear, and his fingers quickly typing away at the keyboard of the impressive computer in front of him.

And squarely behind the older man, working feverishly to find the "asshole" who had killed his wife, was a large black-and-white picture tacked up on the wall amongst many smaller ones.

The picture was from the camera in Seattle, and showed Four walking down a busy city street, following the fifteen-year-old boy he was about to kill.

The look on Four's face was one of malice and hate, and his captured movements showed him ready to kill.

It was that picture up on the wall of the Hunter's office that made the team stay three steps ahead of the task force, and made sure that they protected their best friend, and themselves in the process.

Four smiled at the screen in front of him, and then, as he watched the law enforcement officers from five different agencies work feverishly on the screen, his smile faded.

He remembered one fact that they hadn't mentioned during their planning. He felt the weight in his chest grow heavier and knew that he could still bring this all down. He could lose his two best friends, and his own life in the meantime.

Because the hunters were closer than they thought. And the team was panicking.

Chapter 17

Mayor Benjamin McCabe, or Benji, as his often-disappointed wife called him, had never done much with his life. He was used to disappointing people and had only recently done more than live off of the coattails of his family's name.

He had surprisingly won a second term as Mayor of the small Utah town of Vernal. And he knew, deep in his heart, that him winning, and twice at that, was mostly due to his wife's influence.

That and the fact that he kissed the oil companies' asses in town, at every turn. And he did it often, and publicly. Embarrassingly public.

But the oil companies had put Vernal on the map, and they were the largest source of income in town at the moment. And who had the money, he had learned, got their asses kissed.

Ben McCabe hadn't started out not wanting to accomplish anything with his life. His father, and his grandfather before him had been deacons, and then elders in the local Church of Jesus Christ of Latter-day Saints.

They were both prominent business owners, and they had both, as far back as Ben could remember, ran their families with an iron will, and an even stronger fist.

Ben had just been born with a weaker constitution than both men and had had every intention of following after both men's footprints. But he had just been born weak. And sickly.

In his family, weak and sickly didn't get you very far, and just because you had the McCabe name, didn't mean that you got special treatment no matter what. He failed at proving himself to the two men, and he had failed at even more than that as an adult.

One failure, in both men's eyes, was when Ben was four years old. He had become one of the last children in the country to contract abortive polio.

He hadn't wanted to stand out in that way. He had even been featured on a news documentary about the decline of the disease.

But he had been a sickly kid for all of his four years, and this was just the cherry on top.

He had starting falling down as a toddler, and by the age of four, had full blown, non-paralytic polio. He had spent a year in and out of the hospital, and for one stretch of two weeks, had even had to sit in an old tank respirator, or what most people had called an "iron lung."

The local LDS doctor had dug the iron lung out of mothballs.

Ben could still remember looking up at his father's lined, craggy face and seeing the disappointment on it. His grandfather had not even visited the hospital.

Ben remembered the rejection from both men sharply, and it had led him to be wasteful with the majority of his life, according to them both.

He had recovered and had had a mostly normal childhood afterwards. As a seventeen-year-old young man who was more boy than anything, he had finished his two-year mission. Not being able to call home for most of those two years had made him happy, rather than upset, like the other young men on his mission team.

And he had chosen one of the hardest mission fields in the country. He spent two years and two months knocking on doors and sharing the good news of the LDS Church with the citizens of the poor country of Haiti.

It had been a happy time for the late-blooming boy, and he had hated returning to Utah. But like all good LDS boys, he had returned home, married the girl his parents had wanted him to, a strong-willed girl named Mitzie, and had tried for the next two decades to make something of himself. But he had failed in that, over and over.

The one thing that Ben had going for him over other boys his age from his hometown was a great imagination. And even bigger dreams. But he rarely was able to act on those dreams.

So, he had sat, frustrated and unable to express his imaginative side, for many unproductive years. And having an old-fashioned and overbearing wife didn't help. He had wanted to be so much in life but had not achieved anything he sat around visualizing.

His wife had squelched all of his dreams, and most of his creativity. She was practical to a fault, and he wasn't allowed to be a dreamer. Or an artist.

His secret dream.

Mitzie was not to be trifled with, and as Ben took his long afternoon walk on this Thursday afternoon, he knew that she was not happy finding his one vice. His one small diversion from the mundane and mediocre life that he had been dealt.

His drawings. His art. His reason for breathing, he thought, on most days.

The pictures that he took out of his feverishly creative mind and put to paper. The secret time that he spent in his home office, happily drawing away were the only days he felt like he had a purpose and a reason for being alive.

But not today. She had finally destroyed a drawing, and he didn't think that it would end there. Not for his art. And he wondered why he was going to allow this woman, who was supposed to be the other part of his soul, destroy the only thing that brought him happiness.

She hated his talent, he thought. She hated that something other than her brought him happiness. But that really wasn't it, he realized as he walked down the northern country road out of town. The dog he was walking wasn't doing her business like she needed to. She was just enjoying being outside in the one warm day out of the last couple of months.

His mind went back to why his wife hated his art so much.

It really wasn't that she hated art, or the fact that he was actually good at it. Quite good, he thought. At first she had seemed pleasantly surprised and pleased that he had a natural talent. But then, when she saw what he enjoyed drawing, and yearned to paint, her pleasantness quickly turned to hate and scorn.

He knew he was guilty. He felt both shame and joy in what he drew. But he yearned to put his art to canvas and make a name for himself. He craved it, actually.

So, who cared that he drew nude scenes. He thought they were quite Renaissance-esqe, but Mitzie had called them pornographic several times. They were beautiful drawings of naked women frolicking in a park, laying on benches, playing in water. Naked cherubs, and men doing manual labor in nothing but their sweat. Nude bodies everywhere, but none of them doing anything remotely sexual, other than being bare.

He was quite proud of his abilities, but his wife, and soon, his church, would see them for something entirely different. Just this morning, she had threatened to show the elders what he had been doing with his spare time. And that could never happen.

And so, he had walked out of the house full of hate. Not for her destroying one of his drawings or hating what he liked to draw. No, he hated himself for being so weak to actually capitulate to her demands for him to stop.

He felt like his life was over, and it had never even begun.

For the first time in a very long time, he thought about running away, giving up his position of mayor, and forgetting about his dreams of running for a State seat in Salt Lake City.

No, he wanted to run away to New York or Paris, or Santa Fe, New Mexico. So he could be himself, and live how he wanted, out of his family's and his wife's shadow.

So he could pursue his art.

He yelled at the dog to take a damn shit, followed by shame for cursing. He uttered a prayer for forgiveness under his breath.

The little white poodle with brown marks all over her fur because of a genetic disorder, was also named Mitzie. The name was an inside joke.

Mitzie's father had been Robert Dean Rogers IV, who was the last in a long line of Robert Dean Rogers. But he had only had the one daughter and couldn't pass on the family name.

Which Mitzie had had to deal with her whole life.

And now that she and Benji could not have kids themselves, Mitzie had had a string of dogs all with her own name, which she had adorably nicknamed "Junior." And this damn "junior" wouldn't do her business.

Benji looked around at where he was walking. It wasn't off of his normal route, but he had not wanted to come this far out from town today. It was unseasonably warm, but to him, and the heavy frame he carried around with him, it was unbearably hot.

He was sweating furiously inside his button-down shirt and starched khaki pants. As mayor, he always had to look presentable when he walked out of the house, no matter the mundane chore. Mitzie and his father had made that abundantly clear.

Again, he just wanted to be himself, and be sloppy once in a while. He sighed heavily as he kept walking Junior, waiting for her to do her business, and let him get back home to draw some more.

He liked days off like this the most. His mind wandered to what he would wear if he were an artist, living in an artist world somewhere else.

He would wear canvas shirts, with paint smeared on them. And jean shorts. And straw hats. Maybe even those bright, colorful, and loose cotton shirts he had seen men from Jamaica and the Caribbean wear. With shorts and loose flowing pants that had loose strings on the bottoms where they were slowly fraying away.

He sighed contentedly, thinking of himself wearing what he wanted to wear.

And as he looked down at the sweat stains becoming exposed on his light blue dress shirt, hating that he had to always look his best, and couldn't be comfortable, he suddenly saw and felt a new color appear at chest level. A bright bloom of red.

Well, what do you know, he thought. That was a very lovely shade of red spreading out on his shirtfront.

130

He hadn't feel the bullet enter his chest. But he had felt the impact it caused in the heavy frame of his body. Like a horse had kicked him in the chest, but there was no pain.

He fell to the ground with quite a surprised look on his face. His vision went black, but he still didn't really feel any pain. Benjamin just couldn't breathe.

His chest felt heavy, and wet, and he heard a whistling and squishy sound as he tried to find his breath.

He heard footsteps approach him. His last two thoughts were one of thankfulness that someone had gotten to him so quickly and could help him.

And the final thought of his wasted life was that Mitzie would be so terribly upset that, once again, he hadn't finished something he had started.

Junior Mitzie had never taken a shit.

Chapter 18

"Mrs. McCabe, we at Channel 7 News are so very sorry for your loss, and frankly, to the loss to the people of the great state of Utah. Can you tell me more about your husband?"

Melissa McCabe, who everyone had called Mitzie since she had been a small, headstrong girl, sniffed into her dry handkerchief, looked pleadingly into the bright light over the camera behind the reporter sitting in her living room, and put on the bravest face that she could.

"My dear, dear husband was a visionary. And he was an artist," she said, sniffing again into her dry, unused, and frankly, unneeded, hankie.

She again tried to keep the joy of being in the spotlight off of her face and put on the necessary penitent look she had practiced in the mirror before coming down the stairs to meet the press. It was also the look that she would keep on her face through the state-sponsored funeral that was to take place in Salt Lake City tomorrow.

She was so excited about THAT, that she could hardly contain herself. In the Mormon Temple itself, with the Tabernacle Choir singing for the husband who she had grown to actually despise.

Well, she thought, still with her mourning look on her face, he had come through in the end, and she was going to be somebody. Somebody who other's looked up to and wanted advice from.

The Preacher taking her husband did more for Mitzie McCabe than her fat husband ever did. Secretly, she thanked the killer.

The young, pretty reporter gave her such a look of pity that Mitzie was almost angry. But she went on. She had to. She had a job to do.

Mitzie thought about what to say about Benjamin and went on.

"He always took care of everyone else. Before himself. He had such big dreams. And when we found out that we couldn't have children of our own, why, he went and ran for mayor, because he needed to be a father to us all," she said.

She even managed to squeeze out a tear. It still hurt that she couldn't have children.

The reporter calmly asked another question. "Is it true that he had aspirations for a State Seat?"

"Oh yes," Mitzie answered, excited again.

"We had a plan for him to run next year for a state Senate seat, and after that, maybe even a Federal Seat in Congress. He really had big dreams his whole life to help out as many people as he could. He was almost, I would say, obsessed with it. Even in his art, he showed a spirit of service."

She sniffed again. And wondered if she was sniffing too much. She put her hankie into the pocket of her black dress she wore for the occasion. She had to keep up appearances.

The men in her life, and the men in charge made that face quite apparent to her. But she didn't care about those men. She would be the first woman in LDS church history to lead a charge for change in this country, and in this state.

"Can we see some of his art? I think the public would love to see the great man that he was," the reporter asked. Mitzie jerked back at the question.

"Umm, no, I'm sorry. The family wants to keep those drawings safe for the time being. They are so very special, and private. I hope you understand," she said contritely.

"Of course. Again, we are so very sorry for your loss. He sounds like he was a great man," the reporter answered.

"He was. He really was," Mitzie said. She tried not to roll her eyes.

"And the fact that he was a victim of the serial killer known as *the Preacher*, shows that no one in this country is really safe. What would you say to *the Preacher* if he were watching right now?" The reporter started digging for more sensationalism.

Mitzie sat up straighter. Her white poodle bounded over and started sniffing around her feet. She bent down and picked up the dog and put her in her lap. Stroking the dog gently, Mitzie looked straight into the camera.

"I would tell that coward that HE isn't safe anywhere. He shouldn't have taken my poor, sweet Benji. Now, he has the wrath of the McCabe and the Robert's family after him. And the whole state of Utah as well. We won't stop until he is brought to the justice he deserves. I hope I'm there to watch the piece of dirt fry!" she said vehemently.

"Do you think that there needs to be more social change now that *the Preacher* is targeting politicians as well as his usual unorthodox mode of seemingly random killings?"

"I think the entire country needs to take this situation personally and get armed. Every citizen needs to protect themselves, and band together to find this piece of filth.

We can't be scared to live our lives how we all want to live it. But it will take this country coming together, every single person, no matter color or gender or religion to find this man. Or men. We cannot live like this in this great country!" she said, pounding her fist into her leg, scaring Junior Mitzie off her lap.

Three switched off the television at that last statement. He was smiling. This is exactly what he had wanted. He had no idea that the mayor of the small town in Vernal was so beloved by his community, or that he had had such a firebrand wife who was doing Three's job for him.

He turned and looked at Four and Five. Four was smiling. He had done his part perfectly, and the team felt much safer now that they had a new strategy. It wasn't perfect, and could only be used sparingly, but the more variable changing plans they had at their disposal, the easier it would become to escape after completing a mission.

But it was now time to change the rules once again. This was a month that they had all been looking forward to for quite some time.

"Are you guys ready for a vacation?" he asked his team. The other two men nodded and smiled, looking at each other with a loving smile. Five reached across the small distance and took Four's hand.

Three watched his two best friend' and the love they shared. He was mixed in his emotions. Happiness and jealousy warred within him. But that could change soon.

They were going to take three months off. Another paradigm shift. The country needed to feel a false sense of security, and the team needed to establish more alibis. A rest through the holiday season and most of the winter would do just that.

And Three was going to finally meet Colbie in person.

After two years of chatting online, and then on the phone, they were going to meet, and finally get to know each other better.

He was looking forward to it so much.

His chest swelled slightly at the thought, and he barely noticed the trepidation trying to take over his excitement.

Hunter was tired in his soul. How long could he chase this guy? Correction, he thought, these *guys*. They were certain that the serial killer had at least one accomplice. There was no other way that the scene in Utah could have been established in the short time between the shooting and the discovery of the body.

It had been the middle of the day, it was slightly chilly outside, and the body had not gotten into any kind of a mortis level. So, the shooting had happened, at most, two hours before the medical examiner set time of death. And only about a half hour or so before the body was discovered by a jogger.

So, *the Preacher* had help. And, if it was *the Preacher* who had pulled the trigger, he had skills that the task force hadn't known before. That meant training. A new area of possibilities opened up with that single sniper round.

But how much help did he have? The thousands of questions from the dozens of scenes now bounced around in Hunter's mind, driving him mad. The questions weren't the only thing muddling Hunter's mind.

He looked down at his hand. He was sitting on yet another hard motel bed. The generic multicolored thin bedspread bunched up at the foot of the queen-sized bed. And in his hand, a half-empty bottle of Wild Turkey. And he came to the realization that he had been the one who had drunk the missing half.

Well, he fell off the wagon. Two years wasn't so bad, right?

He knew he was in trouble, but he was finding it harder and harder to care. The work kept him going. *The Preacher*, the son-of-a-bitch who had killed his wife, was keeping Hunter from ending it all.

The man who had taken so many lives was saving Hunter's life. How poetic, he thought, as he took another deep drink of the caustic liquid in the bottle in his hand.

He wiped his mouth with the back of his hand. Looking around the disheveled hotel room, he wondered suddenly what time it was. He stood and noticed that he was wearing just a pair of loose boxers and a white tank top shirt. He only had one black dress sock on. What a cliché, he thought as he ambled over to the window drapes and peeked out. The sunlight hit him square in his drunken eyes, blinding him suddenly.

Shit, he thought. It was daytime. And he had no idea where he was, what he was supposed to be doing, or how long he had been in this room. It was a mess. Empty food containers scattered on the table, and his clothes in a pile at the foot of the bed. He couldn't even find his suitcase.

Most troubling were the empty liquor bottles scattered everywhere.

And more frightening, there was no knock at his door, no partner and friend there to take him where he needed to go or to give him information that he needed to find the bastard called *the Preacher*.

It was just silent, and Hunter had no place in the world. He was lost in a hole of despair, and the drink in his hand the only friend he had.

So, he took a long pull at the bottle, and sank back down on the damp mattress. He realized, as he felt the wetness under his back, that he had pissed the bed. He didn't care, because people at the bottom of a hole they had dug themselves rarely cared about anything.

137

He barely heard the local news on low volume, coming from the TV on the stand in the corner. It was too low, and too far away for his alcohol-muffled ears to pick up.

On the TV, a reporter was interviewing the father of the most recently deceased man, and Hunter would have been very happy to know that the man on the television set was saying that he, himself, would put all of the resources of the LDS church and the fine, fine law enforcement officials in the state of Utah behind a new, better task force, using state-of-the-art tools to find the serial killer who now thought it was a "fine idea to kill innocent politicians."

And the last thing that the addled Hunter should have heard was the derision in the man's tone, besmirching the Federal Task Force, which Hunter had run for two years, and who had not found even one shred of evidence during that time, nor arrested one single suspect, in the ongoing investigation that was rocking the country, every single month.

Hunter passed out again, at ten in the morning, on the day that he lost his position. And his job. And his reason to keep living. He was drunkenly passed out when he lost the respect and concern of his closest friends and co-workers.

Hunter had disappeared, and everyone assumed that he had given up, and gone into hiding. They had no idea where he was.

No one could find Hunter to tell him the news. They had no idea where he was, what he was doing, or how he could be found. They certainly didn't know that he was drunk, in a hotel room, passed out.

And that that hotel room was in Montgomery, Alabama, where Hunter had flown, on a hunch, and a wild clue that only he had known about, and that he had kept to himself. A clue about the man in the photo that had hung behind his desk as an oversized daily reminder to Hunter to find the truth.

He was in Alabama following a lead that he was closer to than he really knew. Closer than anyone really knew. Certainly closer than the team knew, as they sat in the Information Room of the Higgsby's Plantation, less than an hour's drive from where Hunter was passed out drunk, having uncovered who they were.

And uncovered all they had done.

Chapter 19

Three felt hot. The breeze coming off the ocean didn't help much, but the ice cold drink in his hands did somewhat. He knew it wasn't the heat from the sun, high overhead which was making him hot. It was the waiting. It was excruciating.

He was on vacation, and he had been waiting for this trip for almost a full year. The next three months were going to be full of traveling and sightseeing, but for now, these four weeks on this island were the most important.

The island of Turks and Cacaos was an amazingly beautiful and very expensive island to vacation, but it had been worth every penny for the last week of relaxation he had enjoyed. But a week in, the real vacation was about to start.

He was waiting at an outdoor tiki bar, sipping a strawberry margarita, and waiting on the woman who had occupied the time in between the missions for the last twelve months. Colbie X. She was coming to meet him here, and it was making him hot to think about finally meeting the woman he had become quite smitten with.

He looked forward to seeing her waspish grin, and her beautiful green eyes.

He was looking forward to even more than that, with the whispered questions and statements passing between them on the web, and later on the phone and video chatting.

Oh yes, he thought as he sipped the sweet drink, condensation running down the back of his hand, he was very ready to meet the woman of his dreams.

But he had to be careful. He would do everything he could to keep the conversation between just the two of them, and off the topic of *the Preacher*. She was, of course, overwhelmingly addicted to speaking about the killer, and his exploits, and why he was doing what he was doing.

But Three didn't want to let anything slip, especially in her presence, so he had to be sure to control the conversations. He made a mental note to stay strong, and not let anything slip. Not give away something that only the killer would know.

Colbie was too smart, too knowledgeable, and would catch it like a fly, getting stuck in the sticky glue of a ceiling-hung fly trap. She was relentless in her pursuit of finding out who *the Preacher* was. For Three, she was very dangerous.

But at the moment, as he finished his cold drink, and ordered another, he would put that danger aside, and get to know this woman in even more intimate ways than was possible online.

He looked around at the mostly empty bar area. It wasn't quite the height of the holiday tourist season, and so, he shared the tiki bar with only two other couples, both of which were deep into conversations and tropical drinks at tables closer to the beach than him.

He sat at the front of the bar, closest to the doors leading back into the swanky resort he had rented a room at for the next three weeks.

He was looking forward to so much more rest.

He felt a tap on his right shoulder, and when he turned that way, no one was there. He smiled larger than life and turned to the other shoulder.

And there she was.

She was smiling back at him, wearing a gorgeous aquamarine bikini, a light and airy shawl wrapped around her boyish hips, and big sunglasses perched on the top of her dark hair.

He smiled brightly back at her, and as she took a seat next to him, and leaned in to kiss him on the lips, the heat he had felt earlier dissipated, and he felt chills run up and down his spine. A delicious feeling, and one he hardly ever felt.

Oh yes, he thought to himself as he ordered the beautiful young love of his life a drink, he was going to enjoy this as much as he could. He didn't have a single thought for the life back home, or *the Preacher*. And that was just fine by him.

Four and Five were cold. But they were smiling at each other through the chill in the late Norwegian evening breeze. The snow-topped mountains surrounded the valley they were in, and the breeze caught the late summer snows, making for a chilly contact as the wind swept down into the shadowed valley floor. But the two men didn't care.

They drank fancy cappuccinos and wore local wool sweaters, made from the hands of the older women of the village. The sweaters, as well as several other articles of local clothing were the first purchase they had made when the small bus had dropped them off in the village of Geiranger, Norway.

Five had seen a tourist video of the small town, and they both knew that they just had to visit.

When Three had announced a month of vacation, anywhere in the world, for the two men, they had jumped at the chance to visit this beautiful country, as well as spend some of Three's money.

They both knew that it was getting mightily suspicious that the young multi-millionaire wasn't doing what normal young multi-millionaires do. So, now, they were going to do some shopping! The young lovers cherished the thought.

And so, the lovers found themselves in the deep Norwegian valley at the head of the dramatic Geirangerfjord, drinking strong Italian coffee, wearing warm Norwegian wool, and smiling at their intertwined fingers on top of the smooth wooden table.

They were both remembering the day's hike up a mountain trail and finding the small hamlet and wooden cabin that was included in their vacation package. They had walked into the richly appointed wooden shack in the middle of the mountain woods, and with a large wood fire crackling in the stone fireplace, they had made love like they hadn't since they were teenagers.

They were once again remembering each other and finding out new things in each other's eyes. It had been a breathtaking experience, and the life outside of the tiny Norwegian hamlet had just disappeared.

Four had whispered to Five, after their lovemaking, and while they held each other on the comfortable and oversized couch in front of the fire, that this was what life would be after the Plan was finished.

Back down on the valley's floor, they both cherished the memories from that afternoon, and didn't have to say a word otherwise.

The locals let the men have their privacy. All the townspeople knew was that the young couple was beautiful, in love, and very rich. Those three attributes, in this particular part of the world, gave the pair all of the privacy they could want.

All they were was passing through, and no one would remark on anything about them. The pair had spoken about that fact on the first day of their vacation, and loved the feeling of autonomy, and relished the freedom that that had given them.

Like Three, on the other side of the world, they were luxuriating being away from the stresses and hardships they had shared since starting the Plan. They had needed this more than anything, and as Four looked deep into Five's eyes, hands still not letting go, the love they saw in each other would get them through anything.

As long as they could keep visiting this valley, and remembering the times in between the missions, when they could be normal, and relish the love growing between them. Nothing short of death would separate the two best friends. They had been through too much, and witnessed so much more, and their bond could never be broken.

All of that passed through the looks they were giving to each other as the sun sank behind the mountains to the west, and the streetlights came on, their soft orange glow creating an even more romantic scene at the small café table the lovers shared.

And as the waitress came to their table, asking in broken English if the two needed anything else, they decided to order a large and hearty dinner. They would need their strength for the night ahead.

Four winked at his love, and Five smiled beautifully back to him. How their love had grown ever since they were young teenagers, finding themselves in the other. They would need that love and bond for the trials ahead.

They both knew that, and they knew that they needed to make the most of the three weeks they had left on their vacation in Norway, and then onto other northern European sights.

They were going to really live for these three months, before they had to head back to the US, and the Plan.

Chapter 20

Three slept. And as he slept, he dreamed. It was the very first dream in his adult life that he remembered in its entirety when he awoke.

He was home. August, Alabama spread out around him, and he was comforted by the small town in SW Alabama, several miles north of Mobile, in Washington County. The wind was strong in the trees around town, and the sunshine was bright on his face. He looked down and saw that he was wearing one of his favorite western-cut collared shirts.

The one with the pearl buttons. His father had worn shirts like this. Three remembered the pearl snaps the most.

He was enjoying the cooling breeze on the warm day and turned to see that he was standing in the street on Route 43. The entrance to the parking lot surrounding the Dairy Queen was directly in front of him. He felt like the orange GPS guy on Google. The one that showed you the street view.

He watched as five children rode in a pack of bicycles into the parking lot, and parked the bikes all in a row, like race cars before the big race. They had often joked about it.

Three knew exactly what day this was. The day that had changed the trajectory of his entire life. The day that he had lost his first love. And his best friend, her brother. He wanted to scream out to the children to turn and ride home. But he was merely a bystander. A watcher. He knew that he couldn't change what was coming. It had been so big in his life, yet so small in the course of the history of the world. He had worked to change that fact his entire life.

He watched the children walk to the window and order five vanilla cones, dipped in chocolate. They had all loved how the chocolate would harden, turning into a shell of goodness around the drippy vanilla ice cream. He smiled at the group. Although he knew what was coming, he remembered how much he had loved his friends, and they had loved him. He hadn't felt so confident in his life since this very day.

He heard a voice behind him.

"This day, above all others, will change the course of the country, won't it, Harold?" the voice said.

Three turned to find a short, sharply dressed black man standing in the exact middle of Route 43. He wore what Three decided was a white seersucker suit, a Bahama straw hat with a black band, and a cream-colored cashmere scarf. He was holding what looked like a redwood cane, and held himself with an internal power that Three marveled at.

He wondered, distractedly, how the man wasn't sweating his ever-loving face off in the Alabama summer heat. Three decided that he instantly liked this old fella.

"The choices that came from this day changed your life, didn't it, Harold?" the man asked again.

Three finally found his voice. He turned back to the children, joking amongst themselves, licking ice cream like it would melt if they didn't. And it was melting. That was half the fun. The other half was the sweet goodness of the treat.

"Yes, I suppose you can say that it did. Before this day, all I thought about was getting Mary to kiss me, and what car I wanted when I turned sixteen. And after, well, after...all I thought about was vengeance," he answered the sharply dressed man.

The man walked up next to Three, and suddenly, Three felt a presence on the other side of him opposite the well-dressed man. There had been no sound, but he felt a heat from his right side, a heavy presence.

When he glanced to his right, a woman stood with him, silent, beautiful beyond measure. She had blonde hair bound up in a heavy bundle atop her head, a crown of pearls woven within. She was dressed all in white, flowing robes, and a golden light emanated from within her.

Three gulped loudly, and couldn't take his eyes off of her. She just smiled again, and looked towards the Dairy Queen parking lot. She nodded towards the children on bikes in front of them, making Three turn his head back forward.

Three looked back at the parking lot, fear deep in his chest over what was about to happen.

Together the three figures watched the scene unfold in front of them like they were at the Sunday afternoon movie matinee in town. Three felt the woman on his right take his hand, gripping it stronger than he thought was possible from her slight figure.

Together, they watched the police officer drive into the parking lot, and park his cruiser right next to the row of bikes.

They watched him exit the cruiser, and place his baton inside the loop on his gun belt. Three almost looked away, but

147

in his dream, he found that he could not do so. The man next to him watched the scene unfold without saying another word. The woman was just as silent.

Three was glad for the silence.

After the events had played themselves out, and Three and the sharply dressed man had turned and watched Dottie and Floyd pull up in the work truck, load up all of the bicycles into the back, and put the three boys who survived into the cab with them, the pair of men and the beautiful, silent woman, together watched the truck pull out onto the highway, and head back towards the plantation.

Three couldn't take his eyes off of his own young face, full of tears and anger. The woman beside him released his hand, and placed her soft hand on his shoulder instead.

Three was remembering how that truck ride had felt.

And then he remembered talking with Four and Five that very evening about how to pay back the people who had done murder. Three could feel his emotions well inside his chest. He didn't know if you could cry inside a dream, but he felt like doing just that.

Suddenly, all was completely silent.

Not even the wind blew around them, and Three's ears felt like cotton had been stuffed inside them. He looked back at the older gentleman standing beside him, and in his dream, the town around him faded away.

All that was left was the two men, facing each other, in the middle of billowing, pink-hued fog, overtaking everything around them.

Three felt the presence of the woman again, only this time behind him, both of her hands heavy on his shoulders. For a split second, Three felt not a golden aura of peace coming from her, but rather, a deep, black abyss full of pain and suffering. He glanced behind him in sudden terror but only saw the beautiful woman in the golden light, once again.

Soon enough, all Three could see was the billowing smoke. It surrounded him completely. He didn't feel fear anymore. Rather, he felt comforted. He felt calmness soothe the emotions in his chest and throat.

The fog had no smell, and no texture when he swept his hand through it. All it had was the pinkish hue, and it seemed to move of its own accord. Three turned back to the older gentleman, still placidly looking Three right in the eyes.

"What is this place?" Three asked the older man.

"A better question would be, WHERE is this place?" the man said quietly. "This is your dream, Harold. And…..this is my time to give you a message." Three felt the woman's hands on his shoulder tighten.

"What message? And from who?" he asked.

"Only this, Harold Higgsby the Third. Only this: finish the fight. Don't quit. Your path is much more important than you realize," the man said.

"Bigger things than you can realize, or can comprehend, are moving with your actions," the older man said.

He said one last, parting remark, before Three awoke, remembering the entire dream in detail.

"Finish the fight, Three. Don't give in! You are being watched, and your actions, weighed."

Three woke with the heavy feeling of hands, tight on his shoulders still, and a deep sense of motivation in his chest.

Chapter 21

Hunter woke with a gasp, fighting for air. Someone was choking him, and he fought against the hand around his throat. The hand came away surprisingly easy and felt very thin.

It was too dark to see, but Hunter could feel his heart beating out of his chest and he fought against cloth and what felt like blankets, landing hard on a floor.

He closed his eyes against the darkness, and wondered where he was, what day it was, and why he felt like he had been hit with a baseball bat over the head and everywhere else.

His entire body hurt.

He stumbled around in the darkness, banging against furniture and finally a wall. He tripped over some clothing on the floor, and finally groped along the wall he had smashed into until he found a light switch. He hit the switch like it would save his life.

The sudden bright light lit up the seedy motel room that he had been sleeping in since before he could remember. He still had no idea where he was, but he saw the arm that had been choking him. It was a pale white arm, coming from under a mound of hotel blankets on the bed. And then it moved.

A dark-haired young woman peeked out at him, the bright lights making her squint. She looked like a meth head, Hunter thought to himself. He couldn't make himself move. He just watched the woman step away from the bed, naked, looking for a pack of cigarettes.

She was covered in badly drawn tattoos, and her bony body showed the signs of abuse, neglect, and drug use.

Hunter, his mind still foggy, suddenly compared his sweet Karen to this creature and felt nauseous. And then he was sick.

He bounded, naked himself, into the bathroom, the light from the outer room giving enough detail for him to find the toilet and dry heave into it. Nothing but green bile came out of his empty stomach, but what little there was of the junk that came out, Hunter gave it his very best to remove it all from his system.

He involuntarily went into dry spasms, and for almost five minutes could do nothing but let his body purge. The woman yelled something from the other room at one point, but Hunter neither heard nor cared what the creature had to say.

He just concentrated on the purging of his body, and his soul, into the dirty motel toilet. And wondered why he was where he was, and what he was doing with his life.

He heard the door to the motel room open and close, with a yelled curse when the meth head prostitute left. He didn't

151

care. As he sat on the dirty linoleum of the motel bathroom, he didn't care about much.

His brain started unraveling the last few days and he remembered where he was and what he was doing there. He was following a lead on the man in the black-and-white, grainy picture that had hung over his desk, taunting him, for the last several months.

He started getting his thoughts in order, and slowly got to his feet. He felt steadier, but not much. He needed to get moving. He had no idea what was happening in the outside world, and he knew that he needed to check in with Red and his team to see if there had been any breaks in the cases. And he had to tell someone where he was.

And why he was in Alabama, of all places.

He needed a shower, and surprisingly, his stomach was rumbling. He needed greasy food, and lots of it. But first things first. He stepped into the stained bathtub, and ran the water, standing under it. It came out ice cold at first, which shocked him further, but he made himself stand under it until the water warmed enough to be comfortable.

He used the motel issued soap and tiny bottle of shampoo, washing away weeks of grime and dirt and God knew what else. He almost sickened up again when he saw the film of disgust on his body, but he swallowed his revulsion of himself, and finished scrubbing himself clean.

He used a thin, fraying washcloth, also supplied by the motel, and rubbed his body with the cheap soap until his skin was a bright pink. Then he turned up the water temperature to full heat and scalded himself cleaner.

When he stepped out of the dirty shower stall, he felt physically better. Being clean was next to Godly, he thought to himself.

But his mind was a different matter. He couldn't scrub his memories and emotions with a scrawny washcloth, as much as he wished he could. He would just have to deal with that later.

So, clean, and feeling somewhat better, he got dressed in dirty clothes, which smelled like cigarettes and his own filth. He set out looking for breakfast, and a change of clean clothes. In that order.

Sitting at a diner's worn and scarred table, eating a large plate of over-easy eggs, sopped up with white toast, Hunter felt himself a little bit more. His stomach was finally settling, and his mind was clearing.

He couldn't find his cellphone, so had no idea what was going on in the world. But he did finally remember why he was in Alabama.

The lawyer.

It all came back to him while a thick piece of bacon was in his hand, halfway to his mouth. He sat there in the vinyl covered booth, mouth open and bacon hanging suspended in mid-air, as he remembered finally the output photo from the state of New York that had matched the face of the killer that had hung over his desk with a lawyer in New York State.

Hunter put down the bacon, his appetite suddenly gone. As the waitress went back to the counter to prepare his check, he thought back over the last week or more. He remembered everything. And what he had to do next.

His mind went over the fact that not all informational databases in the US were linked. His facial recognition and fingerprint data for known criminals was his main source of information.

But the fallacy in that system is that non-offending people were not in that database. At least, not yet. And he had had no access to other databases like driver license pictures, professional license photos, or passport photos.

Those databases existed, but were not accessible in criminal investigations. It was a damn failure of the system, and he had fought for years to correct that access. But everyone was afforded their privacy and protections under the Patriot Act.

153

In his foray into the world of other known, yet inaccessible databases, he had met a friend. Charlie worked for the Department of Motor Vehicles in Virginia, and he was able to access those databases. So, a couple of times in the last several years, Hunter had persuaded Charlie to run a scan based on an algorithm written by yet another friend. Contacts and networks, Hunter thought as he signed the receipt for breakfast.

A couple of months ago, Hunter had gotten desperate and had reached out to Charlie. Not even Red knew about Charlie. But still nothing had come up. Not until Charlie had called him to meet at a park in Georgetown. Charlie enjoyed the playacting of clandestine meetings and such, and Hunter had learned to play along.

Sitting at a park bench on a sunny afternoon in Georgetown, the birds screaming overhead, and the sun giving Hunter a headache, Charlie had slipped in next to him, and not saying a word, looked around more times than he had needed to.

And then he had slipped Hunter a manila envelope and had quickly stood and walked away. Hunter had not spoken to anyone else since he had opened that envelope.

A year prior, the state of New York had passed legislation that had created a database for state certified and licensed individuals. New York had been one of the last states, surprisingly, that had created such a database, owing to their vast population.

But the money had been available, and it had been a dog-eared legislation bill that had passed the State House, and had sat on the Governor's desk for almost a month. But he had signed it, and the software was created somehow, and in record time. Probably owing to the fact that most other states had had the same database for years.

And that's when Charlie had gotten a hit on the facial recognition software that Hunter had given him years prior.

Opening the envelope right there at the park bench in Georgetown, Hunter looked at a blown-up, 8.5-by-11-inch color photo of the man who had haunted his dreams and his days, ever since the man had killed in Seattle. And Hunter knew exactly who he was, and where he lived.

For some reason, getting the information that he now held made him act outside of his normal tenets. He didn't inform his partner, his supervisors, nor anyone else on the task force of the information, nor where he had to go.

He just packed a bag, and in a mental haze, he took off. He left. He got on a plane to New York State, and didn't inform anyone. He had no idea why. His only thought was his wife's splayed-out body on their sunporch, and how he was going to kill Mr. Christopher Shelly, Esq., himself. He was going to look into the son of a bitch's eyes as he pulled the trigger.

But he had ran into dead ends in New York. He was frustrated that he couldn't find the man in the photos. And then a neighbor of Mr. Shelly had informed him about Mark Sinclair, Christopher's husband, and the fact that they spent the holidays in Alabama, where the men were from.

And so, mind still dulled by purpose and grim determination, Hunter had flown to Alabama, had asked around about the pair of men, and was finally directed to a small town in southern Alabama called August, in Washington County.

Everyone in the state of Alabama seemed to know stories about three young men from August, and their exploits on the football fields, and then their subsequent successes in life.

Mr. Shelly had quite the reputation as a successful, Ivy League educated lawyer. The other two were described as heroes by those who knew anything about them. If only they all knew these men's real passions, Hunter thought, more than once.

Hunter was starting to get a picture of something, but he couldn't yet put his finger on the truth. But he was close. Closer than he had been in the previous two years.

And the night before he was to drive down to the small town, Hunter had fallen off of the wagon, and in the most spectacular fashion. It had started with a small, celebratory drink. And it had ended that morning in a dirty motel room, with a disgusting woman in his bed, and him wanting to die.

Hunter walked out into the late morning sunshine, looked up to the heavens with a silent prayer, and took the deepest breath of his life. It cleared his mind, and he knew his next moves.

He still had not contacted anyone at work, home, or in his life in anyway. He felt free to do what he had wanted to do since Karen had been murdered.

He wanted to kill Mr. Christopher Shelly, Esq. The man the media called *the Preacher.*

And he wanted to do it outside of the law, and outside of bringing the man to justice. Justice for the twenty-two people he had brutally killed in the interim since killing Hunter's beautiful wife.

Hunter didn't give a damn about those people, or their families. He was driven like a bullet towards the southern part of the state, and a dance with fate and death.

A gruesome threesome indeed, he thought to himself, as he headed to a rental car agency he remembered was nearby.

He had no way of knowing what would be in store for him, in August, Alabama.

Chapter 22

"Chris and Mark? Sure, I know the boys. They are both quite something around these parts. Well, them and their third partner, Three," the fat, old man behind the desk told Hunter with a laugh.

"Those boys were the belle of the ball in these parts all their lives, I'll tell ya," he said with another grin and a drink of the iced whiskey sitting in front of him on his desk blotter.

Hunter looked around at the lawyer's large office, appreciating the time and history of the man's small town career that showed on all four walls of the wood paneled room.

He looked back at the old man sitting behind at least twenty square feet of redwood desk and smiled at him. The two men sat there staring at each other until it became awkward.

The lawyer cleared his throat loudly. "Umm, yeah. So, the boys were bright stars in this town, that's for sure. But they had two other friends in their little group. You would see them all riding their bikes up and down Main, and stopping for ice cream at the Dairy Queen. But that was a sadder story than I can tell you," the lawyer said.

"You need to talk to Dorthea, ummm, Dottie. She should tell you the story," the lawyer said, standing.

Hunter noticed that the aged lawyer was about the same height standing as he had been sitting.

"Well, thank you for your time. I appreciate the information. Can you direct me to this Dorthea, please?" Hunter asked.

"Sure, sure. No problem," Mr. Benjamin Rigsby, Esq., said to the FBI agent who had introduced himself as Hunter.

But Ben knew who the man was. He had seen him on the television. Everyone in these parts knew the man who was chasing *the Preacher*.

"Those boys aren't in any trouble, are they?" Ben asked. Hunter just smiled at him again.

"No, no. Just some routine checks. Nothing to bother with. Nothing at all," Hunter told the man.

The old and venerable lawyer gave the FBI agent the directions to Dottie's family home, about a half hour outside of town, and wished him well. Hunter thanked the man, turned, and left.

Mr. Benjamin Rigsby, Esq, watched the FBI agent get into a silver sedan parked in front of his law firm building, and sighed loudly.

It had only been a matter of time, he thought to himself.

Watching the agent drive out of downtown August, Benjamin Rigsby shook his head, and thought that maybe, just maybe, he knew what that had all been about. And he didn't blame the boys. Not one bit.

And the agent didn't even know that he, himself had been fired, and that it had been all over the national news for weeks. He didn't even know that the FBI was looking for him.

Well, Benjamin Rigsby, Esq, wasn't about to be the man to tell the agent, and that was for sure, the older man thought to himself.

The agent was here in August, and that was his own fault. His own funeral, the old lawyer thought to himself, chuckling.

Benjamin walked back to his over-sized desk, picked up the phone sitting on the leather blotter, and dialed a number. A number he didn't think he would have had to call this early.

Taking a last sip of the watered- down whiskey in the crystal tumbler on his desk, the voice who picked up on the other end of the line didn't need to say a word.

Ben told the other end of the call the news, and the connection ended as quickly as it had been established.

It was a much nicer home than Hunter expected. He parked in front of the sprawling ranch style house after driving down a long, tree-lined drive.

It seemed that this Dottie woman had done well for herself as the housekeeper of the Higgsby family, Hunter thought to himself as he got out of the car.

The wind was brisk, and had turned cold overnight. He pulled his suit jacket closer, telling himself that he needed to buy a winter jacket.

He looked up at the Christmas lights twinkling on the ranch home. They were multi-colored, and Hunter felt a momentary pause in his chest, remembering putting up large-bulb, multi-colored Christmas lights with his Karen.

His breath caught a little, and he had to regain a little composure before ringing the doorbell. He hated himself suddenly for how much he craved a drink.

The door opened immediately, like the occupants of the home had seen him coming from a mile away.

A large black man had opened the door and stood in the opening, staring at Hunter with such a look of distrust that Hunter immediately felt unwelcome. But he knew he had every right to be there, so he cleared him throat, and asked after Dottie.

"She's in da back. Whatch'a want wit her?" the man asked. Hunter flashed his credentials and told the large man that he just had a couple of questions.

The large man looked Hunter up and down, not even looking much at his extended identification, and then motioned Hunter to follow him into the house.

The inside of the home was decorated and cared for in meticulous detail. Hunter had spent his entire career walking around homes in poor neighborhoods, ghettos, and the projects. He was used to seeing hardship, poverty, and disdain for living better.

But none of that was apparent in this home. He had not expected it to be anything more than it was, but he was suddenly aware of his own prejudices based on his long career, and a little from his upbringing. He had seen the worse of humanity, and now he expected it at every turn. He liked that fact about as much as the fact that he wished he was drunk.

There were family pictures on the walls, real plants, tenderly cared for at every angle, and a sense of calm over the whole place.

Hunter felt immediately better just for being there. The home radiated calm. He assumed that the mother of the place was the real reason for the sense of home.

The large black man who name Hunter had not gotten, brought him into a back sunroom. The room was so severely similar to the sunroom where his sweet Karen had met her demise that Hunter stopped and had to clear his mind for a few more seconds than was socially acceptable.

The people in the room just stared at him, waiting for him to gain his equilibrium. Finally, he was able to get his bearings, and notice the small woman sitting in the wicker rocking chair in the middle of the room.

She was old. That was apparent. Her tight crop of hair was mostly gray, and her face looked wrinkled as much as a woman's face could be. But she radiated calm, peace, and humor. Hunter instantly felt at peace in her presence. She was one of those people that others always described as a sage. A wisdom. A medicine woman.

Hunter knew who she was and how she had spent her life, but nothing had prepared him for what he was feeling as he stepped down into the sun-filled room, and sat across from the woman.

"Floyd, get us some coffee, dear, will, ya?" she said to the large man brooding in the entrance to the sunroom. The man, apparently this Floyd, gave Hunter one last look of disgust, turned, and walked back into the comfortable gloom of the house.

Hunter turned back to the aged woman, who looked calmly and placidly back at him. Hunter felt like he wouldn't be able to keep much from this woman. Like she knew all the answers to any question that she would ask him. He just got a grandmotherly sense from the woman. It was off-putting, but Hunter was charmed by her all the same.

He started.

"I don't know if you know why I'm here, Mrs. Henderson," he said. She interrupted him sharply.

"Better call me Dottie, son. Let's cut the bull and get ta' why you'se here," she said in a soft, yet commanding voice.

"Yes, ma'am. I'm here to ask you some questions about the boys," he said calmly.

161

He watched her eyes for deception. For anything, really. But she looked back at him calmly, and with a knowing look that was filled with both wisdom and humor.

Again, Hunter felt a strange sense of comfort, and at the same time, off-putting guilt and shame in his belly. He felt like this wise sage of a small woman could see into his soul.

"The boys, huh?" she said. She just nodded to Hunter.

"I guess I better start at the start, so they say," she said to Hunter.

He pulled out a small spiral notebook, and poised a pencil over a blank page. He knew without saying anything that this woman knew exactly why he was here, without him having to ask a single question.

"When Three was born, I know'd he'd be a special kind of boy," she started. There was no way Hunter was going to interrupt this woman's narrative.

"Three come from a long line of special men, but Three was more than any of 'em, you know? Bigger, was going places," she said. Hunter just nodded.

"When that boy was just a little bit of a thing, he naturally surrounded himself with his people. His little group of friends," she said.

She was deep in memoires, and Hunter knew enough about questioning to not say a word. Just take notes.

"First, it was that little slip of a gal, Mary, and her brother, Matthew. Those kids were just the kindest kids I ever seen, and they loved Three, and he loved them," she said wistfully.

She was full of sorrow suddenly, and it threw Hunter off. He listened even more intently.

"When the kids were all in first or second grade, and Three was just as tight with the little girl and her brother, they did everything together, mind you, and then they adopted Four and Five," she said.

162

"Three was always a lonely little thing, but now he had his own little family around him. He picked them kids because they was like him. They all had troubles at the homes, and they all needed each other, that's a for-sure thing there," she went on.

"You'd see them kids riding bikes all over the county, up and down the streets, all five of 'em, thick as pea soup, and wasn't nothing going to separate the lot," she said.

And then Hunter watched her look out the back windows to the sunroom, and the deepening night outside. She signed mightily, and turned back to Hunter, a glint of moisture in her eyes.

"Up until the kids were in the eighth grade. Three had just the biggest ole' love for Mary. He looked at her like a grown man looks at his wife of years, ya know?" She waited for Hunter to say something.

He cleared his throat.

"Yes ma'am, I do know," he said in reply.

"I bet ya do. Well, it was a regula' day, just the same as any other, only there was a evil cast to this day. It was hot as hot could be before noon, late summer, and the kids went to the Dairy Queen out on route 23 to get the ice cream," she grew quieter.

"Three grew up with money, the others didn't, so he was always treating his friends. That boy never did have no problem with that," she said.

She smiled a little, thinking of the boy she helped raise. But then the melancholy look took over her face once more.

"There was no reason, none that that Officer McCrery was even there, looking for a kid that matched Matthew's description. There had been some vandalism at the overpass over at Route 43, and someone said that a young black boy, on a red bike, was seen leaving wit' some cans a' paint," she said.

"So this white man with a gun, came harassing young Matthew, just 'cause the boy had a red bike," she said.

Hunter swallowed. He felt sure he knew where the story was heading.

Just then, the large man, Floyd, came back in with a silver coffee service, and placed it on the wicker table between the two. Both the wise, old woman, and the disenfranchised officer of the law nodded their thanks, and they went about pouring their own cups.

The woman took a sip of the hot coffee, black as could be, and sighed. She continued with her story.

"That man had no business there, but they sure told stories after the fact, that be for sure" she said.

She took another drink of the hot coffee. Hunter felt a little shame for putting cream and sugar into his coffee.

"He walked right up to the kids, took little Matthew off his bike, and throwed him right there on the hot concrete. Ain't no reason for such. None at all. And then Mary got a bee in her bonnet, and jumped over on top of Matthew, screamin'. The other three boys, all big, strong boys, got off their bikes, but I knows they didn't mean nothin'. I knows it!" she said.

She was growing from quiet to angry retelling the story, Hunter thought.

"That police man got spooked, and before you knew what was happening, he done pulled his revolver out, and aimed it at the black babies. Both Matthew and Mary put they's arms up, warding off the man, and he shot them both. Right there in the parking lot of the Dairy Queen. Right on the concrete them kids rode they's bikes on, every day, about," she said.

She was suddenly overcome with sadness again.

"Well, of course, you know they covered it all up. 'Justifiable cause' they called it. Murder, is what I calls it," she said.

Hunter knew from experience what she meant. He, himself, had been on the lucky end of just such a finding of cause. He escaped prison by the skin of his teeth for his own actions.

And as he thought about his own actions, it all suddenly became clear. He swallowed visibly and noisily.

He looked back at the older woman. She was reaching over to a tall, narrow table next to her chair, and picked up a picture frame that he hadn't noticed until she had reached for it.

She handed him the frame. Turning it around, he felt his stomach drop.

It was a black-and-white photo, obviously several years old. In the picture, five prepubescent children sat on bikes, all in a row. Three of the children were white males, the other two were a black boy and a black girl. All of the children were facing the camera with big grins on their faces. Except two.

One white boy, sitting on a white bike in the middle of the line of kids, and the black girl, sitting on a darker bike, with a white basket attached to the handlebars, next to him. Those two children were looking at each other, and the smiles they shared were directed at each other, and no one else.

Hunter now knew the whole story.

He knew exactly why *the Preacher* was killing the way he was. And he suddenly knew that he had gotten it all wrong.

The Preacher wasn't a single man. *The Preacher* wasn't the lawyer from New York State, whose black and white picture had haunted Hunter's dreams of late.

No, he thought to himself, starting to rise from his seat, *the Preacher* was a whole team of people, all with the same agenda. And it had started the day that little black boy and little black girl had been killed by the nervous white cop outside a Dairy Queen, so many years ago. And whose deaths had enraged a group of kids with means and above average intelligences.

Hunter suddenly felt lightheaded.

He looked back over at the little, grayed woman, who was placidly looking back at him with deep, knowing eyes. He wanted to bolt out of the room and run, and never look back. But her voice stopped him.

"Now you know, Mr. Hunter-man, why them boys are a doin' what they's a doin'," she whispered. Hunter nodded. He knew the truth. And as the saying goes, the truth set him free.

The old, dark woman winked at him as Hunter felt the barrel of a gun, pressed against the back of his head.

Chapter 23

The hammer being cocked, loud in his ear, made his blood turn ice cold.

"Slowly reach into the left side of your suit jacket, and remove the Glock 9-millimeter pistol held there with your thumb and forefinger around the grip," a calm, steely voice said behind him.

He had no choice but to obey. He knew one small step, one small movement against what the voice told him to do, and he would be dead without a moment's hesitation. He knew this to be true like he knew that the sun rose and set each day.

He also wondered how the voice knew such intimate details, like what service semi-automatic pistol he carried. That fact made his knees almost give out.

He did as the voice behind him said to do. He pulled out his service pistol with his forefinger and thumb around the grip. He held it out to the side of his body, and met the eyes of the woman still sitting serenely in front of him.

She nodded slightly to him, got up, and walked out of the sunroom. Hunter knew that no one in this house was on his side, especially the old black woman. In a lot of ways, she probably was the catalyst behind the entire situation unfolding around Hunter. A situation he, himself, had no control over.

The voice told him to drop the gun, and he complied. He felt his life slip away as the gun clattered to the tiled floor. He knew that his life was over on this day. A day that didn't really mean anything special. It was just a random Thursday. How very sad, he thought.

A tear fell from his left eye, and he wondered suddenly how much it would hurt.

The voice told him to slowly turn around. When he did so, he looked up into the eyes of a grown-up visage of one of the boys in the black and white picture he had just looked at. The boy who was looking lovingly at the young black girl. Three. The boy that they called Three.

Hunter saw the emptiness in the young man's eyes. He swallowed loudly. He had never been in a tenser situation in his life, and he knew that his life was in this young man's hands, and this young man had already killed dozens of people. Hunter was more worthy of death than any of them. He wasn't going to talk his way out of this.

"We are going for a ride. Outside," Three said to Hunter.

Hunter couldn't find his words. He abhorred showing weakness, but he knew that he had no dog in this fight. He was going to try to control what he could control, but he knew that

Three had no compunction about killing him at all. All Three needed was a proper place to stage his body, for maximum effect.

Three led Hunter out to his own rental car. Parked next to his car in the circular driveway was a forest green Jeep Wrangler with a hard top. Hunter just shook his head at the seemingly normal scene around him, while his insides boiled because he knew where Three was taking him.

Straight to his death.

His mind was fuzzy, his breath was coming in short, quick bursts. He knew that his flight or fight system was kicking in, but he didn't know what he could do to change the paradigm, as he had been taught, years ago at the academy.

But this foe was a professional, and Hunter knew in his soul that he didn't stand a chance against him.

Three never took the heavy revolver off of direct sight with Hunter's head. He told Hunter to get into the driver's side of the car, and Three slid in smoothly in the passenger seat. Not for even a second did Hunter have a chance to get away.

Three informed Hunter of where they were headed, and Hunter almost couldn't make his hands work on the shifter. But he got himself together, and didn't want to die before he could ask questions, or find a way to get away.

So, he cleared his mind, put the car into drive, and pulled out to the long driveway leading off of the property.

They headed south, towards Mobile. Hunter glanced occasionally at the serial killer sitting next to him in the rental car, and every time his eyes met the eyes of Three, a jolt of electricity shot down his spine. He almost peed himself when Three said two words as they pulled out on the highway.

"No talking."

Hunter let his focus move from the thick tree cover outside the window of his rental car, and the gun pointed at him without wavering.

For the entire forty-five minute drive to Mobile, the gun never moved, and Three never took his eyes off of Hunter. Three was poised for anything, and Hunter could tell why he had been so successful in his pursuit of his plan. And Hunter knew that the plan was exactly that.

A Plan for whatever purpose. The purpose, Hunter couldn't figure out. But the means, that, Hunter saw clearly.

As they pulled into the city of Mobile, Alabama, Three gave directions without taking his eyes off of Hunter. Hunter followed the directions perfectly, while looking for a way to change the paradigm. But he never saw an opening. He never saw a way to overcome Three and the gun aimed at his own face.

Hunter pulled the rental car down an alley close to downtown Mobile. He could smell the Gulf, close by. He slowed down as he pulled along a brick building, and stopped in front of a tall, white garage door on the back side of the building.

There was no one around, and Hunter felt keenly alone. He wondered if he could scream for help when they got out of the car. But Hunter never got the chance.

The garage door opened in front of the car. Two men, both dressed in all black, stood to either side of the door. Three instructed Hunter to drive into the dark bowels of the brick building. Hunter refused.

Three pressed the gun into Hunter's temple, cocking the hammer on the back of the pistol, and pushing the barrel hard against his head. It hurt. Three told him that he would kill him where he sat, they had contingency plans for that. Hunter believed him.

So, he pulled the car into the deep confines of the brick building, not knowing what to expect.

One of the men opened the driver's door, pulling Hunter out of his seat. Hunter saw that it was the lawyer from New York State. The man they called Four. The man who was photographed in Seattle.

170

Hunter felt a hatred for the man that he couldn't explain. He was convinced that this man had killed his Karen. So, Hunter started fighting back. But he wasn't the physical specimen as these three men. His meager fighting was hampered by stronger men, and his own abuse of his body over the last several weeks.

Already, even though Hunter knew he was about to die, he wanted a drink. A drink of anything. His mouth salivated at the thought. And he was ashamed of that fact.

The three men, the team, as Hunter referred to them in his mind, manhandled him across a concrete floor, through the darkness of the inside of the non-descript building, and down a flight of stairs against the far wall.

At the bottom of the stairs was a door. When Three opened the door, and the other two men pushed Hunter into it, it became quite clear what was going to happen.

The room was soundproof, as Hunter's ears popped when he entered the room, and it was more of a box than an actual room. Hunter glanced around the dark room in panic. And he again fought against the two men holding his arms. He whipped his arms about, trying to loosen their vice-like grips on him. But again, he could hardly move against the men.

And then Three was behind him, with his strong arm wrapped around Hunter's throat. Three whispered something in Hunter's ear that he could barely hear against the panic thrashing sound in his head.

"If you don't stop fighting, we will just put a bullet in your brain. And you won't get any answers," he said. Hunter calmed down. Enough to see the chair in the middle of the room.

The men maneuvered Hunter into the chair. It looked like an old wooden electric chair from ancient movies that Hunter had watched as a child. And then one of the men besides him confirmed that that was exactly what it was.

Again, panic set in, and Hunter was sure that the men were going to electrocute him to death. But nothing was attached to the chair, and no cables or wires were led to the walls, or sources of electricity.

So, once again, he calmed himself, looking for a way to change the paradigm.

The men moved quickly, methodically, and with practiced movements.

They strapped Hunter's wrists down to the arms of the wooden chair with large leather bands. The buckles looked new. Then they reached down and strapped his ankles in the same way.

Finally, Three walked in front of him, and reached around Hunter's neck and strapped his neck to the back piece of the chair. Hunter was completely immobile. He could only move his eyelids and his mouth. He realized that that was exactly what the team wanted.

Suddenly, a bright, overhead light came on, and Hunter realized that he had been successfully put into an interrogation scenario. He was impressed with the men around him. He had to give it to the young men, they always seemed to have a plan.

Hunter suddenly wondered how they had set all this up, as if they had known all along how things would play out. These men had always been five steps in front of him, and he was damn mad, suddenly, at how they had managed that.

He stared back at the men in defiance, daring them to try to get information from him. He was ready for torture. He was ready for pain. He steeled himself for whatever was coming.

What he wasn't ready for was the abject dismissal of the three men. After making sure that Hunter was immobile, two of the men left the room, and Hunter could hear their footsteps leave up the stairs, and out of the building.

That just left him and Three. Three stood in front of the open door, and eyed Hunter with flat, emotionless eyes. And then he spoke.

"Dr. Hunter O'Connor, PhD, and twenty-five-year veteran of the Federal Bureau of Investigations. Widow to Karen

O'Connor, nay, Mulroney. I have been following you and your career for some time. You are a genius-level forensic scientist, and a sadist. You are a self-professed alcoholic, and passably insane. And this is the last room that you are ever going to see," Three said all in one breath.

Hunter didn't know what to say. He just listened to this serial killer pronounce doom over him.

"For the last month, you have dropped off of the map. We lost your whereabouts after New York, and when you popped back up after using your credit card to book a flight to Montgomery, we knew we needed to act. We all rushed home, and set this little meeting up," Three continued.

"We lost you again after that. Your last cell phone call pinged off of a tower in SE Montgomery, and we knew it was only a matter of time before you showed up in August. So, we waited, and when we got word that you were hotter on our trail than we realized, we had to take action. I hope if you don't mind if we put a plug in this little breech to the Plan in the only way we really know how to," he said with dispassionate eyes staring straight into Hunter.

"We picked up your cell phone location two days ago in Montgomery, and sent a friend to retrieve it. It was in a bundle of your clothes in a trash bin behind a seedy motel. The battery in the phone was almost dead, but it was enough for us to trace."

"Apparently, after you left all of your belongings in that motel, the cleaning staff threw it all away. So, we knew that you weren't traced, or followed, to August. Thank you for that, by the way," Three told him.

Hunter was instantly angry at himself. He should have never tried to take matters into his own hands. He should have followed procedures. He should have told Red.

But he was proud, drunk, and full of rage. So, he had gone against character, and landed himself in this soundproof room, about to die. He only had himself to blame. He knew that suddenly. And he also suddenly knew that these men were much more organized and professional than anyone at the Bureau knew.

Hunter was impressed with the whole situation. He had no idea, in all of his experience, in how these men could do all that they did. The reasoning behind the Plan was outside of his ability to grasp.

"The rest of the world is moving on without you, Dr. O'Connor. Your team at the FBI has already replaced you and your men. The heat has been ratcheted up, but we are prepared for that. The Plan will continue, but on a different trajectory. Like your training at the academy taught you, we are changing the paradigm," he said.

He moved closer to Hunter. His hands were empty, but Hunter felt like this was it. This was the end. But he was wrong. Far from it, in fact.

Three walked up to the immobile man, and ripped his shirt open. Hunter heard the buttons pop off of his collared dress shirt, and hit the concrete floor with tiny pings of sound.

Hunter watched at Three pulled a familiar black tip marker from his back pocket, and still couldn't find his voice. He watched as Three wrote out his doom onto his hairless chest.

Three wrote the number, large, on Hunter's chest, and stepped back. Hunter looked down at his exposed skin, seeing the dark number 96, loud on his chest. He looked back at Three, and barely suppressed a whimper.

Three reached outside of the room and brought a Bible into the light. He was flipping through pages of the worn Bible, and Hunter knew what he was doing. He was looking for the perfect Bible verse.

Hunter was suddenly damned if Three would pin a page to his body. He started fighting against the restraints. But they held, and Hunter was soon breathless with exertion. Three just looked dispassionately back at the agent, and then reached into his front pockets and pulled out a pair of latex gloves.

174

He tore a page from the Bible, after showing a bit of emotion at finding just the right verse. He pulled a pen from another pocket, and Hunter watched as the killer in front of him marked the page, and then held the Bible page against the wall to Hunter's right.

Three stabbed the pen through the page and into the sound suppressant material lining the wall. The page stuck to the foam suppressant, staring Hunter back in the face.

Three didn't say another word, he just walked back towards the door. Hunter knew now how he was going to die. He wasn't going to be shot, stabbed, or suffocated. Not like all the other victims.

No, this sadistic fuck was going to leave Hunter strapped to this Godforsaken chair, and let him starve to death. Or dehydrate himself to death. Or any other ghastly way to die by being left here for God knew how long.

Hunter finally did pee himself. Three looked dispassionately at the puddle spreading out on the floor under the heavy wooden chair. He grinned at Hunter and Hunter was instantly full of rage.

And he finally found his voice. He shouted at the killer before the killer could leave out of the door to the small room.

"Why the fuck did he kill my wife?" he yelled at the back of the killer. Three froze, and turned around.

"Why my Karen? She was innocent, you fucking fuck!" he yelled. The effort took the rest of his strength.

Three looked deep into the eyes of the man who had chased him unsuccessfully for two years.

And Three told him eight final words. The last eight words that Hunter would ever hear.

"He didn't. I did. She was your sacrifice," he said.

Three did some few last-minute adjustments, and walked out of the room, leaving the light on. The door slammed shut behind the killer, and Hunter was stuck in the deepening isolation of the room. It pressed in around him, and he panicked for the final time.

As he panicked, the sounds pressed into his skull, dampened from the foam sound suppressant on the walls, and Hunter became even more terrified in the echoes around him.

Eventually, Hunter regained his composure, and stopped freaking out against the restraints. He could hear nothing. No sound entered the room. All Hunter heard was the sound of his own heart, beating in his eardrums.

He finally glanced around at the room, looking for a way to escape. But it was no use. He was stuck as stuck could be, and he knew that he was going to die right where he sat. If starvation or thirst didn't kill him, then the detox of his body from the alcohol would surely do the job.

His eyes finally found the Bible page stuck to the wall next to him. And as his eyes read the underlined verse, he prayed for the first time in his life. And it was a prayer that asked God to just take him quickly. He didn't want to be stuck in this room with his regrets, and his sins, loud in his mind.

"...I plead with you to give your bodies to God because of all he has done for you. Let them be a living and holy sacrifice—the kind he will find acceptable..."

And for the rest of Hunter's life, his thoughts were on the sacrifice of his wife for his own sins, and how he had failed in all that he knew. How he had failed all those who had come before him. He failed those who were going to come after him. He had failed his wife, Karen. Oh, his sweet, innocent Karen.

And finally, his thoughts stayed on the fact of how his life had been for nothing.

His dying thought, several torturous days later, was on how he had been mistaken about the world, all of his life.

His entire life had been for absolutely nothing.

PART III

Chapter 24

Red walked down the dark stairs hating the fact that someone else was always on the scene first. And he still wasn't used to the smell. Before he even walked into the box-like room, he could smell his old friend. His first thought was that it was a damn shame.

A real damn shame.

He walked into the bright light given off by the spotlight set up by the forensic team, aimed into the dark room. And there was Hunter. Or what was left of him.

Damn shame, Red thought again to himself.

He looked away briefly. He had to steel himself to see his old friend and partner in the last, ghastly, visage of life. Hunter's body was emaciated, and he wore a hideous death mask.

He turned back to the room, and put on his professional face. He would mourn later. But first, he had the first tangible lead of this entire case, and the shame of it was, he wasn't even on the damn task force anymore. But he wasn't going to let this go.

His supervisor had allowed him to travel down to Mobile, Alabama, just to collect Hunter. For old times' sake. But Red was going to take this clue in his mouth like one of his prize-winning pit bulls, and not let it go.

He had Hunter's bank and credit card statements. He followed the paper trail. He had known Hunter had been in Alabama long before the anonymous phone call had come into the task force hotline with the address of where Hunter's body would be found. They were still analyzing that phone call.

It had come in from a burner cell phone, but even those could be tracked, somewhat. Every cell phone in the world, even the ones not linked to an account name or number, were still tracked by the cell towers that they pinged off of.

So, with some patience, and a lot of eye strain looking at long lists of numbers and codes, you could find out where that burner phone was turned on, connected to one of dozens of networks, and you could follow the trail of it, as long as it stayed on, and the network card was used.

He had done that last week, and now knew as much about the link between the phone records, Hunter's financial records, and witnesses at both locations to figure out what the hell had happened to his old friend.

Red stepped into the room and saw his old partner's body again. He looked away from the death mask on Hunter's face, and looked down at his hands, which were bloody, and darkly purple. The nails were cracked and broken, and deep gouges were dug into the heavy wood under his hands. Red shook his head again, a deep sense of sadness blossoming in his chest.

He caught his emotions, but just barely. His friend had suffered unfairly. He had suffered mightily. Red turned away from the other forensic investigators in the room, and pretended to examine the sound-compressing foam stapled to the walls.

In actuality, he was wiping away tears. Tears for his partner. Tears for the lives that had been torn apart by this senseless act. He knew that he would have to talk to his priest when he got back to DC.

"Sir, signatures are the same. But instead of taking the entire shirt, it looks like he just cut a piece from the bottom," a tech told Red.

He had to speak it to Red's back, as Red was still pretending to examine the walls. Red nodded to the man, heard him turn away, and Red wiped his eyes again. He needed to be strong for this.

Red took a deep breath, squared his shoulders, said a little prayer under his breath for his fallen brother, and turned back towards the body of his partner and longtime friend.

He vowed to the man who had suffered so much at the hands of the sadistic killer he would do everything he could to bring that killer to justice.

And he vowed it so harshly that he could feel something snap within him.

Something cleared up in his mind, almost as if a blockage had been removed and he could think and see clearly.

He knew where he needed to start, and he wasn't going to let anything or anyone stop him. Not his supervisor, not his wife and family, and most assuredly not his inability to see the things that Hunter had been able to see.

Red was going on the hunt. Like his ancestors before him, he was driven towards a dance with destiny. A dance with *the Preacher*. And one of them wasn't going to walk away from the dance.

That was his vow to the body of Hunter O'Connor, his partner and friend.

Chapter 25

Three men sat around a dark oak table, surrounded by the workings, the research, the Plan, stuck to standing boards, written on white boards, lines and lines of actionable planning on computer screens.

The men were silently looking at each other. They all knew it was time for a refresh. A re-planning. Time to move on.

It was time to take a deep breath, find their focus, and press on.

"Are we going to be able to keep the contact with Colbie X? I mean, you left her pretty abruptly, didn't you?" Four asked Three. Three was looking at the ground. He looked up at his boyhood friend.

"Yeah, I explained it to her. I had to get home for a business emergency. She is pretty intuitive though, so I'm not sure. I should reach out. But then again, maybe not. The plan needs to come first," he answered.

"Guys, can we please discuss how we are going to keep going?" Five asked. He had a bit of panic in his voice. "Hunter got so close. He knew everything before we showed up," he went on.

"I think we got lucky. Everything we have seen, he didn't tell anyone where he was going," Three said.

"Yeah, but if he could figure it out, so could these new guys on the task force," Five said.

"Well, let's change the paradigm. Let's move from here, find a new base of operations. Cut ties with the people here," Four said.

"We can't do that, and you know that," Three said to both of his friends.

"But we can change the Plan. We can move bases, and we can try a new approach," he went on.

"What's your idea, Three?" Four knew his best friend was up to something.

"Let me show you guys something," Three said.

He got up from his seat, and led his friends over to the bank of computer screens against the north wall. He sat down in front of the main console, and started typing.

"We can look for a new base of operations later. All we need is some out-buildings, a house, and a bunch of land. If you ran that search, we would find a hundred suitable places. We can purchase it through the blind trust that Five set up last year, but this, guys, this is what I wanted to show you," he said.

On the screen was an overhead map of a section of southeast Colorado. Three zoomed the map down enough to show a small town, with only four cross streets, and probably only one stoplight.

"What are we looking at, Three?" Five asked.

"This is Ordway, Colorado. It's just an example of what we should be aiming towards," Three answered.

"I don't understand," Four said.

"Guys, Ordway is just like a hundred thousand small towns in America. Less than two thousand people, not much of a police force, no crime, very few cameras," Three said.

The guys started to understand. The heat was on, so they needed to change the Plan. And the Plan only said that there needed to be 120 victims. Not necessarily where those victims came from. The less chance of discovery, of course, was the key.

"We are going to start changing our research techniques. These small towns have one huge disadvantage. They would notice three strangers wandering around for a week. So, we need to start more disciplined digital research. Find me people in these small towns who live alone. They may be alone all day, working from home. They will have no one coming around. If they live in the outskirts of these small towns, even better," Three told the team.

"And since the bodies wouldn't be found for a little bit, we will start a new strategy. The anonymous call to the press. All of these small towns have one thing in common. They usually have a local newspaper," Three said.

The other two men smiled. This would make the plan a lot more fun, they knew. They would do most of the work right from home. The missions would go from a week or more each, to a single day.

The hard part was getting there, unseen, as it always had been. But they were getting quite adept at the changes they had to make to not be noticed. This was just a new way of accomplishing their goals.

They all knew that before it was over, they would have to change the rules again. The new task force looked serious. Much more serious than the last one.

This task force was much more funded, and had a lot more power behind them. They had already been compared to the Highway Men that pursued Bonnie and Clyde in the century before. They had even employed a couple of electronic investigators to the team. Five, himself, knew a couple of the Federal Computer Crimes Investigators.

They had been a part of the team who had caught the hackers several years prior, where Five had made a name for himself, without anyone realizing who he was, and that he had just been a kid.

Now, Five had to step up his own game. He relished the challenge.

The team would just have to change with the times, as they always had.

And with a simple goal in mind, the men could accomplish the plan using the tools they already had, and learn as they went. They had the confidence in themselves to do this.

All three men walked away from the short meeting feeling a lot better. It was time to get back to work.

They still had several years, several victims, and several goals to achieve what they set out to achieve.

It was time to move into the second half of the game, and press forward to the end.

After all, it's all they really knew.

Chapter 26

Sylvia Deveroux's back hurt. Those damn chickens were getting better at hiding their eggs.

The bastards, she thought to herself, as she rubbed her lower back. And the weather was turning.

Her arthritis was acting up, which always meant snow. She would need to get the boy from town to come and help her move her plants inside.

She hated paying the boy out of her egg money, but he did work hard when he came out to the Deveroux farm. She had to give the boy that much credit.

She put on her tin pot to heat water. Her mother had used the same old tin pot for tea most of Sylvia's childhood, and Sylvia was no different. No sir, no reason to change things up on account of the rest of the world changing.

She was eighty-eight damn years old, for heck's sake, and there was no reason things should be changing on any account, she thought. The water was soon boiling over the gas flame of the ancient stovetop, and she added in the loose tea leaves. A dash of chamomile, some honey added to the water, and one of her last sprigs of lavender from the garden this year. A good, solid tea.

She would enjoy the tea as the weather outside changed though out the day. She looked forward to the cold. It was an old friend. A reminder to slow down a bit, relax, and enjoy life. The rest of the year was so busy, she thought, as she used an old wooden spoon to stir the tea. She was ready to slow down.

The wind was picking up outside, and as she glanced out the front windows, she saw that the sky was graying over. Yup, she thought, snow is coming alright. There wouldn't be time to bring in the plants.

Well, so be it. She didn't much have use for any of them except they were pretty. Well, the peppers she could use. So, she took the water pot off of the stove, wrapped her shawl around her bony shoulders, and walked outside to bring in the cayenne pepper plants in the terra cotta planters. There were two of the pots, and although they weighted quite a bit each, Sylvia had always been a lot stronger than she looked.

Certainly stronger than the two husbands she had buried right here on her family's old farm.

Those two men had been pretty, but not much use outside of the bedroom. Why she was thinking of those two old fools as she trudged in the two pepper pots was certainly strange, she thought.

But, she had been having a lot of strange feelings lately. Like things were coming to a head, and she was just there to see it. A rather bizarre thought. A lot of those lately as well. Thoughts and feelings, she said under her breath. Neither of which would get supper on the table.

185

Settling the pots just inside the front door, Sylvia walked back into the kitchen, and filtered the tea into a tall glass jug. She added three slices from a lemon she had sliced just that morning, and set the jug to cool on the kitchen table.

She would busy herself gathering the fixings for a good stew for that night. A good stew with homemade biscuits.

She would make extra, and send the boy from town home with a dozen or so. His momma would appreciate that. That woman had more children running around their little house than she knew what do to with, that was for sure.

And then she remembered that there was no reason now for the boy to come out, at least not until the snow blew through. Her old mind was slipping, that was sure, and she laughed to herself as she still prepared the ingredients to feed at least eight people. And why not, she thought. She had the food. And the time.

Her thoughts then went back to the woman in town with all the children running crazy.

And here was old Sylvia, out on her farm, childless, and just as happy as a peach for it. She loved her solitude and quiet more than just about anything else in this world. Well, almost as much as fresh biscuits.

Sylvia spent the rest of the late morning, and right through lunch time, putting together the stew. She knew she would make too much, but she would can what she didn't eat right away.

With the snows setting in, here in southeast Colorado, right in the Arkansas River Valley, she would need to rely on canned goods, and the vegetables and pickled fruits down in the cellar.

She never ventured off the farm once winter really set in. There was no reason for it, that was a sure thing, she thought to herself as she set out flouring the table to roll out the biscuit dough.

That night, as the snows outside started really piling up against the barn, shutting out the world, and blanketing everything in a clean, pure white blanket, Sylvia felt content, happy, and very full.

She patted her belly wistfully, and thanked the good Lord for such a good day.

The stew had turned out wonderfully, and she was proud of the fact that she had grown every single ingredient right here on her farm, the last thing in the world that was all hers.

The biscuits had been heavenly, with fresh apple butter from the fall's harvest. Just the right amount of sweetness. She had eaten the biscuits hot from the stove, like dessert before the meal. She smiled at the memory, and patted her belly again.

She sat content in her father's old, battered chair in front of a happily dancing fire. She wore her flannel pajamas, and meditated on her life as she stared into the fire that was just like a thousand other fires in the same fireplace here in the home she had never left.

Thousands of nights, thousands of fires, so much happiness, and a history of family and love. She was content to be alone now. Cherished it, actually.

But this home had kept so many generations of family safe and secure, the world outside hardly ever pressing in. Sure, she thought, wars had taken brothers and uncles away, but the women of her family had always made this farm a home, whether the men came home or not.

Her brother Eli had not. But many had, and now it was just old Sylvia, and she was still alright with that.

Finally, the shadows were stretching, and Sylvia was getting sleepy from watching the dancing flames, and exploring her memories of the last eighty-eight years.

The wind howled outside, but inside her house, she was as warm and safe as a June bug in summer heat.

She could hear the snap of the flames on the seasoned oak logs in the fireplace, and as she was floating off to sleep, right there in her father's oversized chair, a piece of movement caught her attention. Her eyes had almost been fully shut, the warmth pressing in. But the movement brought her fully awake.

She embarrassingly jerked awake, not meaning to show concern. But she didn't need to bother worrying.

The people watching her movements all day knew how strong and independent Sylvia was, and respected her all the more for it.

Sylvia's eyes traveled up from her lap, and saw Death in her living room.

A man stood in front of her, covered head to foot in white military garb. It shocked her that he had made it into her living room without the slightest sound. But she knew deep in her soul what the man's presence in her happy home meant.

He stood out in her home like a peacock in a grocery store. Covered head to foot in some skintight uniform, he was so out of place.

But Sylvia had a sudden, and very eerie feeling, that although the man stood out in her wonderful country home, he was right where he was supposed to be.

And she wasn't surprised, really. She wasn't frightened. For weeks now, she had been having those same feelings her momma had always talked about.

She had known what was coming, just as those with a finger on the pulse of the world always did. Sylvia, herself, had always been one of those people. She always seemed to know what was around the corner.

She looked up into the man's eyes.

"You don't need the mask, son. No one to see you here," she told the figure.

The man reached up, and took off the skintight white neoprene mask, exposing a face younger than she had expected. But it didn't faze her at all.

She had had the best day, and she was ready to leave this world. He was handsome though, she thought.

She wondered whimsically if this man was worth more than just a pretty face. She suddenly felt sure that he was. This man was a catalyst.

Her simple mind, based in her simple life, told her that truth, but not what it meant.

Well, better get on with things. She was ready.

"Well, go on son, do what you came here to do. No reason to jaw about it," she told the man.

The young man only said one thing before he smothered the life out of Sylvia. He simply apologized to her.

She appreciated the respect the man showed her, at the end.

And with those last apologetic words in her ear, Sylvia Deveroux went out of the world the same way that she had come in: silent, thankful, strong, and ready for whatever was to come.

Chapter 27

"I don't give a good goddamn who you are, son, this here is Crowley County, and I'm the big hog around here," the fat sheriff spit into the FBI agent-in-charge's face.

The federal agent wiped his eyes, put his aviator sunglasses back on, and prepared to give this hick asshole a tongue lashing the likes he hadn't had since his momma was wiping his ass.

But Bob Woodyard put his hand against the agent's chest, stopping him in his tracks.

"It's quite alright Sheriff Collins, quite alright. We will just poke around and see if we find anything that will help you fellas out with your investigation," Bob told the fat, balding sheriff.

The sheriff spit out tobacco juice to the side of the road, making Bob Woodyard's stomach lurch, but he held it in, as he did most things concerning local law enforcement.

"I know you federal boys like to come in, swinging your dick like you own the place, but Ms. Deveroux was a local, and she deserves folks who grew up here to find the asshole who done this," the fat sheriff pontificated.

"Damn shame it is. That woman never hurt nobody," the Sheriff said to no one in particular. He was sweating in the cold of the day.

The sheriff was holding his regulation cowboy hat in both hands, wringing it as he looked around the front yard of the dead woman inside the clapboard farmhouse.

Agents and local police were standing off against each other in the yard, trying to get first crack at the scene inside the home.

Luckily, the big name news agencies in 'Springs and Denver were still too far away to have gotten here before the local police and the FBI. There was even talk of Homeland Security sending some boys from Denver and Salt Lake City.

The FBI agents themselves were from the Denver office, so there weren't as "federal" as the local boys wanted to think. But there were still from outside Crowley and Otero counties. And anyone outside the Valley was treated like big-city folks.

The sheriff looked up as his two deputies came riding into the yard on horseback. He had sent them out to find tracks in the snow, but by the look in both men's eyes, they had found absolute shit.

The horses were snorting, their breath clouding up in front of them as they trotted into the side yard. All three men walked over to the two deputies, who were dismounting, rubbing down their sweating horses.

In this temperature, a sweating horse became a dead horse.

191

"Well, find anything, boys?" the sheriff asked his deputies.

The two men glanced at each other, and both shook their heads.

"Well, good goddamn. How does this sumbitch not leave tracks in fresh snow?" the portly sheriff asked the two FBI agents.

"He's a professional, that's for sure," Bob said to the Sheriff.

The older, fat man just shook his head, placing his cream-colored cowboy hat back on it, and walked away muttering to himself.

Bob walked up to the two deputies and started to ask some questions they may not have thought to think about.

"Did you find any kind of back roads, dirt, or gravel?" he asked.

One deputy spoke up, the other man looking at him to do so. "There's an old farm road, about a quarter mile to the northeast. Runs out to Road 17," he said.

"And were there new tire tracks there, son?" Bob asked him.

"Well, yeah, I suppose so. Looked like a couple of different trucks came and went on that old road," he answered the FBI agent.

"How do you know they were truck tracks?" Bob asked, his interest peaked.

"Well, those tracks are a lot deeper into the dirt under the snow. Had to be a truck hauling some hay or livestock," the deputy answered.

"Anything lighter would have stayed up on the snow. At least, in our experience here," the young law enforcement man said.

"Excellent, son, excellent. Do you mind going with my colleague here, and showing him those tracks you found?" Bob asked the deputy.

The man looked cold, but nodded, suddenly wondering where this was heading. Those truck tire tracks, and many like them, crisscrossed this county more than anything else, even animal tracks.

He didn't think they could find out anything from those tracks. But he would humor the "federals" if they wanted to go look at some tire tracks in the middle of some hay fields.

Bob Woodyard watched the three men walk the two hot, sweating horses over to the horse trailer they had come in, and walk them back up the ramp and into the heated interior.

His subordinate, Chase McLean, also watched them stow the horses, and come back down the ramp, and motion the agent to one of the trucks parked nearby. They drove away, heading north.

Bob looked back at the house. He was very cold, but the crisp air brought him mental clarity. He needed to look outside of this situation, and figure out what his own predecessor, God rest him, couldn't. Bob was under a lot more pressure than Hunter O'Connor had been, but he relished the challenge.

Over his own long, industrious career in law enforcement, he had crossed paths with Hunter many times, but they had each made a name for themselves in different areas. Hunter had been the star of the forensic sciences, and the blooming science of profiling.

Bob Woodyard had earned his stripes simply chasing down bad men, and locking them up.

He saw himself as an Old West sort of Lawman. Like Wyatt Earp, or Frank Canton. As a young man, he had even applied for the Texas Rangers. He wanted to be Pat Garrett.

But he found himself a young, unmarred, Christian agent with the Bureau, and his hard nose and quick wit temperament had helped him build a long list of captured criminals who thought there were better than the law. He had showed them all that they were not. Only innocent men were above the law, in Bob's views.

A movie had even been made in the 1990s about a famous case he had been in charge of. *The Fugitive.* And while he was proud that Tommy Lee Jones had portrayed him so well, he really had liked the man, after all, it still stung that he had depicted Bob as a US Marshal, and not a G-man.

Well, this *Preacher* fella was just the next guy who had earned Bob Woodyard on his tail, and that was, historically, not a good place to be.

Bob was also the deputy director of the Criminal, Cyber, Response, and Services Branch of the FBI, and as such, had a much longer reach into the resources, people, and funding he thought he would need to bring this serial killer to justice. And what he now had an inkling about, was to bring in the Intelligence Branch, along with his best cyber investigators, because there was no way this man was doing what he was doing without some serious IT.

It was becoming a brave new world for criminals, Bob knew, and he also knew that like those lawmen in the Old West, he had to stay current with the best evil minds, if he was going to put a stop to the destruction and mayhem those minds brought.

This guy was a little different though, Bob knew, so he relished the chase.

One thing he knew, was that it was almost impossible for law enforcement to catch a career serial killer without that man making a mistake. It was in the mistakes that killers were caught, and this man had not made a mistake yet.

It was concerning, but Bob knew with all of his experience and heart, that all men eventually got sloppy, and slipped, and exposed themselves to those with eyes to see it, and minds to understand it. Bob was the most patient of those men.

With that in mind, Bob Woodyard said a silent prayer in his mind, and walked into the still, cold house where *the Preacher* had done his most recent ghastly deed.

Later, after the techs and other agents had done the best job they could collecting evidence, bagging anything that could be analyzed, and moving away with poor Ms. Deveroux's body, Bob had stayed behind.

After observing the scene, in the cold, drab house, as all the other law agencies' people had departed the homestead, he had an epiphany.

He had wanted this time alone with his thoughts, and his imagination. And as he walked around the chilly, shadowy home, he tried to really get a sense of what the killer had done before, and right after he had ended the life of the older woman.

Bob walked around the home, still not touching anything, but trying to get a sense of things. He closed his eyes, and felt the air in the chilly home.

And then he could see it.

He could see the woman's body in the chair in the living room, fire burning down, fierce wind and snow outside the windows.

Bob watched in his mind as the killer, taller than he had originally assumed, walked around the same rooms he was now in, the woman's body still warm in the other room.

The killer was looking at the family pictures, the cotton napkin-covered dish of fresh biscuits on the old wooden table in the eat-in parlor just off the kitchen.

He saw the killer stop in that kitchen, get a sense of déjà vu as the killer sighed heavily, feeling strangely at home in a country kitchen with water you had to pump, and herbs drying on the sideboard.

The sights and smells seemed to be familiar to the killer. Bob watched inside his mind as the killer touched this and that surface with his gloved fingers, almost reverently. Almost homesick.

Bob could see the still, small signs, and used those to let his imagination work.

195

Bob saw all of this in his mind's eye. As if he were standing next to the young man, a storm raging around inside of him stronger than the storm raging outside the windows on that murderous night.

When Bob opened his eyes, he was standing in the gloom of the day after, but he retained those feelings he got from the killer. And he finally understood the man's hesitancy.

Bob realized that they had been looking at the motivations for the killings all wrong.

The Preacher didn't want to kill.

He knew that from the mercy the older woman in the other room was shown. How the number '95' had been written on her upper chest, almost at her neck, so as to maintain the woman's decency. Her privacy.

And the Bible page had not been stabbed into the body, or stuffed into the woman's mouth, like so many others. It had been placed on the tall round table next to the chair, almost like a love note, left for those to find.

No, this man had respected this woman. He had probably watched her perform her work for a couple of days before committing the act. This was not the senseless killer that Hunter O'Connor had written about in his notes on all the cases previously.

This man had an agenda, sure. And Bob was greatly intrigued by what that agenda just might be. The Bible verse highlighted on the table next to where the woman's body had lain, peacefully, and at rest.

"Being confident of this, that he who began a good work in you will carry it on to completion until the day of Christ Jesus."

Bob saw that their pursuit had been all wrong. They were sniffing up the wrong trees. The last verse had been a message, and Bob felt that it had been just for him.

This wasn't over, not by a long shot.

And he wasn't chasing a cold, calculated and gifted killer. Well, the killer was all of those things. But he also was not any of them.

Bob couldn't quite get that bit right in his mind. But he knew one thing: he was chasing an innocent man. An innocent man who did not want to kill, yet still did, because he had no other recourse.

Bob had never seen a crime in quite this way before. He had always been able to see from a killer's perspective, but never this clearly. It worried him. Quite a bit.

For the first time in his long career, Bob Woodyard wanted to quit, and let this all play out.

But he had a job to do.

He had sworn to uphold the law, and the law would have to keep him motivated for this case.

He just hated knowing this early in, that the feelings in his mind and his heart would be at war when this one was finally finished.

Chapter 28

Three woke up in gratitude, six months later. One of the things that he had started doing every day is watching motivational videos on YouTube to start his day positively.

He had to do this now.

His existence was one that would cause him to quit and give up right now. But he had a job to do before he could quit. He was only halfway there, and now he had to saturate his mornings with reason and motivation to keep going.

Change the paradigm, he thought to himself, as he accomplished his morning stretching and exercises. Five hundred push-ups, sit-ups, and running on his treadmill for an hour. The sweat, and the mental motivation, kept him going, most days.

After a shower and before heading downstairs for breakfast, he got connected online and went to the website that he went to first, every morning. Colbie X's website.

She usually updated her blog every evening, and he waited until the morning to read it. He needed the motivation she gave him to continue the plan, and not just give up halfway.

He felt like he knew a little how Jesus felt in his second year of ministry. He knew what was coming, and could have been happy just doing the bit that he had done, and live the rest of his life in failure.

This morning, like most, Colbie had written a long blog bemoaning the lack of progress the country was showing in coming together against *the Preacher*.

Of course, a lot more was going on in the world than one serial killer, but *the Preacher* was still big news most days. There were hundreds, maybe thousands, of links to websites professing to reveal his identity and claiming to predict that they and only they knew where he was going to strike next.

He had become a cult figure. A rock star of a serial killer, to the younger generation. So, Colbie went on and on about how the next generation was missing the point.

She wasn't wrong.

He logged off after reading her post two times. He needed to call her and try to reignite the spark he had blown out by leaving their vacation so abruptly, and with no warning.

He had literally left her standing on the curb, holding her bags. He was still apologizing for that, six months later. She was coming around though, and believed his lies about a hostile business takeover of the fake company he told her he ran.

Five had set up all of the paperwork and updated the company's social media and tax return information every couple of weeks. So, any digging she did in his holdings, she would see that he was a legitimate businessman. And he was, in a way.

He had feelings for the woman that he wasn't quite ready to accept, or confess.

He walked downstairs to the smell of bacon cooking. Four and Five were actually home this week, and Three welcomed their company.

For two weeks out of every month, they had to travel back to New York to uphold their lives there. It was becoming increasingly taxing on them both, but Three knew that those two men were as committed to the Plan as he was.

He just wondered, as he did about himself most days, if they were strong enough to see it through to the end.

In the kitchen of the large estate that Three had purchased in Southern Maryland last month, Four was cooking breakfast while Five sat at the eat-in table, punching away at his laptop. The view from the windows behind Five was breathtaking.

The house sat on a short cliff overlooking the Patuxent River. The trees were starting to leaf again, as it had been an unseasonably warm spring. The water of the river below the house was green, but the light of the rising sun reflected off it, making it appear like an emerald.

They had a dock that ran out into the river, and Three had purchased a twin engine luxury speed boat, which was moored at their pier. He had even bought a license to hold oyster pots just off of the dock, and they had tried their hand at crabbing the small blue Maryland crabs, but had no luck.

He was hoping to throw in the crab pots again later, now that one of the old men at the corner market nearby the house had given him a secret: frozen chicken necks.

Worked every time, the old man had said.

Three's mind went to the fact that life was like that a lot more than we all realized. Sometimes, bait will snare you every time, and if it didn't, they found a new bait that would. He wondered if anyone was ever truly free, in this world.

Three stood in the doorway leading into the kitchen and watched his two best friends for a couple of minutes. He was grateful for both men. More than he could ever tell them, show them, or give back to them.

He knew that they were a trio based in love and shared childhood trauma, but that wasn't enough to keep them all together through what they experienced. Without their skills, Three knew, the team wouldn't be here today.

He walked into the room, and both men noticed him. Four told him that breakfast would be done in ten minutes, and Five gave him the daily update of the research and updates from those they had hired and cajoled into helping them.

"Hunter O'Connor's old partner is nosing around too close to home, Three," Five told him.

"I hope you have a plan for this guy. He ran into a wall with the burner phone. But he has latched onto the holding company who owned the warehouse in Mobile. He has filed a Freedom of Information Act release for the tax information for the shell company," Five went on.

"I routed the paperwork through Geneva, and into the Soviet Bloc, so he won't get very far there. If he gets to the end of the trail of breadcrumbs, he will find a Mr. Donatello, in St. Thomas, who thinks he works for an American insurance company, and has no information. And if we see Red request or buy a plane ticket to St. Thomas, we will fire Mr. Donatello in an email, and liquidate the office," Five told him.

Three nodded to him, knowing his best friend had it all under control.

"The Bureau still hasn't found my backdoor into their mainframe. It's getting close though. They have ran three sweeps this month alone. This new guy, Bob Woodyard, is no joke. He makes Hunter O'Connor look like a newbie," Five continued.

Three knew that if he was worried about this, then Three should be worried. Five was the best hacker the world never knew about, and if he was close to being found out, Three knew that they needed a different approach.

"Watch your back, Five. Always have two ways out, and erase your footprints," Three told him. Five nodded.

"Tell me about the money," Three said.

"The Japanese Stock Market, the Chinese, and the European Union Exchange are all up at least 2%, and as you've seen on the news, with the Presidential election coming up this year, the Dow is adjusting accordingly. We got a good return on the sale of the land in Alabama, and liquidating the holdings in Switzerland and moving it all to St. Croix, with a 3% uptick in the move, you are sitting, this morning, at a quarterly increase of 4%," Five told him.

"So, give me the total," Three said. They had this conversation every week.

"As of this morning, with all seventeen accounts, three blind trusts, and the retirement funds I set up, your total is five hundred and thirty three million, six hundred and forty thousand, and some change," Five told him.

Three nodded.

They were solid when it came to money. This plan had cost him surprisingly little compared to the financial strategies that Four oversaw and Five incorporated. He had a plan for all of that money. But it would take an army to pull off.

Three sat down across from Five, and Four joined the pair holding a serving platter overflowing with bacon and eggs. The three men dug in greedily, knowing that these times together, when they could spend a day breathing, and enjoying each other, were rare, and were going to become rarer as time went by.

Tomorrow, they knew, they would be driving down to North Carolina, where another victim in a small town was waiting. Five already had the details, and Three and Four would do the recon. So far, after six months, and six victims, all in small

202

towns, on the periphery of those small towns, the new task force was not bringing the heat to the trio quite yet.

Bob Woodyard was under a ton of pressure, they knew, and they were staying three steps ahead, which was the plan. They vowed not to underestimate this guy. They had thoroughly researched him, and knew that he was no joke. He was known to use irregular methods to find his man, and Three didn't need unconventional methods at this stage of the game.

He needed control. Or they wouldn't make it for eighty-nine more victims.

Three hoped that for the rest of the Plan, it stayed this exact way. And he knew that it could. As long as there was no pattern. Nothing that the task force could get ahead with.

He needed to do something about Hunter O'Connor's old partner. But he couldn't kill the man. He refused to do that.

The man was a good man, committed to his friend, and his family. Three wasn't going to be that cruel. He had thought about it plenty, but he couldn't bring himself to do it again.

Plus, the man was being watched, and he was showing paranoid tendencies, and Three knew that Red believed he was next on the list.

He was not. But he thought he was. Especially as he got closer to an answer that Three had set up for the man to find, and hopefully end his fruitless search for his friend's killer.

That would play out the way that Three planned. By next week, Red would stop his pursuit, Three prayed. Three would give him and answer that would satisfy him.

After breakfast, and after all three men helped clean the spacious kitchen, they separated to spend the day doing whatever they wanted. It was a rare free day, and Three wanted to go to the movies. The other two lovebirds were going to go hiking around a lake they had heard about. Three wished the two men a happy day, and went back upstairs to get ready.

As he sat on the edge of his bed in the house that didn't quite feel like home yet, but which was necessary for a couple of reasons, Three got into his head.

This happened from time to time, and he could feel it coming on. He sat on the bed, looking out the window at the river below, and just let it happen. He had tried to stop it in the past, and he knew that ended in disaster. He had to let this play out so that he could get on with his day.

The faces of the victims floated up in his mind, not fast, but not slow either. Like a home-made movie from the early 90s: scratchy, and date stamped.

He saw them all, and how he had left them. He didn't see the deed itself, just the aftermath. The setting of the scene. He put his head in his hands and let the montage play itself out.

So far, thirty-one victim bodies and the scenes they had left behind jammed his mind. He had to see all thirty-one of them, and process them. He had to do this every single time this mental traffic jam happened.

Almost like he was paying contrition for his sins.

This was his way of purging, of confessing, and he knew that when he did this, he would open his eyes, and feel better about himself.

Finally, the memories stopped, and he was able to breathe again. He opened his eyes to the sun shining outside of his window, the leaves on the trees were green, and his day looked more positive. He stood, stretched, and went to find his wallet, and cell phone. He was ready for the day ahead. And especially the night. Tonight could change absolutely everything.

A new romantic comedy was playing at the Tinsel Town Theatre in downtown DC, and he wanted to see it. He had texted Colbie the night before, and she was going to go watch it today as well.

He had told the pair of men he spent all of his time with that he had purchased the home in Southern Maryland so that their drive to New York was easier, and they could be closer to their lives there. But there was more to the move then that.

Colbie had moved to Washington DC late last year, and he was sitting about forty-five minutes from her house at that exact moment. Nobody knew how close they were to Colbie. And he hoped they never found out.

He wasn't quite ready to tell the rest of the team about his true feelings, and what he wanted to do with them. And about them. About Colbie herself.

Because he was in love with the woman, and he was going to tell her who he was.

He was going to tell her tonight that he was *the Preacher*.

And for some reason, as he thought about his plan for the evening, he felt a huge sense of relief.

Chapter 29

Three and Colbie walked out of the movie theatre holding hands. The Washington DC street was bustling, and the warmth of the late evening radiated off of the pavement under their feet. Both Three and Colby wore huge smiles.

The movie had been cute, and both had felt the movement of their relationship as they had sat watching the screen, their hands intertwined between them. They had exchanged glances at each other every time something moving, loving, or funny happened on the screen.

That's why Three loved stories so much. They could really move you if you understood and saw the clever, personal parts.

"You seem different tonight, Harry," Colby said up at him. He smiled down at her and told her exactly how he felt.

"I feel good today. Like a weight has been lifted," he said.

Colby looked up and down the street, watching the crowd of people moving about like ants at work. She smiled again, feeling Three's hand tighten in her own.

"What now, good sir?" she asked him.

"How about dinner? There's something I want to talk to you about," he answered.

"Okay, good-looking, lead the way," she laughed.

He led her down the street, moving around people who were moving slower than they were. Three felt buoyant. He felt great for the first time in as long as he could remember.

He was going to unburden his soul to this woman, and he prayed that she understood, accepted, and stayed. He was confident she would.

She had been the first, years earlier, to understand why *the Preacher* was doing what he was doing. She saw the undercurrents, the deep parts of life. Unlike most people who swam on the surface, always hurt and offended. Colbie saw things different, and he loved her for that very fact.

As they walked down the busy street, Three pointed out a few things to Colbie. He wanted her to be in the right frame of mind for what he had to tell her.

So, he pointed out several police officers standing watch over the people walking through the city in the summer warmth. Many of the police officers were engaged in conversations with tourists, natives, and even children.

The children talking to the police was the biggest change, he knew. Even little black boys and girls talking and laughing with white male police officers was such a huge difference from just a couple of years before.

Three wasn't so egotistical to think it was all due to renewed connections between law enforcement and the public because of *the Preacher*, but he also knew that he had helped in some small way. Fear tended to do that to people, he knew. It brought them together.

For better or worse, people still had a pack mentality. When the entire pack was threatened, they circled up and looked out for each other. People will always be people, he thought to himself.

Colbie noticed this as well, when Three pointed it out. She knew they would discuss this phenomenon over dinner, as they had so often done, online. She was internally happy that she was a part of something like this. Her own life experience helped her realize that sometimes the best things came out of the worse conditions.

A thought entered her mind suddenly, and she was surprised when it burst in her consciousness: "the <u>right</u> ends are always justified by <u>any</u> means."

She realized that she had never looked at it quite that way before, and she was much more introspective during the rest of the walk to a corner restaurant that Three promptly led her to. She wondered the entire way just where that thought came from.

The restaurant was a very nice ramen joint. These kinds of small, bustling places had been springing up around DC a lot in the last couple of years, and Three had been dying to try one.

Luckily, this late in the evening, the restaurant wasn't too busy, and he asked the waitress, who met them at the door, for a back corner booth, away from the leftover dinner crowd close to the front windows.

The waitress led them both back to the booth. The seats were made from dark wood, and had no cushioning. Three knew it was to entice rush hour customers to hurry their meals and get out, clearing room for the next diners. But this late in the evening, they could take their time with their meal.

The atmosphere in the place was soft and comfortable, and both Three and Colbie felt at ease. They were also at least thirty feet from the nearest people, so Three felt comfortable talking.

For a few minutes, both of them studied the short menu, and ordered drinks and dinner when a different waitress inquired after their needs. She smiled at them and collected the menus.

Three asked for a crispy pork bowl, and Colbie got a vegetarian option, with extra noodles.

Three smiled at her as she handed her menu back to the waitress and they both watched the waitress walk away. They turned back to each other, and Three took her hand across the table. He was happy, but nervous.

"Alright, Harry. What's got your attention tonight? What do you want to tell me?" she asked him. He gulped loudly, and looked around the restaurant. He started with a question.

"The District of Washington established a law several decades ago, mostly for corrupt politicians. It states that an informer for law enforcement, at every level, cannot wear a recording device, and if they do, and are asked about it, they must confess to it, or else whatever is recorded cannot be used in court. It's a law that had now been adopted by more than thirty states," he said.

"So, I need to ask you, Colbie, are you wearing a wire?" he asked, all in one breathe.

Man, he was nervous.

Colbie looked at him in shock. She had not been prepared for that.

"I have a real reason to ask you, honey. I do," he tried to diffuse what he just said. He almost whispered that last.

She looked at him, eyes intense, and heart beating. "No, Harry, I don't have a wire on me," she said.

His face told her that he was really worried, so she reached up to her blouse, and quickly unbuttoned the top three buttons.

He tried to stop her, but she insisted. She spread her shirt apart, showing him her pretty white bra, and nothing else.

"Ok, okay. I'm sorry. I had to ask," he said.

"You're worrying me, Harry. What's going on," she said, concern heavy in her voice.

"Colbie, I'm going to tell you something that will change things between us, but I'm tired of keeping it from you. I can't tell you the entire story, but there's some key bits you need to know," he said.

He was looking at the table and couldn't meet her eyes.

"Harry, look at me. Look at me," she said fiercely.

He looked up, meeting her beautiful blue eyes.

"You can tell me anything. Seriously. We have been telling each other practically everything for three years now. I'm not going anywhere," she said.

Her eyes matched her words, so Three relaxed. Not completely, but enough to keep going.

He took the deepest breath of his life, his shoulders raising almost up to his ears, and was about to open his mouth to spill it all, when the waitress walked up, holding their dinner in large, white ceramic bowls.

She set both bowls in front of Harry and Colbie, and asking if they needed anything else, she smiled and moved away to another of her tables.

Three couldn't eat. The noodle bowl smelled delicious, but he was still very nervous.

"Harry, it's okay. Get it out," Colbie told him.

She reached around her bowl and put her small hand on top of his larger one. He felt a lot better with that touch. So, he looked her back in the eyes, drew another deep breath, and told her what he had been trying to say.

"Colbie, I'm *the Preacher*," he said.

He maintained eyes contact, watching her reaction.

She continued looking into his eyes, neither of them moving, as he watched the wheels turning in her mind. He was prepared for her to jump up, and run screaming out of the restaurant to the first police officer she saw.

But, as always, she surprised him, once again.

"Oh, I know that," she said.

"What?" He practically shouted.

He was shocked. Beyond shocked. He practically fell out of his seat. She just sat there, smiling a Cheshire cat grin, driving him almost crazy with curiosity.

"What the hell do you mean, you know that?" he practically shouted again.

"Shhh, not so loud, stupid," she said.

She smiled at him again, but seeing the pained expression on his face, she explained herself.

"Harry, I'm not stupid. Not by a long shot. I got my first inkling of it when we started talking, at the beginning," she said.

She went on and explained it all to him.

"I suspected the first hundred or so people who logged onto my blog. I know that serial killers usually revisited the scene of the crime, or at least, try to get in close to the investigation," she said.

"I knew that *the Preacher* was too smart for that, but what I DID figure, was that he, or she, would become active on any website, or blog post, that talked, or discussed, one way or another, about them," she said.

"Especially, if the person writing the blog understood why he, or she, was doing what they were doing. So, I made sure to give affirmation to *the Preacher*, and see if he, or she, would talk to me," she smiled.

He was impressed with her. Much more so than he had been five minutes earlier.

"Anyway, when you stuck around, and kept talking to me so much about it, and taking the devil's advocate role, I figured you knew more than you were saying," she said.

"So, I did some research. I found out all about you, 'Three,' and figured it all out a long time ago," she finished.

She was quite impressed with herself, he thought, and rightly so.

He didn't know what to say. He was stunned, and shocked, and more scared than he had ever been. She kept talking, and he finally heard what she was saying, the buzzing in his ears slowly going away.

"What I don't know, Harry, is the 'why' of it. I know what you are trying to accomplish. I really do. But why this way, and what started all of this? I have been dying to ask you for months. Ever since you left the island so abruptly last year, and then Hunter O'Connor's body was found a week later," she said.

He was a little embarrassed that she knew then, and that he had been so sure that she bought his lame story about a business emergency. He had hated lying to her, and watching her face as he rode away from her on the island.

He still beat himself up over that. But they had to take immediate action, and there was nothing for it but to leave. He didn't realize that she would connect the dots so quickly and easily.

He looked back up at her beautiful face, and for the first time, outside of his small circle, he felt acceptance. His feelings for this woman deepened in that moment. And so, he told her the rest.

He told her about Mary, and what had happened to her and Matthew. While he was telling her the whole story, he saw tears forming in her eyes. She was finally understanding, he thought.

He told her about his love for Mary, and what losing her and her brother had done to the rest of his small circle of friends. He did not tell her how Four and Five were involved. He couldn't do that yet. But he told her absolutely everything else. More than he had planned to, actually.

When he finished, and she was holding his hands with her own, their food forgotten, she said the words that he had been waiting for years to hear. It gave him a renewed sense of acceptance, love, and motivation to keep going.

"Harry, I get it. I really do. And I know you aren't some psychopath. I know what you're trying to accomplish, and I'm so proud of you for doing it. I'm here for you. Whatever you need," she said.

And then he told her the rest of the story. He told her the part where he had fallen in love with her.

And she said it back to him, making his ears ring again, but in a good way. The words she repeated back to him made his heart sing, and his mind reel with gratitude and relief. He felt at home.

Finally, he felt at home.

That night, back at her apartment in northwest DC they showed each other just how much they loved each other.

As they fell asleep late that night, Colbie watched Three breathe, and thought about how much he reminded her of her late twin sister. And how she felt that their paths seemed to be the same trajectory.

And finally, how she still needed to protect herself, so that she wasn't as crushed as she had been when her sister was taken.

As for Three, for the first time since he was eleven years old, he slept the whole night through.

Chapter 30

Red now knew fear like he had never felt it before. He felt panic. He felt his bladder and bowels loosen. All he could think about was Renee and the kids. And how they would get through the rest of their lives without him.

A burlap sack had been thrown over his head. He could see light through the mesh of the material, but nothing else. And he was strapped into a chair, just like his old partner, Hunter, had been at the end of his life.

The thought of dying the same way Hunter had is what loosened his insides the most. He was sweating. And he was angry as all hell. How in the hell had he gotten himself ambushed this way? His thoughts went back to Renee and their two teenage daughters.

The twins wouldn't know how to process losing their father. Red gulped loudly, straining against the restraints.

He could hear nothing. He tried to get his bearings. To use all of his senses to garner as much information about his surroundings as he could. It was how he had been trained. But whoever had abducted him controlled any information he could absorb.

So, he thought back to where he was, and what he had been doing when he had been taken. He wondered mightily if he had been on the correct course, and the killer had nabbed him because he had gotten too close.

He took a little pleasure in that knowledge. The fact that he was strapped to a wooden chair, not being able to see or hear a thing, told him that he had been close. Apparently as close as Hunter had been.

Over the last half a year, Red had not stopped pursuing his new hobby. Finding *the Preacher* on his own. To exact revenge for Hunter, and Karen, and over thirty other victims. But mostly for Hunter. And the sworn oath he had given his partner's body, before they had taken it away to be analyzed and then cremated.

So, on his off hours, his weekends, all of his vacation time, he had pursued the paper trail. He knew that Hunter had gone to Alabama after spending time in New York. But before that, he had been back in Washington DC for a while.

So, Red went to these places as well. Asking questions, trying to follow his partner's last movements. Who saw him? Who talked to him? What in the hell had Hunter been doing, and following? Why he had fallen off the grid, against all sense?

It hadn't taken long for Red to discover that Hunter had been following *the Preacher* on his own. He had gone against protocol, and led his own path of revenge. The same that Red was doing now, actually.

The Bureau had no idea that Red was doing his own investigation. And while not as thorough as Hunter's had been, resulting in his death, it was more than Red had done at any other part of his career.

The truth was, he had spent most of his career following Hunter's lead. Hunter had been the brains behind the duo's successes. He had been the one with the gift.

Red just followed him, and fathered him, and watched over his genius. He relied on Hunter's abilities for his own advancement in his career than he had his own resources and gifts.

But now, without Hunter, Red was lost. He didn't know what to really do in his new position as a deputy agent in charge. He had moved into the Organized Crime division of the FBI, and he hated it. He didn't know the people, the techniques, and he felt like no one wanted a black and white patchy faced veteran around the offices. He couldn't put his finger on it, but he felt lost.

The only thing that kept him going was what he did with his free time. He had neglected his family, his church, even his own needs, to follow Hunter's footsteps. And those footsteps had brought him home, to Washington D.C, and to a park bench down by the National Mall, watching busses and cars whiz by on Constitution Ave.

And waiting for someone that Hunter had never told him about.

As he waited for the man, he wondered at all the secrets Hunter had kept to himself. Like the drinking. The cheating on Karen. The demons he carried every day.

Red sat on the park bench, standing out like a sore thumb. A large black man with vitiligo marking his oversized features, looking around himself with apprehension at what he was about to learn.

Anyone watching him, and he felt the eyes on him like an itch between his shoulder blades that he couldn't quite reach, would see someone who didn't belong where he was, and what he was doing. He hated standing out so much. But there wasn't anything for it.

This is where the man had told him to wait.

The man who had called Red's cellphone the day before. The man who had told Red why Hunter had been killed. The man whose phone number had matched one of many that Red had been following up on.

Red had finally gotten the information he had requested from IT. Hunter's cellphone records. They didn't have his actual phone, but they had all the information they could get from the carrier, after a judge's warrant had made the national carrier give up what the law required them to.

A friend in IT had sent it to Red as a courtesy. Most in the Bureau knew the bond that the two men had shared.

So, after going through hundreds of phone call records, thousands of text messages, which only showed the numbers the texts were exchanged to, not the actual content of the texts, and his movements, recorded by his Google Maps account, Red had found the one man who may have the key to helping Red solve the killing of Hunter, the killings of so many others, and the identity of *the Preacher*.

And then that man had surprisingly called Red right before Red himself was going to reach out. Like a Divine connection, Red thought.

A short, portly white man scuttled up to the park bench, and sat down like he was giving the secrets to the White House to Red. Red just watched the show with a smile on his lips.

"Ain't no one watching you, Charlie, you can relax," he told the nervous man.

But the man didn't hear him, or didn't listen. He just sat there, scanning the surroundings like there was a sniper's bullseye on his chest at that exact minute. And for all Charlie knew, there was. He was more scared than at any other time in his life.

And since Hunter's death, he felt cold, icy hands around his throat every waking minute. In truth, he didn't know if what he was doing today would be the thing that put the mark on his own head, but he had a very strong sense of right, and he wanted to give Red the same information that he had given Hunter.

He owed Hunter. After this, Charlie would never tell another soul. He had too much to lose.

And so, that's what he did. He started talking to Red, and a half hour later, he handed Red a slip of paper out of his side pocket, and got up and left, still scanning his surroundings, waiting for a black-clad boogie man to jump out and end his life. Red could give him no relief of his fear, as Red's fear was close to the same.

He went back over in his head what Charlie had told him. How, a couple of years prior to *the Preacher* killings, Hunter had approached Charlie with an offer. Money, an algorithm, and a request for information.

Hunter had, apparently, been obsessed with databases of information that he could not access on a daily basis without a judge's warrant. So, Hunter had set up backdoors.

People like Charlie, who had daily access right at their own work computers. Hunter had had a friend of his (Red was starting to think it had been Squibb, the IT specialist who had almost lost his lunch in Arizona upon discovering victim #2), write an algorithm to connect facial recognition software to be used on any national database.

It had been brilliant, actually. Red was impressed.

And it was that exact software that had given Charlie a hit, and that had led to Hunter's death.

Red now held that information in his hand, and he wondered where it would lead him.

He got his answer two days later outside of a hotel in upper New York State, when a burlap sack was thrown over his head, as he walked down a deserted side street, looking for an apartment building.

Strong hands, stronger than his own, had grabbed him, kept him from reaching his gun, kept him from defending himself. And the next thing he knew, he was tied securely to a chair.

He had no knowledge of where he was, what his fate would be, nor how his children would cope without their father. He had screwed up, and he now knew he was going to die.

Something, or someone, moved in the room near him. He had assumed that he had been alone, but he hadn't heard a door open, he couldn't sense the change in the room to indicate that someone had entered.

So, someone had to have been in the room the entire time with him. He couldn't believe that he had not been able to sense that presence. Who was this person? A ghost?

A voice broke the deep silence. It was flat, monotone. It gave Red chills he couldn't explain. He usually was never fearful of anything. Let alone another person.

He was a big, strong man, and his childhood had been rough. He had grown up a freak of a black boy, in one of the toughest neighborhoods in the country. He had never been as scared as he was when the voice broke the silence.

"Mr. Jerome Lionel Jackson. 'Red' as you're known to everyone in your life. Deputy Special Agent in Charge of Organized Crime in the Washington DC office of the FBI," the voice said.

It continued giving Red all of his own information.

"Husband of Renee Marie Jackson, née Parker. Father to thirteen-year-old twin daughters, Rose and Juniper Jackson," he said to Red.

Red jerked at his restraints as his family members' names were mentioned.

219

"Twenty- two-year veteran of the Bureau, and deacon at First Baptist Church in Rockville, Maryland," the voice continued.

Red wondered if this was how Hunter's last days on the planet came to pass.

"We have watched you as you have pursued us. We have watched as you've gotten as close as your ex-partner, Hunter O'Connor, had gotten. And we are going to give you incentive to stop your private little investigation," the voice said.

He heard the voice sigh loudly. For some reason, that confused Red more than at any other time since he was strapped to this chair.

"As you can no doubt understand that this moment, Mr. Jackson, your life is quite squarely held in my hands. As are the lives of your wife, your children, your pastor at your church, and anyone else close to you that I choose," the voice said.

Red just nodded his head inside of the burlap sack. He felt more helpless than at any other time in his life.

"I don't want to kill you, Mr. Jackson, nor your family and friends. I don't want to kill you because you are a good man. You are a man of integrity, and you have overcome so much in your own life, that I respect you, Mr. Jackson." The words shocked Red.

"But for the sake of the Plan, and for the sake of the changes this Plan is to make in the country, I will kill you without hesitation, as well as your entire family, and add them to the list, numbers drawn on their chests, Bible verses of their own. Do you understand me, Mr. Jackson?" the voice asked.

Red just nodded his head, absorbing all of the information that he could.

The voice continued. What he said next put Red into such mental convulsions of confusion, he felt lightheaded.

"We stopped spraying the smiley faces close to the victims over three years ago. We went in this new direction because the country needed help in moving forward with changes that were long in coming. And even now, those changes are taking place. Fear of us, and what we can do, wasn't achieved with the happy faces, so we tried this new tactic," the voice said.

Red was instantly dumbfounded.

He knew all about the Smiley Face killings. Everyone at the FBI knew about them. It was a deep conspiracy theory that had gone around for decades. A long string of drowned college boys killed over several years, all the bodies found, face-up, near a paint-sprayed happy face on a wall, or a bridge, or a building.

Was *the Preacher* saying that he, and his cohorts, were the Smiley Face killer, as well as *the Preacher*?

Red was suddenly overcome with chills, goosebumps, and panic. If that was the case, the current taskforce had no clue what they were doing, who they were chasing, or how very far away from the truth they were.

It had been considered, for years, that the Smiley Face killings were done by a group of sophisticated, online players who communicated via the dark web, and that no one had even a clue as to how to start looking for these people.

The only leads that the Bureau had was eye-witness statements about how each of the eighty-plus slain young men had been followed, and drugged, by a man and a woman in an old car. But these cases went all the way back to the early 90s. What the hell had Hunter stumbled upon?

He had no way of knowing that, in that moment, Three was trying to confound and confuse Red off of their scent. Three knew all about the Happy Face Killers, as well, but he and his team were not the same people. But Red did not know that.

The voice shook Red out of his thoughts.

"We are going to let you go, Mr. Jackson. And we will watch you. We will watch you physically, digitally, and everywhere you go. We have eyes everywhere, and we have resources that you can't imagine. My advice to you, Mr. Jackson, is to give up this pursuit, and enjoy the changes the Plan will bring to law enforcement, as well as the general public, by the conclusion of it. I advise you to enjoy your life, and your family's lives."

Red nodded again, scared straight. He knew he would never pursue this again. He would leave it up to others, and he would protect his family. He believed every single word the voice said. And he believed with all of his heart that he was a coward for it. But Renee and the girls came first. They had to.

Red had no other choice but to agree.

He woke up the next day, in the hotel room that he had booked in upstate New York, and after the confusion of how he had gotten there wore off, he drove straight home to Washington DC.

He hugged his family close, absorbing all of the sights, smells, and feelings his family surrounded him with daily. The way his wife's hair smelled. The way his daughters felt light and innocent in his arms. The way their home felt comfortable and known. Their smiles aimed at him as he walked through the front door could change any bad day into a precious one. His family was his everything, and he knew it, in that moment.

He didn't let any of them go for several minutes, until they all asked if he was okay, and what was the matter. He couldn't talk. He could only weep.

He wept for Hunter. He wept for breaking the promise he had made his old partner.

And he wept for getting so close to ending the killings, and selfishly picking his loved ones instead of the victims to come. It was just too big for one small black man to stop.

And he felt like a failure for that fact. But, as he looked at the beautiful and precious faces of his family, he knew that he chose correctly. He couldn't lose these people.

Even if it meant allowing eighty-nine more people to die over the next seven-and-a-half years.

Even if it dammed his soul to a hell of his own making, for the rest of his natural life.

Part IV

Chapter 31

Six years later, Bob Woodyard stood in the middle of a Category 5 hurricane. Not the kind of hurricane that destroys homes and uproots trees. No, this kind of hurricane destroyed careers. Lives.

The pressure of it could drive a sane man right out of his mind. But Bob just stood in the midst of it, like a smooth, round boulder in the middle of a rushing river. He let the sound, the pressure, the intense upheaval wash over and around him, to no effect.

Ninety victims in ninety-seven months. It was staggering. It was mind-blowing. It was grotesque in ways not quantifiable to rational men. The sheer number of victims, bodies splayed out for the world to see, changed things. Of course it would change things.

Like bodies left on a battlefield of war, in hopes that the changes would be positive. And so, the entire country had changed because of the onslaught, the consistency, the continuing horror. And rightly so, Bob thought, watching the whirlwind of activity around him. Rightly so.

Even after so much evidence, so many clues, so many scenes to process, they were still where they had been five years prior. *The Preacher* was a consummate professional. In fact, that piece of information alone would narrow down the list of suspects. How many people in the world had this level of training? he wondered. How many ex-soldiers, Special Force veterans, hell, even cold-war era spies, could summon this level of discipline and consistency?

But they had run into dead end after dead end. Bob felt a gaping chasm between where he and the task force stood, and where *the Preacher* was doing his business, completely unhindered.

And to be honest, Bob Woodyard, himself, wasn't a young man anymore. His thirst for the chase, his hunger for the capture just wasn't what it had been in the previous decade. And he still had that pervading feeling that he didn't really want to catch this guy.

Against all of his morals, his ethics, and the sworn promises he had made himself and his community, he wanted this guy to reach number one. It was a thought that gave his mind dissonance and confusion, and kept him up most nights.

He just knew that his heart wasn't as invested in this case as it was in others, in other times, at other places. He wanted to see how this damn thing was going to turn out.

So, for the millionth time, he wondered if he was pulling his punches, so to say. If he was slacking in the job that had been his driving passion for so long.

He wondered if he was letting those who relied on him to extract justice, or at least to start the process that would bring justice down, and if doing so, he was damning his own soul.

So, standing amongst the hurricane of activity, trying to find the heart to put himself completely into the search for the man (or men, he thought ruefully), he squared his shoulders, took a deep, cleansing breath, and started shouting orders.

He would at least make a show of doing his job properly.

A bold and brash young man approached Bob amongst the bustle of the loud FBI offices. He was an up-and-coming nephew of so-and-so, and Bob despised his whole generation.

"Mr. Woodyard, sir," the young, dark-haired kid said, in a way Bob thought was smarmy and servile. "I was scouring the internet last night, and I may have found a lead, sir."

Bob was distractedly disinterested, but had to make a show of doing his job, which he had just thought about moments before the kid walked up to him. So, he sighed heavily, and asked the kid what he had found.

"Well, sir," the kid, whose annoying name happened to be Richie, started in.

"There is this blog all about *the Preacher*, called DeathX.net," and Bob stopped him there.

"Son, what's a blog?" Bob asked him. The kid sighed loudly himself, annoying Bob even further.

"It's short for 'weblog,'" the kid said. When he saw the look of confusion on Bob's face, he went on. "It's kind of like an old-time newspaper column, where a writer gives opinions about just anything, really, and people read and can respond to it," the kid explained.

"Okay, I'm with you, go on," Bob said.

"Well sir, this blog is written by a woman named ColbieX, umm, Colbie Marie Porter, and sir, I think she knows more than she should about *the Preacher* killings," he said, a look of smug satisfaction on his young face.

Bob had a desire to punch the kid in the kisser, but refrained. And then he was mad at himself, because he had the same feeling at least twenty times a day with the young agents around him.

Not for the first time, did he think about hanging up his shield and retiring to a stream in Wyoming, worrying only about catching dinner.

"Alright kid, I will put someone from IT on it," Bob said, dismissively.

The kid got a look of defeat on his face, suddenly. Bob could tell that he wanted to pursue the lead himself, and crack this whole thing open from a — what did he call it — a *blog*?

So, Bob went against his own judgement, and agreed that this kid could pursue the lead he had found, with the caveat that he got help from some IT guys, and kept Bob in the loop. The kid walked away with a smile on his face and a spring to his step.

Bob watched the kid walk through the hurricane of movement and panic-driven busy work around him, and knew that he, himself, had at one time that same look on his own face and spring in his own step.

For the rest of the day, Bob sat in his office, staring at the many pictures, internal decorations, and the proof of a life-long career, and just lived in his memories of better times, and the motivation that he had leading up to this, his last case.

He sat in his memories, and lived there that day, and the next. And didn't do what he had promised himself he would do. He didn't put himself into this new case the same way he had always done.

And as he kept more to himself, and people on the task force started whispering amongst themselves. Bob was just fine with it. He couldn't put his finger on it, but something moved in his life, and in his choices.

And an outside force gave him peace and quiet in his questing mind, and showed him a closure to his own career, and enjoyment of things internally, rather than externally, through this case.

At that moment, where the Material could not see the Spiritual, two ArchAngels looked down, and manipulated a man who could ruin the entire plan, before it was brought to fruition. Before the world would be changed, once again, by the deeds and sacrifices of one.

They took away the man's Will, and replaced it with a tiredness for his passion. It was easily done, with humans, but an ArchAngel must be careful to not take away the Will to live.

And so, Bob knew in that time, on that day, that God, or whoever had maneuvered him through his life, and had renewed his motivation to keep going everyday through his career, was gone from his mind, and he was just fine with it.

He was just fine with *the Preacher* doing what *the Preacher* was going to do.

Chapter 32

Three was reading a recent article by ColbieX concerning the social and economic changes in the US that could completely be connected to the fear raised by *the Preacher's* long killing streak.

As he read her words, he was reminded of why he was doing what he was doing, and the reasons the plan needed so badly to be finished. And then, he started thinking of the reasons that it didn't need to be finished at all.

He could walk away today, and for the rest of his long life, enjoy the life that he had been given. But he also knew that he would never rest. Not now. Not when he was so close. But still, the reasons to quit were quite important.

In fact, both reasons sat on chairs across their comfortable living room, and both were engaged in their own research. Their research just happened to be cartoons on their iPads.

He cleared his throat loudly, making both twins look up at him, and smile at their father.

Five years earlier, he and Colbie had been blessed beyond belief to be given the gift of their two children.

Emma, Three's daughter, had gray eyes and looked like her mother. She was studious and gregarious, seemingly at ease with both contradictory qualities.

Jack looked like his father, and he was the smartest, most physically gifted child that Three had ever seen. Jack just seemed to do everything early, easily, and nothing seemed to bother him. Emma was the emotional one of the set, but even she was happy more often than not.

And Three's heart burst in his chest every time he saw his children do something new.

When they walked for the first time, days apart. When they said their first word, Emma beating Jack to that feat by more than a month. When they both won their age group swimming competition at the local youth swimming center, at the young ages of four.

Jack's time in the fifty-meter was a little better than Emma's but she was determined to beat him next year. Three had no doubt that she would.

And he also knew that the twins were what brought him back to somewhat of a normal life, every time he came home from the road.

For a week after each mission, he was in such a deeply emotional hell, he could hardly keep going. But his children's laughter always made him feel better, and the love of Colbie, his best friends, and the family that he had scratched out of the muck and mire of his life gave him reason to keep going.

The future for his children would be so much freer than the darkness of his own childhood, and the country that had fostered so much fear and hate that it had seeped into the very genetic code of the generations leading up to the birth of Three and his friends.

He knew that the plan needed to be finished. But man, he thought, was it hard to imagine how this thing was going to end now that his family and his circle had grown by two.

Four years earlier, when Colbie had surprised him with the news that she was pregnant, he was more hesitant than at any other time in his entire life. But she assured him that everything would be okay. They would protect the children.

So, she gave birth to them in a private concierge medical clinic in California, having flown there by private jet the week before her due date. It was a clinic in the middle of the Mojave Desert, where generations of Hollywood elite and the rich could receive medical care in absolute privacy.

The twins were given Colbie's family's name of Porter. Both of their middle names were Higgsby, however. Jackson Higgsby Porter was two minutes older than his fraternal twin sister, Emma Higgsby Porter.

And they were perfect.

Both of their parents doted on the twins, as well as their uncles, and the extended adopted-family in southern Alabama.

They had all lost Dottie late last year, but she had helped raise a third generation of Higgsbys before she left the world. The day before she passed peacefully in her sleep, she had bounced both three-year-old gangly toddlers on her skinny lap, grinning like she had won the lottery.

Three liked to think that Dottie had died happy. He buried her in the old family plot on the Higgsby plantation, which he still just couldn't seem to sell. His best friends had, at first, thought that the plantation had sold.

But in reality, Three had purchased it through a shell company that he, himself, had set up, outside of the knowledge of his team. He was doing that a lot more than he was really comfortable with lately, but the end, Three knew, would dictate that he did some things alone and kept the details close to the chest.

By now, the plantation was overgrown, and no one went there anymore, except to bury the dead. But it would stay in the family.

Somehow, he knew that the property would be an important part of the culture that would arise after he finished what he was set to do.

Memories and emotions cascaded in Three's mind suddenly, but he was at peace.

After four years of having time with his family, his progeny, his best friends, and his purpose in life, he was ready to finish the plan.

No one, except Five, knew how Three planned the ending to come about. His final statement to the world at large.

He knew, before he had killed Karen O'Connor so many years earlier, how it would all climax. He had just kept it to himself, letting those close to him think whatever they wanted to think.

Most of them just saw the conclusion of the plan as a stepping off point for lives to be lived, knowing that they had changed the world. And it would be changed. For most of those that he cared so very much about. Especially his children.

When he told Five what he needed from him, it had been a knock-down, drag-out fight. But Three needed him, and only him, when this was all finished.

Five finally begrudgingly agreed to help, but ever since that conversation, sworn in secrecy, Five couldn't quite meet Three's eyes anymore.

He shook himself out of his emotional roller coaster, knowing that he still had almost three years, and stood up, walked over to his serious twins, and picked them both up, giggling, and walked them out to the swimming pool in the back yard.

He threw both children into the water, which glistened in the noon time sun and heat. Both children were excellent swimmers, and they both spurted to the surface, treading water as they grinned up to their father.

Emma was the first to complain that her clothes were now all wet, and "Momma isn't gonna be happy."

Three's heart burst at his children's smiles, and for a little while, all was well with the world.

And for today, and the next year and a half, he thought to himself, sun beating down on his bald head, that was enough.

Just barely enough.

Chapter 33

Lung's aching, feet pounding the concrete, splashing through rain puddles, Three ran for his life, and his freedom.

He screamed into the com unit in his ear for Five to execute "Escape plan Alpha, fucking Alpha!" but heard only static back.

He was in Plainview, Texas. A shithole little town where he felt reasonably safe to pull off a mission. They had stayed out of Texas for the simple fact that every person was armed, and enjoyed using their guns, or so he had heard.

But good candidates for successful missions were becoming scarce.

They had really had to start thinking outside the box, and were working in places that they had not been before. Hence, Plainview, Texas. And it had gone to shit, right from the beginning.

As Three's feet beat the pavement in staccato bursts, he saw an alley ahead, catty-corner on the other side of the street next to the U.S. Post Office.

The alley was next to a run-down building with faded lettering on the side of the white cinderblocks: "Your Parts & Machine Center" and next to it, "Carlisle Motor Machine."

The plan was designed for there to always be three exits from the mission curtain. His military and special-ops training from years prior was now as natural as breathing for him, and so far, they had had a 100% success mission rate. Until now.

So, on the small map against his wrist, this alley was designated spot #3, right across E. 8th St. He hoped like hell that Five and Four had gotten his heavy-breathed message to enact the diversion he would need to disappear. He knew that creating a diversion with a federal building would stop any would-be pursuers.

This damn country around here, he thought as he approached the post office, running down the sidewalk on N. Ash St, listening to the sound of running boots behind him, was too damn flat, and too damn open. This exit would have to go off without a hitch, he knew.

He wondered, not for the first time, if this was the final stand down. It certainly wasn't what he had planned, but he could handle it. The Plan would just be moved up a year and a half.

He ran past the stairs in the front of the post office, the overhead lights on the front door glinting off of his military spec night vision goggles, and he pushed his tired body even further.

As he passed the front glass doors of the post office, even with the sidewalk in front of the old building, he saw the block of C-4 with the remote detonator pushed into the middle of it, stuck to the bottom left side of the right-hand door.

He smiled. He just needed to get across the wide, brick street, and the rental car down the alley would be awaiting him. He knew that Four and Five were in another car, in a parking lot near where he would exit the area, and would detonate the bomb when he was safely by it, but not the people chasing him.

Then, the plan was for the team to make it to the airport only a few miles away, where a private plane was waiting for them, the pilot an old friend.

As he passed the post office and moved across the deserted E. 8th St, the alley approaching him, the explosion behind him surprised him, and lit up the night, and the invisible shockwave of the blast launched him against a wooden fence on the opposite side of the alley.

He heard something crack in his back as he flew through the heavy wood of the fence. The last thing he thought was that this particular mission had gone right to shit.

Three days prior, they had arrived into a small, dusty, dirty town in the Texas Panhandle. They looked at each other as they drove the non-descript small hatchback car into the town.

The sign that ushered them into Plainview, Texas boasted a population of some seventeen thousands residents.

But as they drove through the cracked and potholed streets of the town, they figured that the actual number was massively outdated. There was no way there were seventeen thousand people still living in this dying town.

Even better, Three had thought to himself as they pulled up to the hotel along US 27. They were risking a hotel this time because they had all received brand-new aliases and identifications with the institution of the new federally mandated Identification System that had been instituted the month prior.

Three smiled, thinking that he may have had a hand in the creation of the new REAL ID system.

They were posing as oil field workers, passing through on their way to Odessa or Midland, towns to the south, smack dab in the middle of the Permian Basin. As always, they had done their homework.

Three's tactical packages would be arriving at the post office the next day, so the evening that they arrived in the small town, and for the next two days, the team would focus on surveillance, recon, and planning.

The team tended to overdo it with preparations, but they knew you could never be too sure. The more you planned, and the more exits and entrances you had into a mission field, the better the outcome. They had learned this the rough way over the last eight years.

Five, who was driving the small Honda hatchback, dropped Three and Four off at a truck stop called Flying J, more than twenty miles outside of town, and the two men got into the rental cars (rented under different names than the ones they were using for the hotel) that had been parked at the truck stop a few days earlier by the rental agency.

All three members of the team had perfect credentials with the rental agencies. Luckily, the federal agents had not thought to look into rental cars and vans and trucks over the years. Three smiled as he got into the white Ford F-150 he had rented for the week.

A couple of times, he had even used Colbie to rent various vehicles, to really throw off anyone following them. He had not been happy to include Colbie, but she always insisted on helping in any way that she could.

He usually just dictated the blogs and messages that she would put out into the world, to throw off the agencies he knew monitored her output.

The three men of the team then drove into Plainview from different directions, Three coming in last as he had to drive the farthest to come into the small town from the east.

I-27 went north to south through the middle of the small town, so therefore, to come into the town from the east, Three had had to drive several miles out into the country of the Texas Panhandle to join back up with main Route-70, which bisected Plainview going east-to-west.

After the three men arrived at separate rooms in the dirty Days Inn next to I-27, they met in Three's room to start going over the plans. They would wait until nightfall and scout the town for a likely target, as well as the many avenues out of town they would have to take.

All three men had flirted with the front desk woman, complaining about their job working out in the fields, and how they needed a soft bed, etcetera. This was a skill that all three men had developed with the understanding that it would make them all forgettable to the woman, should she ever be questioned.

The team assumed that the FBI pulled no shortcuts anymore, and any person in town was a likely eyewitness. So, they always kept their heads on a swivel when inside a mission area, and became as unremarkable as possible.

This was always easier for Three than for the other two men, but all three had done a remarkable transformation over the previous decade or so. They had honed their skills of disappearing inside a crowd. And using disguises and never dropping character helped a great deal.

And so, they set out, as they had done every month for the last several years, to do their homework on the small town they were in and to pick a target. They would find the perfect opportunity, successfully complete the mission without giving away any clues to their pursuers, and return home, without anyone locally being the wiser.

And two days into the five-day mission, things started to go from bad to worse.

It had started with Three noticing a blue, unmarked sedan being in three different locations around the small town of Plainview.

And while that wasn't an occurrence to worry about, strictly speaking, it had still stood out to the watchful eyes of Three, who had the most training in the group.

The fourth time he noticed the car, he hid around the side of a building close by, and watched as a young, dark-haired man in obnoxious mirrored aviator glasses left the safety of the large window-fronted building across the street from the car, and causally look around for the three men that he had been tailing before climbing back into the car and pulling away.

Three marked down the license plate number, noticing the single radio antenna on the rear of the sedan, and felt a weight settle into his belly and a knot form in his throat as he realized that some form of Federal agent had somehow stumbled onto the team, and was watching the men, who in turn started watching the agent.

And so, it became a game of cat and mouse. Four and Five were adamant about aborting the mission in this small Texas town, but Three didn't want to waste any time. If the agent could find them in Podunk Texas, he could find them, or follow them, anywhere.

So, it became increasingly obvious that the team was going to have to do something about the lone agent that they saw around town a couple of times over the next two days.

The team still did their due diligence in obtaining the necessary information for the mission to succeed, but they had to do it even more circumspectly, and with greater care.

At the end of the five days of the mission parameters, when all the intel was gathered, and the plan was set into place to perform what they had arrived in town to do, it became much more a hastily put together, fly-by-the-seat-of-their pants accident, than an actual military spec operation, which is what they had always planned for.

Meaning, Three had fucked up, rushing to do the job on a person who wasn't even the original target, and then found himself running for his life from a group of gun-carrying rednecks, hell-bent on bringing the most famous serial killer in American history to justice. Texas-style justice.

And it had all begun with a game of pool.

Chapter 34

The original target in the small town of Plainview, Texas, had been a small-business owner who was obviously armed at all times.

The thinking was, when the team had picked the older man, that taking out a target who owned a gun store and indoor shooting range, would show the prowess and ease at which *the Preacher* operated unchallenged.

But the plan had gone horribly wrong from the beginning of the day they had set aside to perform the mission and get the hell out of Dodge.

A light rain, a steady cold drizzle, had soured moods, and made their efforts that much harder to accomplish. As the team situated themselves in the mission window, put themselves in a position for success and then extraction to the small airport a couple of miles away, bad luck and unexpected situations made them almost abort the entire operation.

First, the target changed his routine for the first time in the five days they had been in the small town. Usually, he closed down his business on Columbia St. at 6 pm, got into his beat-up blue pickup truck, and headed downtown to a pool hall situated two blocks south of the post office.

But on this day, as Three sat at the small, dank bar inside the pool hall, regular clothes covering his military battle cloth and gear, the gun store owner did not appear. And as Three grew increasingly paranoid about the change in routine of the large fat man, the blue unmarked patrol car that he had noticed half a dozen times around town pulled up in the street out front.

A young, dark haired man stepped out of the car wearing mirrored sunglasses, looking like a wannabe movie adaptation of a federal agent. Three gulped visibly, and turned back to his warm beer sitting in front of him on the scarred bar top. He heard the bell attached above the only entrance to the bar jingle, and he started sweating.

He sat, and watched the beads of condensation run races down his beer glass. His senses told him that the young man who had gotten out of the unmarked car had taken a booth at the other side of the small, dingy bar.

A few patrons were scattered throughout the smelly room, and he knew that two others had gone into the men's room within the last two minutes.

Time slowed down, and Three's ears and eyes were straining for everything he could take in.

The whooshing of the twin ceiling fans above him, not doing much good moving air around the warm, black-painted walled room. A fly buzzed at the light over the mirror above the bar. Three's eyes focused on the mirror, but couldn't see the man behind him, as his own reflection was in the way.

That meant that the agent knew what he was doing, and he was as aware of the room as Three was at that moment. Or, Three thought to himself, he had gotten lucky. Lucky was a lot worse for Three at that moment than smart.

Three quickly pressed the red trigger button taped to his inner arm, under the light, loose over shirt he wore. This would trigger a light in the car in which Four and Five sat at that exact moment, three blocks away.

When the rest of the team saw the light, they would begin formulating an escape plan for Three. It was a contingency that they had enacted several years prior, when Three was unable to use his voice to raise the alarm. Five had fashioned the simple button-receiver tool, and Three never went into a mission field without it.

A voice sounded in Three's ear, where the hidden microphone and speaker were held in place by his ear canal. It was Four, and he was telling Three to calm down, and that Five was calling up the schematics of the building, once again, to give Three an escape plan.

"Just act cool. Why don't you get up and start a game of pool? That way you can keep your eye on the whole place?" Four suggested to Three.

Three agreed, and got off of his stool, carrying his still-full glass of beer with him, and walked over to a simple, coin-operated table at the back of the dark bar room, near the bathroom doors, and another door that led into the back kitchen and employee areas.

He took four quarters from his pocket, where he had placed them for just this very reason, and racked the balls when they came to the end of the table, in a slot at knee level. After arranging all of the pool balls in the correct order in the plastic triangle frame, he walked over to public-use cue sticks lined up in a rack on the wall.

And when he turned back around to begin a slow, solo pool game, the young agent was standing at the opposite end of the table that Three had racked the balls. He was smiling and holding a cue stick from a rack on the other side of the room.

"Hey, I didn't see you playing with anyone, mind if I play you?" the young man asked Three with a grin.

As he said it, he pulled four quarters out of a front pocket, and placed them in the coin rack on the side of the table made for the use of calling a next game.

Three gulped quickly, feeling sweat fall down his spine, under his tactical military harness over jet black, unmarked clothing. He simply nodded at the young man and watched as the agent lined up the cue ball from a hole at knee level on his side of the table, and line up to break the racked balls at Three's end of the table.

The cue ball hit the racked rows of multicolored balls right in front of Three with a loud crack, making him flinch back. But he held his ground and watched as three different colored balls fell into pockets around the small pool table.

"I'll take solids," the agent said nonchalantly.

Three just stood on place, waiting for the young man to arrest him, or at least start asking him questions that he couldn't answer honestly. He had no idea what this young agent knew or didn't know. Three knew that he could give nothing away.

The agent sunk two more solid balls in quick succession before missing on the one ball in a corner pocket. As he stood up from his missed shot, he smiled at Three, revealing slightly misaligned, but very white teeth.

"Guess my run is over. Your shot, man," the agent said to Three.

Still not uttering a word, Three bent down and took aim at a stripped purple ball and sunk it soundly in the same corner pocket that the agent had just missed.

And that's when the agent started asking questions.

"So, you from around here?" he asked, innocently.

"Just passing through, going on to Odessa," he answered back, using a local, longer drawl than his usual Alabama-tinged accent.

"Ahh, for work, or is that where you're from?" the agent asked, feigning interest. Three decided to take the rough guy act.

"What's it to ya?" he asked in return.

"Nothing, nothing, just making conversation," the agent said, holding up a hand in a warding gesture, as if he meant no offense.

Three continued to sink his stripped balls in rapid succession, trying not to take his attention off of the agent. The agent, to his credit, stayed cool, calm, and collected.

Three wondered if he really knew who he was talking to. If the agent knew that Three was *the Preacher*, Three knew that every law enforcement car, truck, SWAT van, and helicopter between here and Dallas would show up in the wide, brick street out front.

And that's when Three started to relax. There was no way the task force would send in this young agent, alone, to take on the famous *Preacher*.

Three started wondering just what this guy was doing in this particular pool hall, in this particular small Texas town, on this particular day. He knew this agent had gotten extremely lucky, or he was doing what the other agent, Red, had done, and gone off solo to make a name for himself.

He suddenly grinned at the agent, throwing the young agent off his game of trying to remain calm. Three did not take his eyes off of the soft brown eyes of the young agent as he lined up a shot on the eight ball, and sunk it smoothly in the corner pocket directly in front of the agent.

The agent tried to save face, muttering a quick congratulations under his breath, and turning back around to take a seat at the bar. Three smiled at the agent's back and regained much of his confidence in return.

He clicked the red button strapped to his forearm again, turning the light in the car with the rest of his team off. He heard a sigh of relief in the small earpiece.

He confidently walked back over to his seat at the long, scarred wooden bar, and sat back down. He was now two seats away from the agent who had just lost the game of pool, but to Three's estimation, had lost so much more.

Because at that moment, Three decided to change the target, and kill this handsome, young upshot of an agent.

And he was going to do it right here in this pool hall.

Chapter 35

Three's heart was beating out of his chest. He had sat at the bar, making small talk with the young man two seats away, as well as a few other people who came and went over the next hour.

The sun was setting outside and the original target never came into the bar. Three distractedly wondered what happened to change the man's schedule. But he shrugged it away and waited for one single thing to happen: the young agent's beer to force him to visit the men's room.

And then it happened. The young agent excused himself. He got up off of the stool in front of the wooden bar, and made his way, slightly stumbling, to the men's room at the rear of the dark bar. And as he passed by Three, Three got up off of his own stool, took the young man by the arm, and offered loudly, to help him.

They walked together to the restroom, and Three saw most of the eyes of the patrons follow them to the bathroom. He suddenly realized that this was a small Texas town, and he and the young agent were strangers. So, as with any social situation where something seemed out of the normal, people would notice.

But Three was in a zone where he felt reckless, and he wondered at his sudden impatience. He noticed a spike in adrenaline. He was going against so many of the precautions and plans that the team had put into place over the last eight years. He was going against the norm, and he knew, deep in his heart, that this was against everything he felt safe doing.

But something drove him. Something or someone had their hand on the part of his brain that warned caution. And for a fleeing second, he knew that this wasn't the first time that it seemed that an external force controlled his actions. But he put his attention back to what he was about to do.

He felt like he couldn't control what was about to happen. He just prayed that whatever it was that was pushing him to be so reckless would get him out of danger once the deed was accomplished.

He and the young agent pushed into the dark interior of the men's room, and Three knew that the people outside would expect him to come directly out, after having helped the young man into the room to do his business.

But Three couldn't do that.

Which meant that the patrons outside, in the bar, would automatically assume some hanky-panky was going on in the men's room. They wouldn't tolerate that, this being a town dead-center in the Bible Belt. But there was no help for it. Three would just have to be as fast as he could.

And so, as Three locked the door behind him, the agent drunkenly turned to see why Three had followed him into the single room, Three hit him with a sharp jab, straight to his nose. He knew that would make the man's eyes water, and pain explode in his addled mind.

The agent, to his credit, took the hit, and instead of crumpling in pain, covering himself as one normally would, he started swinging right back. Three blocked all of his attempts with his fists.

Three knew he had to finish this quickly. Messily.

He backpedaled, throwing the young agent off balance, and Three used that opening to aim a straight kick at the agent's solar plexus.

A satisfying thud sounded, and the air whooshed out of the agent's lungs. He went to his knees, silently holding his midsection as he struggled for air. Just as Three knew would happen.

Saying a silent apology to whoever was listening, Three pulled his black-bladed, serrated K-Bar from under the overlarge shirt he had been wearing, and plunged it straight into the agent's throat.

The agent's eyes became bigger than saucers, his breath never returned, and a nasty gurgling sound erupted from the hole in his throat. Three removed the knife, allowing the agent to fall over in an increasing circle of blood.

Three quickly got to work as soon as the young man stopped twitching. He tore the agent's shirt off, finding an FBI badge hanging on a chain around the man's neck under the shirt.

Three made sure enough blood had soaked into the light blue colored shirt, and stuffed it into a waterproof case on his side. He removed the loose, baggy clothing that hid his own tactical gear, and threw them into a corner. There would be no evidence gathered from off of those clothes.

He quickly wrote the number on the chest of the agent, and stuffed the Bible page, pre-marked, into the agent's hand, which was already tightening up in mortis.

248

After making sure that the scene was properly set up, Three opened the single, frost-colored window in the room, seeing outside that it had become dark, and actually had started raining.

He didn't know the rain had started, but was thankful for it. It would cover his scent.

He pulled himself up, through the window, and out into the wet, dark night. He crouched under the single window above him, and he found himself in an abandoned side yard to the building he just left.

The yard was in-between two tall buildings, and was enclosed in a chain-link fence with a gate. He was three blocks from the rest of his team, and his own get-away car. He would make it, quietly, quickly, and the team would drive to the small airport, three miles away to the south.

As he got himself ready to climb the chain link gate, and make his way to the waiting car, he heard something behind him that shot adrenaline and bright lights through his brain.

Someone was kicking the bathroom door open. How that was possible? Three wondered to himself as he started running for the fence.

What Three did not know, was that the bathroom was such a small space, and the agent's blood was pooled around him.

The pool of blood moved much more quickly than Three had anticipated, and had traveled under the bathroom door, out into the bar. A patron passing by the door had actually stepped in it others noticed it.

As Three made his way to the fence blocking his escape down the road in front of the pool hall, several shouts and exclamations blew up the night behind him.

"Hey!"

"Hey you!"

"That dude killed this dude!"

"Get 'em!"

They had discovered the body too quickly! Three had to make his way as fast as he could to the waiting car, and get the hell out of Dodge

He had a contingency plan for being followed out of the mission envelope, he just needed to get there.

The last thing Three remembered, as the fire and debris rained down around him, and the rain was cold on his face, was that he couldn't move his legs.

The explosion was so much bigger than it should have been, and he was truly, and royally fucked.

Chapter 36

It was distractedly hot, Bob Woodyard thought to himself. He looked up at a bright blue Texas sky, the sun shining down on his face, entirely too joyfully. Bob was more annoyed than he ever remembered being.

Standing in the middle of a brick-lined, wide street, he looked in front of him at what remained of the Plainview, Texas post office building.

Shit, he thought, for the thousandth time that day. Just shit, shit, shit. A litany of curses went through his mind.

He looked back to his left, down the wide street to the pool hall on the right side of the road, about three blocks to the south. There were dozens of people down there, both law enforcement and lookie-loos, standing behind the police tape, keeping them back from the horror of the small bar and the tragedy within.

Shit, Bob thought again. His mind went to the kid. Richie, he thought. The young man that he had so easily dismissed a few weeks previously. He had given the kid free rein to pursue the lead that he had found on his own.

And now, they were in Podunk Texas, and the kid was lying dead, on a dirty bathroom floor, his throat ripped in half by some kind of large blade.

The eyes of the dead still haunted Bob's imagination, as the body looked up at him from the middle of a large, congealed pool of blood.

Shit.

Come to find out, and Bob had just learned the fact this morning, Richie was the nephew of Don Strickland, Deputy Director of the Bureau. More and more shit, he knew.

For the thousandth time, as Bob looked up at the blown-out front of the Plainview Post Office, he considered hanging it up finally. The breeze of whisperings around the office certainly showed that many around him felt the same thing. About him. He was done, they said. He was washed up.

He wasn't doing his job. He could concede that much. He really was not doing his job the way he had done it for decades, moving him up in the ranks, making him immortal in the eyes of the younger generations of agents.

That much was true, Bob thought again, and he still couldn't find the fire in his belly to do a full-court press on following *the Preacher* down to Mexico. He sighed deep in his soul, and started walking down the middle of the wide, brick street, towards the pool hall, and the accusing eyes of the young man dead on a black tile bathroom floor.

They had tracked the killer to the small airport nearby. A cross connection of radar information showed a small, twin engine private airplane, with a registration in Canada, had taken off twenty minutes after the post office had been blown to hell.

The plane had flown straight south, with obvious entry permissions to Mexico. They were still following up with that.

They had lost the plane when it had landed at the *Aeropuerto Internacional Benito Juárez*, in Mexico City, where it had fueled up, and took off within fifteen minutes.

They had lost it again as it passed into South America, headed towards Brazil.

There was no way for the US government to track a small, privately owned airplane into Brazilian airspace. You could thank the current president of both countries for that fact.

But the FBI was working closely with the CIA to try to find out what the occupants of the airplane had done once they had landed. Word would come in about that soon, Bob knew, or word wouldn't.

The way *the Preacher* had covered his tracks for so many years, Bob had little doubt that the CIA would come back with jack shit.

He had more pressing concerns. He knew, deep in his soul, that this was all going to end dramatically and tragically. Everything pointed to that fact, and he didn't know how he felt about that, or what he was going to do. He was swimming outside of his normal lanes in this, and some force outside of himself seemed to be holding him back. He knew that much, at least now.

As he arrived at the purple-and-black painted pool hall butting up against the surrounding buildings, and surrounded by police tape he once again, saw in his mind's eye what he felt had transpired.

He saw the black clad young man climb from the window on the side rear of the building, hop the dilapidated and leaning fence in front of the side clearing of the pool hall.

He saw regular citizens burst from the front of the pool hall, and start chasing after the young man running down the sidewalk towards a post office building that was still intact.

Outside of his mental purview, he vaguely heard his name called by someone walking out of the pool hall and towards him through the ghost silhouettes of the mental projections he was seeing with his third eye.

And what the hell was his third eye anyway, and where had that thought come from, he wondered distractedly, as he uncharacteristically walked away from where he had been heading. But he was following a video in his mind, and he knew that what he saw in his mind was much more important than what was happening outside of himself at the moment.

And so, he ignored the shouts behind him.

He started to sprint down the road. Back the way he had just come. The sun beat down on his bare head, and his loafers slapped the brick road in staccato beats that jarred his entire body. He was getting on in years, and sprinting to keep up with a mental apparition was not what he had become accustomed to.

But he was out of control. Hands guided him outside of his human senses. Guiding him from within another existence. He couldn't even catch his breath.

The apparition ran hard, and he tried to keep up. He watched from a growing distance as the black-clad young man ran towards the post office on the corner, two blocks away. Then one block away. And then right before him.

His out-of-control body came to a screeching halt, and he felt something pop in one of his knees. That forced him to kneel, right in the middle of the wide street in front of the destroyed post office. And he watched the ghost scene unfold.

The black-clad figure ran right in front of the post office, and headed out into the bisecting street, towards the corner opposite the post office.

As he cleared the street, and the white building across from it, Bob Woodyard saw in his mind's eye how at least three men who had been chasing the figure reached the front of the post office, and Bob had to shield both his real and mind's eyes, as the blast from the explosives he had not noticed before blinded him.

Tears leaking from both eyes, kneeling in the middle of the empty street, Bob looked back at the ghost figure in his mind, who was running across the street, and Bob saw him suddenly fly through the fence next to the white building, and then saw his prone body, laying out in the yard beyond the fence. He suddenly knew what had happened.

Bob felt hands on his shoulders, heard his name being called from far way. Like from the end of a tunnel. And not a short one at that.

His body was on fire, his knee wouldn't quite work, and he was having difficulty catching his breath, as those hands lifted him from where he had slumped over in resignation in the middle of the heat-baked red brick street.

And as he saw the juxtaposition of the real and the apparitional scene in his mind, he could only mumble one phrase.

"He is hurt, he is hurt, he is hurt," Bob repeated under his breath.

But luckily, the mumbling was heard by the young agent who was assisting him. The young agent who had chased him down the broad avenue because they had all instantly assumed that the great Bob Woodyard had finally lost his mind.

The young agent had kept pace with Bob as he sprinted down the middle of the West Texas street. And the same young agent who had witnessed the great man fall to his knees, and then to his side, mumbling.

Bob Woodyard's face was dry. No sweat, and not an ounce of color to it. Pale as a sheet, the agent thought to himself as he helped Bob Woodyard to his feet.

"He is hurt. He is hurt bad," Bob was muttering to no one in particular.

The agent still had no idea what he was talking about.

Chapter 37

Three awoke to silence. Not all at once, but rather, in stages. First, he perceived only darkness. His eyes were still closed, and there was nothing around him that he could sense. And then he felt his body. Or rather, he only felt half of it.

The last stage of awakening was his memory returning. It all came back to him in a rush, and not like in the movies, where the hero, after being injured, awoke with a start, and his memories came back to him only after a beautiful woman, who was nursing him back to health, reminded him what had happened.

No, Three was alone.

It was still dark, and he remembered everything. The loud groan that escaped his lips, and the tears that started falling down his face was all the proof anyone would need of his internal anguish. Anguish as he mentally felt down his body, trying to move every limb. His arms and hands, fingers and elbows moved when he commanded them to.

But nothing below the waist seemed to want to do what he asked his body to do. And in that, he knew the truth. He was paralyzed, and the plan was now shit. It was done. When they were so damn close, it was done.

He let himself mourn for a few more minutes. He let the tears fall, and the feelings of failure wash over and through him.

And then he straightened his shoulders, metaphorically, and started using his greatest gift, his mind, to figure out how to keep the plan from failing in the fourth quarter when he was down by six.

It was the middle of the night, wherever he was, and he was still very tired. As his thoughts went through plan after plan, and idea after idea, his eyes started drooping again. His mind was going fuzzy. He lost consciousness all at once.

And then he dreamt.

He was still alone, in this dream. He felt alone.

He opened his eyes. Looking around, the sky was bright and blue, the air was warm, and it smelled like early summer.

He was lying on his back in a field. He could feel the springy grass under his body. It tickled the back of his neck as he pivoted his head around to see where he was.

He immediately recognized his surroundings. He was in the overgrown fields of his ancestral home. He could make out the family cemetery surrounded by the short wrought iron fence surrounding it to his left. As he turned his head to the right, he could make out the plantation home off in the distance. Both were perpendicular to his vision, as his head still rested against the soft ground under him.

He looked up at the sky. He sighed heavily. Even in his dream, he couldn't move the lower part of his body. What cruelty, he thought. He closed his eyes in his dream, wishing it away. How he was cognizant of being in a dream, he didn't know.

But he knew he was in two places at once. His body, caught up in traction in the real world, and laid out below a cheery sky, here in his dream.

It felt so real.

He wondered if he was really dreaming, or if his consciousness was somewhere else. Not on the same earth, but a juxtaposition of earth, at the same time. His mind couldn't comprehend it.

He suddenly heard soft footsteps.

Oh for hell's sake, what now? He thought to himself.

He opened his eyes, having to raise his hand up over them to block the sudden glare. The glare wasn't coming from the sun, but rather, from the two people approaching him. No, he thought. They weren't people. This pair couldn't be human.

He sat up as well as he could, just using his arms to support him. He took his eyes off the pair approaching him long enough to look at his dead legs. They already looked skinnier to him, inside the pressed white pants he wore. He saw that he also wore a startling white chamois shirt.

Looking back up at the pair of figures approaching him, he assumed they were angels. What other beings wore light colored long robes, and had eight-foot long, outstretched white wings behind them?

He felt strangely calm, even if the figures were glowing and had to be over seven feet tall. They drew close to him. A soft, gentle breeze whispered over his face as they came to a stop, their wings folding in, but not disappearing.

He distractedly wondered why he assumed the wings would disappear.

And then the wings, which to his eyes were not made of feathers like the books showed, did disappear. Both figures, almost simultaneously, seemed to shrink down, until a well-dressed man, and a beautiful woman, also splendidly dressed, stood before him.

He still had to look up into their faces, but at least they weren't glowing like the sun anymore.

"Harold," the older, black man in the pressed seersucker suit said to him, nodding.

Three nodded back slowly. The man looked very familiar. Three couldn't put his finger quite on where he had met the man before.

"Three," the woman's voice was like a song. His heart leapt in his chest when she smiled down on him. He smiled back, momentarily forgetting all of his ills.

The well-dressed, stately man spoke first. The woman knelt down next to Three, taking his hand in hers, almost seeming to hold him up with it. He couldn't take his eyes off of her face.

"It's been a long road, hasn't it, Harold?" the man asked him.
He only nodded.

"You began a movement here. The world watches. The currents of change follow you. What do you plan to do now?" the man asked.

Three could see the man turn his head around, gazing out over his surroundings, and talking about the world as a whole, and not just their present location.

Three took his eyes off of the woman's smiling face, and looked up at the man. He looked so familiar. They both did..

Three found his voice.

"It's over. I can't walk, let alone finish the plan now. And I can't ask others to take over for me. This was my doing.

260

It's mine to finish," he said. He tried not to sound bitter, but he heard it creep into his voice nonetheless.

"Well, Harold, you're in a pickle, that's for sure. I think we can help with that. But if we do, Harold, you MUST finish the plan. The fate of this country depends on it. It's on the brink, ready to be pushed over the edge. Can you not feel the pressure in the world?" he said.

The man had extended both of his arms, encompassing the world around him. Three knew exactly what the man meant.

Three could feel it. He had been feeling it for quite a while. That's how he knew he was still on the right path, and had yet to be condemned to a burning eternity.

He wasn't a religious man. Had never been, really. But he had the same faith in a higher power, and an equal fear of an eternal damnation as the people who had raised him.

With the plan unfolding over the last several years, he had always felt that, as evil as his actions were, he was on a good road. He had always felt justified.

"How can you help?" he asked the man, who simply smiled and nodded his head in the direction of his companion.

Three's eyes traveled back to her serene face, and all tension left his body. She smiled fully at him, and he couldn't help but to grin back.

"Three," she said.

He was all ears for her. He felt stupidly inadequate for her, but her hand never left his. He drew strength from that.

"This is going to be painful. Not more painful than the accident in the first place, but the same pain as the injury. All must be in balance. It's God's eternal law. So, prepare yourself," she told him.

He didn't really know what she was talking about, and didn't have a chance to think it over.

A bright white light escaped from between their enjoined hands, and as the flash hit his eyes, forcing them to

261

close involuntarily, a pain blossomed from the very middle of his body, forcing him to throw back his head and scream.

He could literally feel his broken body form back together. His torn muscles re-knit in an explosively painful way.

The tear in his spine where one of his vertebrae had shattered and severed the cord joined back together, and painful shoots of energy ran up and down his legs.

The bones in his back and the shattered vertebrae bonded back to their original condition. That pain was almost too intense to take. His scream continued until his body was whole again.

He had felt every single part of the knitting back together of his broken body.

For celestial healing, it sucked big time, he thought. But he also felt such an overwhelming feeling of gratitude that tears ran down his cheeks like rivers through a hot, dry desert.

It was difficult for him to find his breath, and during the healing, he didn't think he took a single breath.

And then it was over. His scream echoed over the land around him, and he was panting with effort and a sudden lethargy. He had to take a moment to find his energy. To find his voice.

And as he moved his legs under him, trying to stand like a newborn giraffe, more tears came. He could feel his whole body once again.

The part of his mind that knew he was in two places at once hoped that this healing miracle took in the real world as well. Something deep inside him told him that it would. He smiled.

He rose to his knees as both Archangels helped him stand. He found his feet under him, and even though the accident was only hours earlier, he felt like he was learning to walk all over again. His body felt weak, worn, and hardly able to support itself.

But support itself, it finally did. He stood firm, and looked eye to eye with the two beings who had just saved his life. Saved the plan. Saved him.

All he could do was mumble a small "thank you." He didn't have words otherwise. How could he? Any words felt inadequate in that space.

When he was fully steady, his energy renewed, and his eyes clear, the man spoke again.

"We are not permitted to interfere more, Harold," he said.

"But we can encourage. We can direct. And as I told you once before, you need to finish the plan. The world hinges on it. Press on to the finish now," he said.

Three felt emboldened, once again.

The woman's singsong voice hummed in his ear.

"We will be with you, Three. To the end, and especially AT the end," she said.

He knew her words to be true. And he suddenly remembered another dream, now superimposed over this one, where he had met this duo before.

He had forgotten that dream until now.

He looked on the pair with new eyes. A familiarity rose in his chest and he felt light and free. He knew, finally knew, that he was doing the right thing.

A sense of love emanated from the pair, and he knew in his heart it would be enough to see him through the end.

If ArchAngels were helping him, he thought as his surroundings disappeared slowly around him, then he must be doing something right.

And it was time to finish what he started.

He came awake slowly. He was still in traction, his body strapped to the thin mattress under him. He reached down and unbuckled the wide, leather straps holding his body to the

263

rotating bed. He swung his legs to the side of the bed, and awkwardly rose to his full height.

It was difficult, and a little bit painful, but when he stood fully, his legs under him, he knew the single miracle that had just happened while he was in the place where the material could not see the spiritual was real.

And it was finally time to finish the plan.

He felt a ping of apprehension, but was instantly calmed from a source outside of himself. The ArchAngels were still with him, and would see him to the conclusion of this plan. He now knew that with all of his heart.

He smiled, felt his legs grow stronger under him, and walked out of the hospital room he had been in.

His head was high, his energy was strong, and his body was healed. He was walking towards history, and even though he knew how it would end, he wasn't afraid.

Not anymore.

Two beings looked down on the man who was about the shake the world to its core. Neither could be prouder as they watched him walk towards destiny.

Part V

Chapter 38

"It's time, gentlemen," Three said as he entered the living room of his home in the Maryland suburbs of Washington DC.

Four and Five looked up from where they sat on a couch, holding hands, discussing a bit of an unknown future together. Five was holding back what he knew, and he had been feeling like shit about it for weeks now.

Apprehension filled the room. The three men were alone in the house, and since this day had been planned for so very long, they were ready. But there was sweat on brows, butterflies in stomachs, and shaking. hands.

265

Four had no real idea what was coming. Five thought he knew the entire plan moving forward, as he had been the most instrumental in making sure the final steps happened successfully, but he still couldn't predict the entire ending.

Three alone knew what was to come, and it was he who felt the most apprehension. Conversely, he thought to himself, it wasn't for himself that he feared.

It was for his family that he was most fearful. But as was happening a lot lately, his tension calmed, his shoulders relaxed, and his belly quieted. He just had a little bit more to go.

The couple sitting on the couch rose as one, and they followed Three down the stairs off of the living room, moving into what had once been a large, unfinished basement, but which the team had transformed into a new base of operations.

Most of what was to happen next had already been planned ahead of time, but Three had some tricks up his sleeve, and the rest of his team was going to have to go along with it.

At the rear of the large open basement, stood a new bank of computer monitors, suspended from a framework of a heavy, grid-like structure.

There was a large table, covered in planning materials, maps, and classified information that Five had procured from his ventures into government resources and hacked accounts.

They would need all of that scattered information and more, Three knew.

Five took his customary seat in the front of the large bank of monitors. The system was linked into every node across the globe that they could gain access.

Five had run the IP address for his work through so many back channels and lone alleyways of information, that any hacker or cyber security expert on the planet would find it impossible to trace what Five did here, on an almost daily basis, since Three brought them all together weeks before.

Across from the bank of computer monitors, hung several flat screen televisions that Three and Four monitored with as much vigor as Five worked on his final creation at the computer station.

These televisions showed every major news network around the United States, as well as several international media outlets. The team had always believed that in order to stay ahead of their adversaries, it had been paramount to stay informed.

And that's really what had kept this team ahead of the most progressive, expensive, and time-consuming manhunt in human history: information.

And the third wall of the semi-square, open area at the end of the basement was made up entirely of a Hercules Organization System.

This kind of system usually made up the garages and workshops of people who could afford it. This particular system, however, did not hold tools and working implements. It held weapons.

Every conceivable weapon that the team had needed over the last nine years. Every job that had been accomplished, every death obtained in stealth and secrecy, had been accomplished with the over-stuffed organization system making up the third wall of the basement.

From firearms, knives, military grade weaponry, and explosives. Every tool that Three had used to kill so many people hung on the wall, clean, sparkling, and ready for further use, if anyone needed it.

Luckily, as the team had agreed to, no more death was needed. At least, not from their hands.

Not unless they were pressed to make an example, and Three was worried the most about that exact situation happening. He had lost his taste for killing long ago, and he was ready to feel clean once more.

That, he knew, was coming soon.

Standing behind Five, Three held a single sheet of paper in his hand. Four was just watching, knowing how critical the next steps were going to be.

They were about the make the final changes needed for the plan to work, and for the work to stick. This was the tricky part, and all three of the men needed their whole wits about them.

The Intel had been gathered, the plan had been worked and re-worked until no one saw a kink in it. But, as they knew from so much experience, nothing usually went as planned once the first bullet flew.

Three started reading off a list of twenty-eight names to Five. As he read each name, Five sent a series of commands that enacted his final project. His opus. The magnificence of his experience, his training, and his brilliance all rolled into one single-use cyber weapon.

Five had created a twin-sided virus that was both a Trojan horse, and a worm file. It was untraceable, unstoppable, and could wiggle past any firewall built to keep these kinds of things out.

It did so by mimicking the security system's own code, being welcomed in as a part of said security system, blowing past the firewalls, overcoming the final defense of encryption and delivering its messages before it self-destructed, leaving behind nothing that could be traced by the heavy arm of every law enforcement agency in the country.

Because what they now did, was no longer the purview of the criminal arm of government enforcement. They were now moving into the deep, dark, entangled world of terrorism, and the entire world would now try to beat a wide trail straight to the front door of *the Preacher*.

The men knew that you could kill regular citizens, without so much as a whisper from the government, but to bring about real change, you had to fracture the very foundations of safety for the men and women who enacted policy from the highest offices and rooms of the venerable US Government.

And when you shook those particular foundations, it was no longer considered serial killing. It became abject

Terrorism, and the entire weight and resources of the Government would be used to protect their own.

And all three men knew, at that moment, that nothing could possibly be traced back to them. And their families. And of course, their community. They had to be quick, precise, textbook perfect, and then hide for as long and as remotely as they all could.

"Speaker of the House, Ronald Whittaker, 22125 Independence Place, North Potomac, Maryland, IP 212-445-321115, email on the House's server mainframe, enter 234-PH-4412," Three read off his piece of paper, and Five entered the information into his data server.

"Senator Jane Fillmore, 345 Rockingham Rd, Concord, New Hampshire, IP locator 456-986GH-45T, email on Senate data server code Alpha-Foxtrot-886." Five's fingers flew across his keyboard, data in front of him on the main monitor flying by faster than the two men standing could read.

"Chief Justice Tony Calliope, 54 Market Street, Georgetown, Washington, DC. IP 43FO-654-54786548, Supreme Court Server, 567 locator 456, internal memo selection, Chief Justice Menu, enter encryption code Alpha, Beta," Three read.

The list held the personal data and avenues to be able to send personal emails straight to the highest, and most powerful movers and shakers in Washington DC. The people who, with the right amount of pressure, the right amount of threat, could enact bold and sweeping changes in law.

Some of these changes were already being put before legislative bodies, and were held within heavily marked and overheavy bills. Three and Company simply wanted to speed up the process. By decades.

With each package of data delivered to each of the twenty-eight names on the list, a separate file was uploaded just for the twenty-eight marked "your eyes-only."

269

These were proofs of data that the team had collected. Skeletons in closets, secrets held close to the chest, and in one particular case, the sensitive data of a secret girlfriend, tucked into a nice apartment outside the Beltway, and who did not possess an American citizenship. She happened to only be seventeen, as well.

That particular Minority Leader of the Senate would not want that information getting back to his constituents in Utah. A state which frowned heavily on marriage misconduct of their elected officials.

Along with all of the data being presented to the twenty-eight members of government was a simple threat. *The Preacher* knew who they were, where they lived, all of their secrets, and how to get to them.

So, *the Preacher* offered a truce.

He would stop the killings around the country, as well as refraining from killing these twenty-one members of government, in exchange for sweeping legal changes in specific laws that needed to be revamped, thrown out, or downright reversed.

And, if they did what they he asked, *the Preacher* would turn himself in.

That piece of the final plan did not sit well with the team. Not one bit. Several lengthy, loud arguments were performed in the kitchen and bedrooms of the home over their heads with that last bit of the plan.

Three simply ended it all with a promise to not do anything that the team did not agree on, well in advance.

The team offered the twenty-eight members of government the single opportunity to do the right thing. They hoped and prayed that over the next six months to a year, those changes be signed into law, and that real change could be effected, all with the simple act of holding a knife to each of the politician's throats.

It was a long shot, the team knew.

The government had a firm stance on refusing to negotiate with terrorists, but as they had proved over and over, the government did just about whatever the hell it wanted — threats, bribes, and integrity be damned.

Three was simply using the history of the last nine years, the deaths of so many innocent people, and the chance for these twenty-eight public officers to do the right thing and be heroes.

They could end the almost decade long terror episode of *the Preacher*.

He knew it was things like that that got politicians re-elected. And that's all those scumbags in DC were really worried about.

And the final coup de grâce? Three made sure that in the individual emails, the recipients all knew who each other were. He wanted them all to know that they were on a list, and that they should use each other as allies to enact these sweeping changes. They would need each other, Three knew.

Because he was betting that they all jumped to his tune, and did so with miraculous punctuality and effort.

In fact, he was betting his life on it.

Chapter 39

"Come back here, you silly goose!" Colbie yelled to Emma. "I'm going to get'cha!"

Giggling, the little girl ran towards the warm water of the beach-lined lake. Three smiled from the deck of the log cabin situated less than thirty yards from the crystalline waters of the sun-glinted lake, as the mother of his children caught the young, bathing suit-wearing girl right as her feet hit the warm water.

Colbie picked up the squirming six-year-old child, and tossed her further into the water, where her cannonball quickly formed as she flew through the air, splashing her brother, Jack.

Jack, for all of his serious nature, laughed with glee as the water hit him in the face. And then he, along with his two favorite uncles, started splashing water back at Colbie and a just-surfaced Emma. It was a game of boys versus girls, and Three had money on his two favorite girls in the whole world to win this particular splashing game.

Three smiled down at his family, feeling only a gentle tug on his emotions. He, alone, knew what was coming soon, and he soaked up his children's laughter like a dry sponge soaks up cool water.

He was drinking a cold beer, and the grill behind him was smoking with the steaks and burgers cooking for his guests and, of course, the blackened hotdogs that his children enjoyed so much.

The smell of cooking meat emitting from the mahogany deck of the tri-level log home enticed all who played and wallowed in the water nearby. Three knew that everyone would soon come up to the house for lunch. One of the last lunches of the summer they had all spent together.

He watched as his family laughed and played. He watched his children's faces full of glee and happiness. He took in the sights of the several people he had grown up with, his closest people, all gathered together at the tail end of the best summer he had ever had.

He took in all of the sights like they were food to a starving man. The sun smiled down on his world, at least for this day, he thought. Today, at least, was warm, happy, and full of possibility for those he loved.

He knew that he must savor these images. These memories. The tail end of the best time of his life.

He caught himself thinking of the changes in Congress, which had been the front-page story on the news several nights previously.

After the team had sent the information packages containing the deal along with their demands to the government officials in all three branches, and tied up some loose ends concerning some other preparations, Three had brought everyone here, to this house, on Governor's Island in New Hampshire.

Since then, those twenty-eight souls, who had come public with the threats that *the Preacher* had sent them, still decided to make the sweeping changes to long-held laws that were made to divide the country, rather than bring them together.

There were some last-minute decisions and changes made for this year's fiscal budget that was to be enacted at the end of September, but which included so many of the changes that *the Preacher* had asked for.

Three's attention came back to the present. He needed to stay present, he knew. He thought about how he had found this place.

During his travels, he had come to Lake Winnipesaukee once, and had fallen in love with the area. He had been scouting the area for a possible target, early on in the plan, but had decided to stay away from New Hampshire as a killing field. He didn't want to spoil this place. Because he had vowed to himself many years prior, that if he could get his family up to the large lake in the middle of the state, he would do it.

And when this log home had come available to rent for a year, he had jumped on it.

And so, right after Christmas, which they had all spent in the Southern Maryland home, they had packed up, and made the trip north.

At first, it was just him, Colbie, and the twins. Four and Five and showed up several times through the end of the winter, for a weekend away from the City a couple of times, and Three had flown his extended adopted-family from Alabama up a couple of times as well. But his own small family had been able to spend so many weeks alone with each other, and to savor time together that Three knew would not happen again.

Once the summer was in full swing, everyone he loved on the planet had stayed around the clock. Almost like they all knew what was about to happen.

But they didn't, Three thought to himself as he got out of the comfortable Adirondack chair, and resumed his duties at the charcoal grill.

He had a mind full of memories of the last three months, and his heart, at least, was at peace.

Looking back down at the beach between the house and the gentle waves of water, he saw each of his loved ones, laughing, and playing in the warm New England sun. He couldn't help it. He was soaking up their faces, their smiles, the joy they all showed, being here, in this place, at this time.

Pretty soon, he knew, things wouldn't be so lovely.

Towards the water, always near the water, were his children. He worried the most for them. They were the only people on the planet connected to him through DNA. He hoped that they had hid that fact well enough for the kids to have a normal life.

He was assured by the medical team that had helped bring them into the world that their true identities were hidden, never to see the light of day.

Since that day, Colbie had been careful to show the world that she was a single mother, and that the children didn't have a father that they knew about. They had trained the children on those facts from the time that they could talk, but Three knew that it would never be enough for the twins. They would need so much more family after what was to come.

He knew that Colbie was estranged from her own family, but he felt that separation would not last too much longer after this year. At least, he hoped for that.

Colbie was never far from the kids. He knew that she suspected what was to come. She had been his champion for so long, but the things that he had done must come with a reckoning.

He knew, late at night, as he lay awake, thinking of the end of this plan, Colbie lay next to him, thinking the same. He also knew that she held out hope that they could just disappear into oblivion, after he had done the job set before him.

She didn't know that for the plan to stick, and make permanent changes in this country, one final sacrifice would need to be made.

His eyes took in his two best friends in all of the world. Four and Five shared a love that he, himself, envied. Not that he wasn't in love with Colbie, but for Four and Five, their love transcended time.

They had known each other since birth, practically, and that bond would last for the rest of their lives. Three certainly worried the least about those two.

Whatever happened, he would make sure that they were protected, and that their parts in the plan were never brought to the light of day. They had each other, and Three knew, that no matter what, that's all the two of them needed. He was beyond happy for his two best friends. He always had been.

He also felt like he had clipped all of the branches of their involvement in the plan, but one last thing must be done to protect Four. Three swallowed at the lump in his throat thinking of how Four would take that particular piece of information.

Looking back towards the house, he saw the only family that he had known for his entire childhood. Dottie was gone, and he truly missed her, but he still had Floyd and Chester.

And he still had Harmony.

Floyd and Chester got on well with each other, as they always had done. They lived together now, down in Alabama. They had taken over Dottie's house, and Harmony, who had been Dottie's estate planner, had made sure that they two men would never want for anything.

Chester still always had a ready smile for everyone around him, and Floyd was still the most like a father that Three would ever have. He loved both men fiercely.

Over the summer they had all spent together, Three had spent time alone with both men, talking, reminiscing, and making sure that they knew how much Three appreciated them so very much. The sentiment had been returned many times over.

Those two men, Three knew, would accept what was to come with the most grace, and have the most peace from it. They had both known where this was heading ever since Three had approached them with the plan to handle Hunter O'Connor.

Three's eyes then found Harmony, sitting on a checkered blanket under the trees close by the water. Her own family surrounded her now.

Harmony had married soon after Three had let the four of them go, so many years earlier. She had secretly been dating a man named Daniel Manning from August.

Three had known the man well, and thought that the match was made in heaven. Without even realizing it, Danny had become a member of Three's family, almost overnight, and especially after he had helped with the "Hunter situation," as they liked to call it.

Harmony and Danny had had three children by the time they had been married for five years. The three children were Three's own children's closest friends.

And it made Three's heart soar to see them all together, and to know, that the next generation of children would be raised with so much less racial hatred as all the ones before.

Those five children, Three knew, reminded him of his own team of best friends, from his own childhood. The team that had been so tragically split with the deaths of Mary and Matthew. Their very own One and Two.

Three vowed to himself over the smoking steaks and the blackened hotdogs, that this team of five would not be split for anything.

And so, for the last three months, Three had had his entire family under a single roof. He had paid for everything, and even made sure that Harmony and Danny's jobs would allow them both a leave of absence.

This summer was more important than any job, Three knew. But he also knew that when it was over, his extended family had to go about their lives. He wanted to leave them with as many wonderful memories as he could before that happened.

Before the end came.

He called everyone together for lunch. He knew that the warm winds that had blown all day would turn a little less warm in the afternoon as the days turned over to the quickly moving fall of New England.

He wanted everyone to enjoy the sun as long as they could. And so, they ate outside, in the sinking sun, sitting on either side of a long, wooden picnic table. The kind of table made for a large family.

The children laughed and giggled over the blackened hotdogs, splattered with ketchup and mustard. The men enjoyed the steaks and the salad that Colbie had prepared earlier. The women ate the hamburgers that Three assured them were organic.

He smiled at the concern they showed for wholesomeness and health. It brought joy to his heart to know that all would be well handled, when this was all finished.

And as the family ate, Three and Colbie stole quick glances at each other over the food, and around all of the laughter and banter back and forth over the long wooden picnic table that took up most of the large deck.

The food was laid out on top of a red and white checkered tablecloth, as it had been all summer, and it was plentiful and delicious.

Once again, Colbie's eyes caught his own, and this time, a lump formed in his throat, and he found it difficult to swallow a bite.

She knows, Three thought to himself. She knows, and she can't stop me.

He almost lost his appetite, but regained it after listening to Four and Harmony tell the children a story from when the

278

three men of their little Alabama team played a rival basketball team in the seventh grade, and how they had snuck salt into the opposing team's Gatorade bottles.

Five smiled a secret smile, but even he couldn't keep his eyes and his concerned face from getting into Three's mind. Five alone knew what was to come, and Three had sworn him to a secrecy unlike anything he had ever made Five promise.

Five had agreed, and he had agreed to his part in the final plan. But he didn't have to like it, he had told Three on several occasions as the summer flew by with fun and laughter.

There was nothing for it, Three knew. The summer was now coming to a close. The government had done exactly what they had asked of it, and now, Three had to finish the final part of the plan. The part that, had everyone known what was coming, they would have done absolutely anything to stop.

Even to the point of turning Three in as *the Preacher.*

The children, more than anyone else, would remember the laughter from that day, and all of the days leading up to it. They would grow up to remember the bright sun, the blue water, and the happiness of the warm summer that the entire family had spent in the lakes region of New Hampshire.

And they would remember the somber yet cheery face of their benefactor, Harold Higgsby the Third, who would go down in history as one of mainstream media's "Most Evil Men."

There just wasn't anything for it, Three thought to himself, glancing around at his family and loved ones, knowing that it was all coming to an end.

He finally did lose his appetite.

There just wasn't anything for it.

Three sighed heavily, and mentally prepared himself for October 14 of this year. The very last time that an October 14 would be memorialized by him, or anyone else who remembered Mary and Matthew, and why that date was so very important to the team.

After this year, October 14th would mean something else entirely.

It would mean something else entirely to the United States of America.

Chapter 40

On September 30, Three disappeared.

Five knew that it was going to happen, but no one else did. Up to that point, everything had just been on cruise control, and the family had felt like this was how it could always be.

Of course, the adults were always aware that the overwhelming resources of the law enforcement arm of the government continued to try to locate *the Preacher*.

But the team knew that they would find nothing. They had tied up all of the loose ends, put blocks up in front of the task force to the point that there were rumors that the task force was funneling down to a skeleton crew after nine and a half years of absolutely nothing happening.

The task force had processed, catalogued, and gone over with a fine-tooth comb ninety-one separate crime scenes. Each victim had had the same markers on or around them, like the Bible pages, and the numbers drawn on their chests, to pinpoint *the Preacher's* involvement, but to this day, no further clues as to his real identity had surfaced.

They all also had had one other identifier that had stayed out of the media. All of the victims were all either missing their shirt, or a piece had been cut from it.

For some reason, and to a lot of the crime scene technicians who processed the deaths, that detail was the most chilling. They could deal with numbers and Bible pages. A killer keeping trophies gave everyone the heebie jeebies.

And for those who knew, or thought they knew, the identity of *the Preacher* were either silenced permanently, or were too afraid to come forward.

Also, a year before, the famed head of the "new" task force, Bob Woodyard, had suffered a partial stroke, and had been ceremoniously retired from his legendary career as a lawman. He had not been seen or heard from since.

Many on the force actually thought he had passed away, quietly, away from the spotlight that at the end, he seemed to shy away from.

Many people who had known him throughout his career whispered over beers that Bob had lost his fight with this last case. And who wouldn't, they would say. *The Preacher* was a sick fuck.

And then the twenty-eight separate packages of information, threats, and promises had come to various high-level members of the government, who were all too happy to put a stop to the killings, and to make the changes that actually made sense to a majority of the public.

So, together with the ninety-one bodies and the final twenty-eight victims who had been threatened, but who had held onto their lives, the final tally of victims associated with *the Preacher* rested squarely at 119 souls.

And had done so, for the better part of an entire year. An election year. A quiet year of massive changes in the legal systems of America.

Three and his family had settled back into a life that was still very cautious. Colbie maintained her and the kids' lives in the DC suburbs of Montgomery County. She had bought a house from the proceeds of her now famous website DeathX, and she and the kids lived a blissful life on a quiet cul-de-sac, in the country, near a wonderful place called Butler's Orchard.

They had picked tons of strawberries at the Orchard that early fall.

Three would visit many times a week, but always arrived through the woods at the back of the home, and always at night. They had maintained their level of care ever since they had returned from their summer in New England.

The kids just thought it was a game. Later in life, they would look back on the sinisterness of it, but by then, they would understand the whys and whats that had made up their father's entire life. They would come to know their father much more than most kids knew their own parents.

Four and Five had settled into marital bliss in upstate New York where Four maintained a new practice that he and a fellow Harvard Law acquaintance opened up in Albany.

They relentlessly fought for LGBTQ+ rights all over the country, and were making quite the name for themselves in the new, ever-changing society of the United States.

Five finished up the preparations he had made at the urging of Three just a couple of nights before Three disappeared. He was to be poised in the basement of Three's Southern Maryland home on October 14th of that year.

Even Four had no idea what was to come, and Five's only knowledge of the events were sketchy. He had been told a broad plan by Three, but he had suspicions that everything wasn't what Three had described.

But once Three disappeared, Five wasn't sure if he should go along with the plan. Only a hastily scribbled note on Five's computer screen left by Three made him relent.

The note only contained four words. Five shed tears when he read it, and when he learned, less than an hour later, that Three was missing.

"Remember Mary and Matthew," Three had written before he disappeared.

The entire family spent the next week frantically calling each other. Harmony and the kids arrived three days into the week to stay with Colbie and the twins.

The kids were having the time of their lives, as their mothers didn't make them go to school for almost two weeks.

The two weeks it took for Three to be located.

And they would never have had located him, if he had not released his manifest to the world.

The rest of the events played out like a movie. A movie that the two women sat on the couch of Colbie's house, watching unfold on the 5 o'clock news on Monday, October 14th.

They held hands throughout the ordeal, and cried together the rest of the night through.

Every single news outlet in the country, and probably the entire world, by the time it was over, got a copy of the manifest. Every newspaper printed it, and every news website on the globe put it on their front page.

Within an hour of its release, it had gone viral in ways that no other story in the history of the internet had gone. Months later, after the clamor had died down, and it had been analyzed every which way it could be, the analysts found out that *The Preacher's Manifest* had racked up so many views in its first twenty-four hours that they couldn't even be counted.

Whole databanks had been jammed from the number of people downloading the fifteen-minute video clip. Transcripts of the video were typed out and transmitted within five minutes of the video being released.

And it was all due to what Three had asked Five to do.

Two months prior, Five had created another virus. This one was much simpler, yet broader in scope, than the one that he had sent to the twenty-eight members of the government the year prior.

This virus simply took over the internet.

It took control of the internet for the single purpose of telling the world just who *the Preacher* was, where he could be found, and why he had done what he had done. Five had argued vehemently against it, but Three had talked him into it, as he had done all of their lives.

The virus that Five had created was a battering ram of code that forced itself into every fire-walled website on the internet that dealt in information sharing. Every news agency website, almost a billion hits on Google within the first hour, and on sites like Reddit, Yahoo, Facebook, Instagram, and Twitter.

The virus then downloaded the video of *the Preacher* telling the world about himself, and then erased itself, never to be seen again. Five called it the 'pound and play' virus.

The video was simple, straightforward, and began differently than how it finished. When the initial viewing of the video was accomplished by the first hundred million or so viewers, the news channels switched over to a Live, Breaking News, show, with all cameras pointed at the Mall in the middle of Washington D.C.

What they didn't know, as they all zoomed onto the lone figure in the middle of the lawn near the Carousel on the National Mall, was that five separate cameras in the trees and four drones hovering nearby, were controlled by Five, who sat, resolutely, in the command chair in the basement of the Southern Maryland home, and who, at the conclusion of what unfolded on that crisp October afternoon, walked away, the house burning down behind him.

His job that day would be to make sure that what happened next was shown to the world, and not covered up, or erased by the very body of people who needed the change the most.

Who the entire plan had been aimed at.

That group who would be forced through blood and bond, to change the way they had always done things. And change for the better of everyone, regardless of sex, age, race, or religion.

Because the entire Plan had been aimed at Law Enforcement at every level in the United States.

The manifest, along with what transpired soon after its release, changed the world as they had come to know it.

Chapter 41

"My name is Harold Higgsby the Third. But most people throughout my life just called me 'Three,'" he said in the video.

He was sitting in a chair, in a dark room, a single light aimed at him. He was wearing a simple black t-shirt, and khaki pants. His legs were crossed in front of him, his hands were folded in his lap.

"I am *the Preacher*."

Here he paused, as to allow that statement to settle into the minds of the millions watching him. His eyes never left the camera. His bald head shone with moisture in the bright light that shown from above him.

The room remained shrouded in blackness. Nothing moved behind him, around him, and nothing about the scene changed over the next fifteen minutes.

"I never wanted to kill anyone. I hate violence. But sometimes, as I have learned in this life, someone must do violence to stop a greater evil," he said calmly.

His voice, the analysts later would recount, never changed in octave for the entire video, and some speculated that he may have been on some sort of downer drug, or was being pressured to give this statement.

That theory was soon thrown out, however.

"The plan that I enacted ten years ago has been in my mind since I was eleven years old, and I witnessed my two best friends being murdered right in front of me, in broad daylight, by a member of law enforcement, simply because of the color of their skin," he said.

At this point, many viewers responded that *the Preacher* started sweating more. No other changes could be seen in his demeanor.

He went on for several more minutes talking about Mary and Matthew, and the bond that they had all shared, and even admitted to being in love with Mary.

At the mention of her name, his words paused slightly, but no other noticeable change came over him, or his voice.

He then spoke about how he enacted the Plan at the death of his father, and that he had acted completely alone. It never came out, on any channel, or in any conversation, that *the Preacher* had NOT worked alone.

For some reason, it was a lot easier for the country to accept that he had acted alone. It made people sleep better at night.

There were those, however, who had come out very early on, like one of the first law enforcement officers who had worked on *the Preacher* case, who said that in no way did he work alone, but back then, law enforcement's position in the communities across the country had not changed, and no one quite trusted them yet.

Those rumors fell on deaf ears, and those who spoke them eventually faded into obscurity.

"I grew up in a community down south who still taught, if not practiced, segregation. But I was raised in a home that also saw color, but didn't care," he said into the camera

"The people who raised me, taught me that love came from those different looking than me, but in no way less than me," he said.

"And that love was the same love, no matter your skin color. So, in the end, I actually cherished those with black skin more than white, because those were the people who actually loved me."

The world was starting to listen.

"And so, I killed dispassionately. I killed fairly. Rich, poor, white, black, Asian. I killed for a simple and single reason," he said, about halfway through the video.

"I killed to instill fear in this country. Because, my brothers and sisters, terror brings together those of different backgrounds more cohesively than any kind of celebration or joy." He said it matter-of-factly.

"Over the last ten years, police departments of all sizes and shapes have increased awareness within their communities. They have enacted community outreach programs the likes this country has never seen before. And you citizens, responded to those outreach programs because you all shared a single thing. You were all afraid," he said into the camera.

He had no way of knowing, when he filmed the video, that many heads were nodding, watching him speak.

"Over the last ten years, the numbers of police killings have dropped by over sixty percent across the board. White cops killing black people, black cops killing white people, ALL

289

classifications of police brutality have steadily decreased. And with the new legislation enacted by Congress and signed by the President, those numbers will hopefully fall to zero in the very near future," he said.

He then spent about five minutes reviewing why he had made threats to the members of the government to make the changes to the laws that were needed.

"Every year for the last two decades, the Government spent nearly forty-seven billion dollars annually, on the War on Drugs," he explained.

"And now that cannabis, and small amounts of all other drugs have been federally legalized, a law which goes into effect after the November elections of this year, all that money is now going to be directed towards rehabilitation and education," he said.

"Half of that almost fifty billion dollars a year will go towards education incentives for students to pursue degrees in social work, mental health, and proper law enforcement techniques," he went on.

"And the new, sweeping laws affecting police at every level, which were just passed through the Supreme Court, and found to be constitutional, will automatically make all law enforcement fall under their own laws," he went on.

"If a cop kills an unarmed suspect, they are automatically arrested, and must face a bond hearing before an internal review hearing. Along with mandatory body camera use, the number of police killings of innocent people should be eradicated," he said into the camera.

"Finally, in the last year, over 1.4 million Americans were arrested and incarcerated for drug possession only."

"As of December first of this year, those who are currently still incarcerated for drug possession charges, over a million souls, will receive a Presidential pardon," he paused at this statement.

"Of the over 2.3 million people in some form of incarceration or another, over half of them will be freed, rehabilitated on the government's dime, educated and reformed," he went on.

"The new annual budgetary gain that has been generated by legalizing all drugs in the US is over 107 billion dollars, and most of that is made up of tax revenue, and the erasure of prohibition by law enforcement. That surplus will now go towards education and safety programs," he said.

"And this was the only way that I could make sure that those changes were made, that people trusted their police forces again, and that there would be generational changes made towards racial hatred and divide," *the Preacher* said.

"I know it won't end with me here. It can't. This movement must go on until this country loses its memory of racial divide and embraces the equalization of absolutely every person on this planet," *the Preacher* said by way of closing.

As the video would down to its final minute, the real ending of the *Preacher's Manifest* began.

"As this video is playing out to the world, I, Harold Higgsby the Third, *the Preacher*, am ready to turn myself in. I deserve to face punishment for my actions," he said quietly.

He then hung his head, the only movement he made the entire video.

"I am currently at these coordinates," he said to the ground.

His voice was lower, but in closing, a single, last sentence could be heard on the video.

"I am so sorry." He looked back up at the camera, a pained expression on his face, at the end.

The video faded to black. *The Preacher* was gone from the screen.

All that remained was a set of numbers and letters in white, emblazoned across the video screen, until even those, faded to darkness.

38.8875° N. 77.0364° W.

Chapter 42

The sounds of sirens were drowned out by the helicopter blades, circling overhead. Three looked up from where he stood on the grassy area very near the middle of the National Mall.

It was early evening, on October 14th, and it had been twenty-four years since Mary and Matthew had been murdered in front of him.

Three looked around him. No one was near. That was a lucky thing, but he knew once the show started, people would come running to see what was to happen.

As he thought about that, and as he heard the sirens getting closer, he looked up into the tree closest to him, seeing a glint of metal, high up in the branches. He nodded towards the shiny metal, and a small, red light turned on.

293

He was now being viewed, in real time, by the same people who had started watching his video several minutes prior. He knew that it had gone viral, and people would catch up to this situation very quickly.

Five was monitoring the cameras situated all around Three, and would make sure that what was about to happen would be shown to the world.

He said a quick prayer under his breath as the sirens became deafening. He felt calm and peace emanate from the middle of his chest, and his breath, which had become labored without him realizing it, as he became so exposed to the world, slowed back down. He knew that he was not alone.

The police cars were the first on the scene, right on the heels of the increasing number of helicopters flying overhead. He knew that the world was watching him.

Tires screeching, feet pounding the street nearest him, front and rear of where he stood, and the unmistakable sound of gun hammers being cocked, and bullets being readied inside chambers.

How familiar the sounds were to his ears, he thought.

He started to walk towards the middle of the grassy area that surrounded him. He didn't want the world to miss what was about to happen next. He could feel eyes on him, guns aimed at him, and history judging him.

He would show history just who he was.

As several cameras were trained on him, the police were rushing out of their cars, vans, and trucks, with all weapons drawn. Three stopped in the middle of the open expanse of lawn. And faced the crowd of police vehicles only fifty or so feet from where he stood.

As he had predicted, only a couple of minutes had passed, but a large crowd of people was already there, watching events unfold.

He felt more exposed than at any other time in his life.

And so, to compound the exposure, he slowly, ever so slowly, reached up to his head, with all eyes on him, and the police screaming at him to get on his knees, and he removed his mask.

Later, analysis would show, that the mask that *the Preacher* had worn, both on the video screen where he had told his manifest to the world, as well as live on the National Mall, was the same face that he had been seen in and photographed in, several years earlier in Seattle.

While that picture was grainy at best, the mask was of the best quality the world had to offer. It had made *the Preacher* look like a completely different man.

And now, the world would see the real face of *the Preacher*. Live, and in color.

The real Harold Higgsby was still bald. He had bright blue eyes, and he wore a short beard.

The cameras around him zoomed in, and the watchers near him on the Mall, and the millions that caught onto the video streaming around the world later would see, was that he was a rather good-looking guy.

He was in his mid-thirties, in terrific shape, as the viewers would come to see very soon after he removed the mask, and a lot of people would later compare him to the likes of Ted Bundy and the Nightstalker, Richard Ramirez, for his good looks.

People would liken his good looks to how he was able to get in and out of all the places he had killed his victims. All that would come later, of course. At the moment, the scene was too tense to allow for that kind of analysis.

The police were staying behind their vehicles until the SWAT team arrived, as was standard practice. There were so many cameras on *the Preacher* at that moment, that what happened next would never be discounted, over-ruled, or erased.

It was livestreamed around the world, and even if the government or law enforcement tried to cover it up, the sheer number of copies being recorded would always make sure that the video would be available to the world's masses, at any time, for free.

The police continued to shout for the tall, well-muscled man to get on his knees. He watched the police carefully, and stood stock still for about three more minutes.

And then he took off his shirt.

The watcher's, behind computer screens, on smartphones, in front of televisions, and even watching on giant jumbotron's around the country, all gasped as one.

The Preacher's muscular torso and arms were not what made the viewers gasp in shock. It was what he was wearing under the sweater that he had removed. And what was painted on his chest.

Around *the Preacher's* neck, not unlike a deranged soldier from some Vietnam War movie who was wearing a necklace of ears, he had on what most would describe as a scarf of many colors.

A long, multi-squared scarf was draped around the killer's neck. It was made up of a patchwork of three-inch by three-inch pieces of fabric, and every one of them, as people zoomed in and looked, appeared to have blood on it.

The lab technicians, later on, and law enforcement officers who were in the know, knew exactly what the killer wore around his neck.

And it was brilliant, they thought.

There was no doubt now, that this man, standing out in the open for all the world to see, was really who he claimed to be. This man was the real *Preacher*.

Every single square making up the vulgar scarf around his neck, was made from the shirt of one of his victims. Ninety-one squares of different cloth, in different colors, and all containing a blood stain that could be matched to the victims.

There was no better proof that this man was *the Preacher*, and that he acted alone.

Every police officer at the scene knew exactly what it was. And every single finger drew tighter on the trigger of the guns aimed at *the Preacher*.

And after a single minute of showing the world the scarf of many colors draped around his neck, and hanging in front of his body, he threw it off, and it landed in a heap at his feet.

All eyes followed the scarf as it hit the ground, and as a single unit, every eye then travelled back up the killer's torso, to his chest, to see what he had done to himself.

In big, bold, solid tattoo black, still shiny from whatever medicine he had rubbed on it to make it stand out, was a tattooed number, directly in the middle of his chest, extending from the bottom of his neck, down to right above his belly button. And now the world really gasped in shock.

It was the number "1."

The next ten seconds went by slower than time itself. All eyes on the killer were in shock at seeing the tattooed number on his torso, but the police closest to him were recovering more quickly than the watchers online and on television.

They knew what it meant.

He meant to be his own, final victim. That question had finally been answered. *The Preacher* was here to offer himself up as his final sacrifice.

But the cops recognizing that fact didn't stop what happened next.

They again yelled for him to get down on his knees, to raise his hands over his head, to lay down. So many commands were screamed at *the Preacher*, that he couldn't do any of them. They were cautiously approaching him, trying to end this situation as quickly, and as quietly as they could.

The killer simply stood, for the next ten seconds, looking at the cameras in front of him, knowing that he was being broadcast to the world, at that exact second, in real time.

The world would see what happened next with their own, innocent eyes.

As the encircling police officers moved towards the half-naked killer, still screaming at him to get down, to put up his hands, to get on the damn ground for God's sake, Three looked into the camera closest to him, a drone, hovering not even twenty feet above the heads of the encroaching police. He raised his hands up even with his head, his fingers loose, and his body rigid.

The analysts, three days later, were able to determine what he mouthed right before he lowered his hands for the final time.

He had looked right into the camera, knowing his family was watching, and he simply mouthed, "I love you."

He then threw his right hand down, and into the large pocket that was attached to his belt on his right side. No one had really noticed it until right at that moment. But with snake quick reflexes, his hand dove into the large pocket.

And as he drew out the contents of the large pocket, the police around him opened fire.

Harold Higgsby the Third, better known to his friends and family as Three, but the world knew him as *the Preacher*, had pulled forth a Bible. The pages were colored red, the cover was black and thin.

And he was hit with more bullets than even Bonnie and Clyde had borne in their own spectacular end.

The video screens around the world zoomed in on his lifeless body, laying prone on the ground, riddled with bullet holes, and the stark number "1" pointing straight up to the heavens, where his soul was now departing to.

And in a room, many miles to the south from the dead body of his best friend, Five wept openly in front of the monitors. He had just witnessed Three lose his life, in the same way that Mary and Matthew had lost theirs.

His head down on the table in front of him, he loudly wept at what he had just seen. And what he had just figured out.

And he knew the truth, finally.

Three had planned this exact ending, the entire time.

Soon, Five realized that he had one last task to perform, and he was running out of time. All of the electronic circuitry that they had used to link the live feed with the internet could be traced back to this home, and Five needed to be far away when that happened.

He opened a red folder, and read the single sheet of paper that was inside. Three had labeled the folder "Phase III." Five smiled at the simile. Looking over the instructions, and seeing that they were plain enough to enact, he started. His fingers flying over the keyboard, Five enacted Three's final wishes for his estate.

Over the last decade, Five and Four had both helped Three amass a staggering fortune that they couldn't hope to spend during the Plan. But now, with Three being gone, his estate being the sole responsibility of the government, Five needed to divvy up the money how Three wanted.

His first act was to enable a multi-faceted withdrawal and deposit into ninety-one separate accounts. It had been Three's wish that ninety-one million dollars of his fortune would go his victim's families.

All of the deposits made into their accounts came with an automatically mailed email describing what the money was for, and if the family did not want to keep the money, then donations should be made to the effort to end [police brutality.

Five had no idea what those ninety-one families would do with the money. He was simply the messenger. In truth, he really didn't care. But in life, Three had cared greatly.

That left the bulk of Three's fortune, which, according to his instructions, was to be divided in half first, with the first half going into trust for Colbie and the kids. Five happily typed away, assuring the financial future for Three's immediate family.

299

The second half of Three's remaining fortune, roughly two hundred million dollars was to be divided into four equal parts, to be shared between him and Four, Harmony and her family, and a share to both Floyd and Chester.

Five smiled as he punched away at the keys, moving the money around according to account preparations that Three had set up before he had disappeared.

Soon, Five was finished. He had done everything exactly according to Three's wishes, and the way that he had set it all up, it could not be traced back to him, to Three's offshore accounts, or to be used against Three's estate or family.

Five was happy with the work that he had done to make sure that Three's family were all taken care of.

He wiped his eyes, erased the information stored on the computers around him in a few, simple commands, and on his way out of the now-empty home, lit the incendiary devices that Three had left tied together in the middle of the living room.

Five then drove straight home to upstate New York, six hours away, and ran straight into the arms of his love, who wept with him, for the loss of their best friend.

They held each other in their shared grief, throughout that dark night.

A couple days after the horrific ending of the serial killer known as *the Preacher*, a lone man hobbled through the cemetery, limping with a cane, slowly making his way through the headstones.

It was a bright, early fall day, and the man appreciated the turning colors on all of the trees surrounding the peaceful grounds of the large cemetery in northern Virginia. He wore a long coat, and could feel the chill deep within himself.

The slowly walking, limping figure finally found what he had been looking for. A double headstone, set close to the row of trees that was the demarcation of this area of the state-ran cemetery. The area for fallen men and women in the line of duty. The law enforcement side of the grounds.

Bob Woodyard looked down at the headstone and read the names printed on the black marble.

"Karen Ann O'Connor" with the dates of her life below. And "Hunter Patrick O'Connor" with dates of his own.

A final Bible verse was written below the couple's name on their shared headstone. It was out of the book of Second Timothy. The fourth chapter. Verse seven.

"I have fought the good fight, I have finished the race, I have kept the faith."

Bob looked at that verse for a very long time. He read it over and over to himself. And he thought long and hard about the couple in the ground in front of him. He had to.

He had failed them both.

After his stroke, he had disappeared from the world, but also deep within himself. He had spent so many days, laid up in the hospital and then in a recovery ward in a nursing home, thinking not about his long, distinguished career, but about his last failure.

And it was a final revelation that had shaken him out of his weeks-long depression and melancholy.

He had just been a puppet, strings held by someone or something larger than himself. He was convinced that he couldn't have done anything to ward off what had happened. It needed to have played out exactly the way it did.

In a way, he was quite proud of the man they called Three. Bob had seen the man in his mind, something he had always had the gift of doing, several times in the final years of Bob's career. That gift, whatever it was, and wherever it had come from, had given him the advantage of bringing the right people to justice, time and time again throughout an industrious and long career.

It had also been what had saved Three's life and freedom for the final years that the man had needed to accomplish what he had set out to do.

In a way, Bob knew, he was just as guilty for the deaths of so many people. But he tried not to think of the sin and wrongfulness in that. He, instead, had been given the revelation that he couldn't have done a thing to stop it, and that had given him peace.

It had also brought him here, to this beautiful, peaceful corner of the world, to say his last respects to a couple of people who had not deserved the fate that had been handed to them, but who had given everything they had, against their wills, for a greater cause.

Bob prayed that this couple found peace at last, and were held firmly in the bosom of the Almighty.

His prayers finally said, and his guilt eased, he slowly limped back to his rental car and headed for the airport.

Four days later, he was standing in the middle of a slow-moving river, wading boots up to his thighs, fishing pole held between two still-strong hands, and a smile was plastered on his face.

Oh, how beautiful the Montana wilderness, retirement, a satisfaction of having done what he was set on this earth to do, and many years of rest to look forward to.

Jerome Lionel Jackson, "Red," as his friends and colleagues called him, sat in his office in the J. Edgar Hoover FBI building in downtown Washington DC. He had been staring at the photo of his wife and two daughters that sat squarely in the middle of his desk for the better part of a half hour.

He, too, had felt an overwhelming sense of guilt and shame after what had happened to the man they had labeled *the Preacher*. And now, more than anything, Red was just pissed off.

That man had made law enforcement all over the country look like fools. And worse still, a cult following and a couple of copycats had already emerged since the man's death. Or as the left-wing media dubbed, his "martyr."

Red was also furious with himself. He had chosen his family's safety over the lives that had been lost since his abduction. It had been easy to pick his family over strangers. But now, after the danger was gone, he only felt anger. He didn't know a better way for the events to have unfolded, but he was still angry.

He got up from his desk, and decided to take the rest of the day off. He needed to walk.

And so, he left out of the front entrance of the tall, white stone building, and started walking down the streets of DC. He didn't know where he was going to go. He just walked.

Almost a half hour later, as Red angrily stomped the pavement with his dress shoes, still unconsciously enjoyed the mid-autumn air of the beautiful city around him, he found himself somewhere he had only been once before.

And then, as he walked further into the mostly unfamiliar park around him, he came face to face with a tall, granite white statue.

He had found his way to the memorial for Dr. Martin Luther King, Jr. And Red looked up into the man's face, portrayed so powerfully in the stone.

Dr. King's arms were folded, and Red had always thought that the man was holding the tide of hatred and divide behind him in the uncut stone of the rest of the statue. A pillar of strength and resolve standing against the wrongfulness in the world.

But as Red looked up into his idol's face, carved resolutely in the granite, his anger dissipated. Dr. King's resolute face took on a new image in Red's mind. His face showed strength, and even anger, yes, but it also showed Red peace.

A peace that he had done all that he could have done, and there was nothing left for him to do but simply soldier on. He saw his own emotions finally, in the face of Dr. Martin Luther King, Jr. And a final truth hit Red square in the face.

Dr. King had been the real Preacher.

And so, Red knew, and could see the truth in the eyes of the real Preacher's statue, that there was still work to be done.

Red said a silent prayer, and as he started walking back towards his office, he saw the last inscription carved on the side of Dr. King's statue.

"Out of the mountain of despair, a stone of hope."

Red felt a new sense of hope well up within him, and knew that he would be just fine.

He was ready to take on a new fight, and make sure that all of the sacrifices of the victims, as well as his best friend and his best friend's wife's sacrifices would not be for naught.

Red was ready to keep up the message of both the Preacher, and *the Preacher*.

He saw the truth, finally.

Smiling, and whistling a tune from between his lips, his steps were lighter as he walked into the future, and whatever that held for him, and millions of others just like him.

And then the next morning dawned beautifully bright and sunny, with birds chirping outside Mark and Christopher's kitchen window.

A cool breeze blew into the two men's bedroom, and they both awoke feeling refreshed, and if not happy, at least at peace. They had cried all of the tears that they were going to cry through the dark night behind them, and it was time to move forward.

Four had the most crippling guilt tear through him for most of the night. But at last, able to sleep, he was given peace from his best friend's sacrifice for him. And he was finally able to put what he had done in Seattle behind him.

304

Later that morning, after a solid breakfast and a short walk in the crisp air of upstate New York, the couple started talking about the past, and hopes for the future.

Within that conversation, they both said goodbye to their friend and brother, Harry Higgsby. And they both resolutely agreed to retire the nicknames "Four" and "Five."

There were no longer five best friends in a tight-knit group.

It was just the two of them left, and it was up to them to remember what the group had stood for, and what they needed to do to continue to fight for justice for the downtrodden, and make it up to Harry for all he had done for the couple.

The couple, who, that evening, sat in front of their fireplace, logs burning fragrantly, and remembered their friend's mission in life.

Three had taken care of everything, even the picture of Christopher that had been taken in Seattle.

Harry had taken the blame for absolutely everything, and the couple could finally rest.

And, to respect Three's wishes for his two best friends, they didn't fight it anymore.

They were finally going to let the dead lie, and get on with their own lives.

And as the rest of the world awoke on the 15th of October, unbeknownst to many, the country was changed completely compared to the day before, and all because of the very public death of a killer.

A killer who had never wanted to kill in the first place.

Chapter 43

The young boy had never been to a funeral before. He didn't know how onerous they could be, or that you had to get through the bad, boring stuff to get to the good stuff later on, like the food.

The boy's stomach rumbled. He was hungry. But then again, his sister had always joked with him about how he was always hungry.

Jack stood next to his twin sister, Emma, looking down at the hole in the ground. A pastor was droning on and on about how his father was in heaven now, and how God forgave even the worse sins.

The boy didn't care about any of that. He knew who his father had been. In the two weeks since his father had been killed, he had learned all about his father from his mother, who had known him as well as anyone had.

They sure all were surprised that his father had been killed by the very same police that he had been trying to change.

But Jack understood it.

His father's death had nailed the coffin shut for the police in the United States.

They had called it "Justifiable Homicide" or some papers had called it "Suicide by Cop," but Jack could see the writing on the walls.

Like how there were, right at that moment, more than fifteen cops in the small cemetery at the back end of the property where his father had grown up.

They watched the funeral with sad, downcast eyes, but they were still there. One cop in particular stood out to young Jack.

He was in a sharp, black uniform, but he stood out because of his age. All the other cops in cop uniforms were young. This guy was old.

His name badge said "McCrery." And he smelled like Jack's mother's rubbing alcohol that she always rubbed on his sores when he fell. Jack, in his young age, wondered why the man smelled the way that he did.

He had heard the old cop tell his mother how sorry he was, but he didn't say it was for her loss, like everyone else did. When he said he was sorry, he sounded like he had done something wrong, and was making up for it.

Jack had had to apologize like that to his mother more than once.

Emma got his attention by tugging on his hand. He could almost hear her thoughts. Almost.

He turned back around, and a few minutes later, was handed a white rose, which he then threw down into the grave where his father's body would be kept for all time.

That's how Jack's young mind thought of it.

Later that evening, after everyone was done saying their goodbyes, and Emma, Jack, and their mother, Colbie were left alone in the large house, Jack went exploring through the many rooms.

And that was how he found his father's boyhood room.

He walked into the room reverently, knowing exactly what it was. He took his time, looking around at the drawings, the trophies, the awards.

Jack got up on the bed, and laid his head back on his father's pillow. And looked up at the ceiling.

And that's when he heard something crumple, like paper, under his head.

He got up, picked up the single pillow under the bedspread, and found what his father had left there.

A couple of days later, Jack was sitting in the back seat of his mother's car, next to his twin sister, Emma, when they pulled up to a large brick home.

It was one of the largest houses that young Jack had ever seen, and he wondered why they were there. His mother turned in her seat, looking at both twins with tears in her eyes.

"You guys saw where your Daddy grew up, right?" she asked. They both nodded in unison.

"Well, this house is where your Momma grew up. With my sister. And my parents. Your grandparents. And your grandparents can't wait to meet you," she explained.

And just as she said those words, a nice-looking older couple walked out of the front door of the house, and waved towards them. The older woman, especially, looked a lot like their mother.

Emma waved back with a smile.

Jack just kept his hands in his pockets, his left hand pressed up against the thing he had found under his father's pillow.

308

Much later that night, and for more days than Jack could remember after, he took out the picture he had found under his father's pillow.

It was black and white, and old.

And what Jack saw in the picture always made him smile. Sometimes with a tear in his eye, but always a smile.

It was the picture of the five kids, all sitting on bikes, all grinning at the camera.

All except the two in the middle.

In the middle of the line of children, smiling from ear to ear, was his father, staring at the girl that Jack could only assume was Mary, who was smiling back at Jack's father.

And Jack knew Mary to be beautiful, like his father before him had felt.

Jack would always smile at the look on his father's young face.

It always told Jack that at some point, early in his life, his father had known happiness.

And that, he would tell himself whenever he had a really bad day, or felt like he couldn't go on because he missed his father so much, was what it had all been about.

Because in the end, what his father had done through the entire ordeal, had been worth it all.

The End

Joshua Loyd Fox

June 2020 - Feb 2021

Epilogue

Three rather tall, splendid looking Beings looked down on a changed world.

The Being in the middle, the One for whom the universe sings, was smiling.

The Father knew that what had been done was good.

Chamuel looked at the young boy left behind, gazing at his father's picture, and knew that that boy would grow up in a world that only knew love for others and no more hate.

It would take a couple of generations, like the Israelites in the dessert, who had had to wander around until the old generation had all died out.

But this world would finally know balance.

He knew, as did the Father, and his Sister who stood on the other side of the Divine, that the Ends had justified the Means.

As they always had.

The Father of All placed His heavy hand on the shoulders of His children to either side of Him, and the two ArchAngels felt complete peace and pride emanating from their Father towards His favored Children.

And it was there that Chamuel left them, to go and find some rest.

The Father's Will had whispered to Chamuel that he had earned it. He was looking forward to doing some traveling through the many realms of existence.

And so, Chamuel slowly faded out from above the peaceful world below, and disappeared in a slowly moving, pink-hued mist.

Azrael watched, amused, knowing that her next assignment would tax her considerably. And like Chamuel had done when given the assignment below, Azrael reached out for help.

The Father smiled one last time at her, and slowly disappeared as well. He left it to His favored Children to do His Will.

She closed her eyes. And let her soul expand throughout all existence to reach her Brothers and Sisters, the entire Host, who were spread all across Creation.

And her soul finally locked onto the one she was desiring above all others.

A mighty yell greeted her in the cosmos, and a beam of pure rainbow-colored emotion rushed at her with dizzying speed.

She merely accepted it, knowing her Brother's strength, and let the rainbow-tinted wash of emotions hit her like a high tide on a lonely beach, bringing relief, and joy, and deep understanding, as was the way for this favored Brother of hers.

Her Brother's gallant and true soul arrived before him by mere seconds, but in the place where the Material cannot see the Spiritual, it seemed like it took eons for him to arrive.

At last, she spoke into the glowing light that surrounded her. She was fortunate that this Brother took an extreme liking to her.

Or, at least, to her countenance that ruled death and department from the Material.

"Hello Raziel. I am in need of your help, and your wisdom, for what is to be done with a world far from here," she said to her Brother.

His knowing smile, and the deep knowledge of secrets and understanding washed out of his countenance, and again, she was soothed.

ArchAngel Raziel had that effect on every one of the Heavenly Host.

Well, except maybe Gabriel and Michael, she thought, amused.

But none of the Host had not seen that duo in millennia. A question to ponder later, she thought as she and Raziel prepared to depart.

She took one last look down at the smiling boy below gripping an old picture, who knew, deep in his young heart that he would, one day, see his father again.

And the boy was right, Azrael thought, thinking back on the question that Harold had asked her as she had guided him through the vail.

"Will my children be okay?" Harold Higgsby the Third had asked.

And she had been permitted to answer him in the affirmative.

Together, she and her brother, Raziel, the ArchAngel of secrets and wisdom, moved off to an older world.

A world that was to end in cataclysm, and to begin anew.

As new beginnings were the primary task for all ArchAngels, this charge was nothing new to them both.

But this world would tax Raziel and Azrael like nothing else had ever done before, because this Mission would come with a cost, as did most choices, chances, and advancements, they knew.

And what tower, reaching towards the heavens, wouldn't be built, without first calculating the cost? She wondered at the verse asking that very question.

And what cost would this old world's new beginning exact?

A cost that would tax the Heavens, and the entire Host, in more ways than they could count.

Joshua Loyd Fox is the author of three novels to date. *I Won't Be Shaken*, *Had I Not Chosen*, and *Amongst You*. All three novels are available on multiple platforms and in several styles from Watertower Hill Publishing, LLC.

All of Joshua Loyd Fox's novels can also be found and ordered at www.jlfoxbooks.com.

Look for his next novel, *To Build a Tower*, available from Watertower Hill Publishing, arriving summer 2022.

This work of fiction was formatted using 11-point Times New Roman Font, on 55lb cream stock paper. The page size is 5.06" x 7.81". The custom margins are industry standard, 0.5" all around, and 0.00" inside, with no bleed, and 0.635" gutter, with mirrored pages.

The cover is full color paperback in a glossy finish.

The binding is 'perfect.'

Made in the USA
Middletown, DE
08 July 2022

68332498R00198